BROKEN FENCES

Visit us at www.boldstrokesbooks.com

BROKEN FENCES

by

Jo Hemmingwood

2023

BROKEN FENCES

ISBN 13: 978-1-63679-414-3

This Trade Paperback Original Is Published By
Bold Strokes Books, Inc.
P.O. Box 249
Valley Falls, NY 12185

First Edition: May 2023

CREDITS
EDITORS: ANISSA MCINTYRE AND CINDY CRESAP
PRODUCTION DESIGN: SUSAN RAMUNDO
COVER DESIGN BY TAMMY SEIDICK

Dedication

For Chelsey, who is everything.

CHAPTER ONE

Seneca shifted the pack. The shoulder straps were padded, but after hours of walking, even the plush straps of her Bushcraft were apt to chafe. She'd walked nearly clean across the state of Idaho before coming into the small town. It wasn't on her main route to Seattle. Hell, it wasn't on any main route as far as she could tell. There had been a scenic little state highway crossing I-90 and disappearing between two mountains. Something about the sight had called to her. Maybe it was the huckleberry bushes with their ripe, dark fruits. Maybe it was the way the red cedars creaked beneath the shade of the mountains. Maybe it was that she had eaten the last of her nutrition bars.

The little square was pleasant and the small businesses around the courthouse seemed aimed at basic needs. *Speaking of needs*, her stomach rumbled cavernously. The last place she'd landed had afforded her the fortune of working as a custodian for a few weeks. Once she'd padded her wallet and supplies, the road called to her once again and, dutifully, she took up her pack. It seemed it was time to settle in and roll up her sleeves once more because her wallet was near-empty.

Shading her eyes against the sun, she squinted at the apothecary sign, then slid her gaze to the advertisement for small engine repair. Seneca stepped across the quiet street and struck out toward the other side of a gas station advertising a discount on Marlboros. Surely there was a vending machine, or something, somewhere nearby. As she approached the northern side of the square, a smell hit her, and her steps faltered. Barbeque. There was no mistaking it.

Seneca's slightly accelerated pace belied her excitement. She crossed another street, and the establishment came into view. *Jack's,* the simple sign read. The aroma coming from the bar and grill was anything but simple. It smelled like home. Seneca let herself in.

As she entered, anticipation bubbling in her stomach at the prospect of a good meal, she checked the time. When she looked up again, it was to find the entire assemblage of patrons regarding her curiously. The glances were not unkind, but neither were they polite. Seeming to realize this, the customers collectively turned back to one another and continued their conversations as though nothing had happened.

Seneca mentally shook her head. Some things would always be the same—like summer rain, slow-paced Sundays, and small-town curiosity. She made her way to the bar as though she'd walked the worn boards a hundred times. She sat and the bartender set a glass of whisky in front of her.

She frowned. "I haven't ordered yet."

He tilted his head. "You weren't going to order whisky?"

She looked into his dark eyes. "Well, since you've poured it." She took the tumbler, swirling its contents before bringing it under her nose. "Nice."

"Maker's." He placed a coaster and napkin near her glass. "I'm Earl."

She flashed a smile. "Well, Earl, I came in because I smelled the barbeque."

"Ah," he said, nodding. "Great choice. What would you like with it?"

"Whatever the cook likes." She shrugged. If it was food, she didn't care.

Earl raised his thick black brows but made no comment. "I'll get that order in for you." Earl made his way to the back, presumably in the direction of the kitchen.

As Seneca waited, she casually studied the bar. Wooden shelves were mounted in front of a mirror and stocked with more whisky than vodka. The top and bottom shelves needed dusting, but the mid-level scotch and whisky saw a lot of action. While reviewing the popular choices, she unhappily noticed in the bar mirror's reflection that she still attracted a considerable amount of attention.

Seneca knew how she looked. Dusty from the road, a large pack at her feet, a stranger to all. She forced away the tension already accumulated in her shoulders. No matter how many towns she hiked into, this initial experience put her on edge. The familiarity of being a stranger. Her eyes flicked back to the mirror. Seneca didn't blame them for staring, but that didn't mean she enjoyed it.

There was a creaking sound as the door opened and two dusty men came into the establishment. They must have been regulars because many a patron raised a hand in greeting and several people called to them. After a very social path to the bar, the two men—one short and one tall—claimed barstools.

Earl poured them each a beer. "How's ranching, friends?"

The taller of the two men, who'd answered to the name of Win, said, "Same as always." He had a bit of a whistle in his speech and his mustache seemed to flutter with the sound.

"Getting ready for our big drive soon," the one called JD said. He was well-built, if aging, and his white hair still held a touch of gold.

"Oh, that's right. It's about time to round 'em up and bring 'em back in." Earl leaned on the counter. "How're those new hands you hired?"

Win and JD exchanged a look. Seneca avoided Win's glance along the bar at her; she quickly busied herself squinting at the menu. "Well, they seem to know what they're doing, but they need a lot of supervision."

"They're lazy?"

JD nodded. "That's one way of saying it, I suppose," he said. "I've not been impressed so far. They're fancy cowboys and I need working cowboys."

"We need ranch hands with some get-up-and-go. Folks that can get a job done well without me or JD having to explain every step. It's gotten to where you can't find help with that skill set, anymore."

"I hear you, friend." Earl traveled the bar to check on Seneca, who patiently sipped the last of her liquor. "How are you doing over here?"

Seneca's interest was piqued. She'd done ranch work before and made a mental note to check out the opportunity before looking for other work in town. Giving nothing away, she looked into his inquisitive eyes. "I could do with a refill."

"What's that you're drinking?" Win called to her from the other end of the bar.

Slightly surprised at being addressed so friendly, so soon, Seneca nodded toward the bottle on the shelf. "Maker's Mark. Neat."

"Well, listen to that accent!" Win smiled. "You from Georgia?" His tone was respectful underneath his playful guess.

"Alabama." She corrected him with a smile of her own.

"Alabama?!" JD rejoined the conversation. "How'd you get here?"

"Walked." She sipped her refill as a second of silence ticked. Even Earl seemed to react—if a slight shift in stance could be counted as a reaction.

"You walked? From Alabama?"

She nodded slowly. "I made a few stops along the way."

"Well, I'm Win, and this is JD." Win hitched his thumb at JD just as a large man appeared in the doorway of the kitchen with a plate in his hand. He wore a greasy apron and the loop around his neck was pinned together with a paperclip. Seneca wasn't sure if she was impressed or alarmed that this was the man who had obviously cooked her food.

"Who ordered the chef's choice barbeque?"

Seneca raised a hand as the sight and aroma of her meal walloped her senses. The portion was clearly meant to feed the cook, but she and her hunger were up to the challenge. Her mouth flooded in anticipation of the meal. She replied around her drool.

"That would be me."

The cook set the plate in front of her. "I hope you like beans and coleslaw."

"There's not much I don't like." She eagerly picked up her fork. "This does smell mighty fine, though."

"Good," he grunted.

Despite his gruffness, Seneca could tell he was pleased that she was. She ate a bite of beans with some barbeque. *So good.*

"So, how long did it take you to walk here?"

Seneca couldn't fault JD for being curious and wasn't about to spurn an excuse to talk to a potential employer. She forked another bite of barbeque, this time with the slaw, and chewed slowly. While she chewed, she readied her sandwich, and anticipated the next couple of questions. She may not have a better work opportunity in this small town. Swallowing, she turned to him. "Well, I've been walking for about three months, but I've made some stops here and there for work." She picked up her sandwich. "Gotta eat."

"What sort of work do you do?"

"Pretty much anything." She tried for casual as she calculated how much money she would need to get back on the road. "I mostly work with my hands. I'm fine with heavy labor, and happy to be outdoors. I've farmed some, landscaped, and can work equipment. But if I've needed to, I've washed dishes, waited tables, and cleaned toilets."

Win and JD wore identical expressions of surprise. Seneca figured her story sounded a little suspect, and so she grinned. "I'm not on the run, if that's what you're thinking."

Win waved a hand as if waving off the idea. "We try not to assume anything."

"Do you know anything about horses?"

There it is. She hid her reaction to JD's question in chewing her food slowly. She sipped her drink before replying. "Well, my grandparents had a farm, and I spent many summers there. They had horses and cows. I can ride." JD and Win were quiet, and so she added to her explanation. "I've mostly dealt with work horses like Clydesdales and quarter horses. I don't look fancy in the saddle."

Her humility was honest. She was familiar with ranch work but knew little about the showmanship some cowboys practiced.

"The work we do isn't fancy." Win glanced at JD. "What do you think?"

JD sipped his beer. "I think we could use another hand to help prepare for the drive. Especially if we might be in position of letting some others go." Seneca met JD's sharp gaze while he studied her. "It would only be temporary."

Seneca nodded. "That works great for me. I don't usually stick around for long."

Earl, who had been unobtrusively cleaning glasses behind the counter, spoke up. "Are you a wanderer?"

"Right now, I am," she answered him, unsure as to how much he unnerved her. *Yes*, her feet and mind, at least, were roaming with no real destination. How was it this stranger seemed to intuit a truth of her journey when she barely acknowledged it herself?

She turned back to JD. "So, when do I start?"

JD smiled briefly. "Seven o'clock tomorrow morning." Win stepped aside to speak with a few patrons. JD pointed at the door. "Just take a right out the door, a left at the light, and then walk until you smell horses."

"That many, huh?"

"Cattle and chickens, too." Seneca detected a note of pride in his voice.

"Wow, y'all must do good business."

"Well, there's more to it than that." JD tapped his foot on his barstool and Seneca saw a cloud of dust shake loose from his boot's tread. "We also function as a group home for older boys in the system."

Seneca hesitated. As a rule, she tried not to get involved with the goings-on and gossip of the communities in which she stopped. "That's interesting." She took another bite of barbeque and savored the flavor while she quickly considered her options. She could search for other opportunities tomorrow and hope for something better. Or she could explore what sounded like a sure thing at the ranch. "A right out the door and a left at the light, you said?"

"That's right. I've got a form you need to fill out, and then we'll see what you can do."

"Sounds good to me."

❖

Finished with her meal and drink, Seneca paid her tab. She slid a small tip across the bar to Earl. When he nodded his thanks, she casually asked, "Where would be a good place to pitch a tent?"

He didn't seem surprised at the question and found a bar napkin and pen with which to render a little map. "We're here. There's a wooded area just east of here and a little path that leads to a grove of oaks and the creek. It's been a long while, but I've camped there before."

"Thank you," she said and gathered her pack.

By the time Seneca exited the building, it was the golden hour. She sighed. She'd been comfortable sitting at the bar and scolded herself for losing track of time. Since leaving Bear Lake near the Utah border, she'd been walking for almost two weeks without a real meal or shower. She'd grown accustomed to civilized accommodations while working as a custodian at the state park's camping facilities. Her little cabin hadn't been glamorous, but it was cozy, and she'd had access to the bathhouse. The creek would be too cold and probably unsatisfactory for a full wash, but maybe tomorrow she'd get a chance to scrub clean again. It had certainly been *good* to relax and eat simple, well-prepared food. Worth the delay in getting to a campsite.

Besides, she'd not had barbeque like that since she'd left the south.

She turned right to head east, glancing at her rough map. The tree line was just where Earl had drawn it. She squinted for the path and found it easily. It might have been hidden from the casual observer, but she'd spent so much time in the woods growing up that the path seemed clearly defined.

The sun sank slowly and tinged the sky with a rich, orange hue. Seneca gathered firewood as she pushed forward to her destination. No reason she couldn't build a small fire to keep away the chilled night air. The crisp, cool nights were something to which she'd only recently become accustomed. She looked forward to a fire, because it would mean a bit of warmth in the night.

❖

She had a good bit of kindling in her arms by the time she reached the grove of oaks. She cleared a bare patch of ground with her foot before dropping her bounty, and then pitched her tent quickly. She retrieved her camp ax to dig a trench and then started the fire with practiced motions. Circling into the surrounding area, Seneca came upon an oak that had fallen some time ago. Pleased with this discovery, she lowered the hatchet from her shoulder and started to work.

The cracking sound of the tool cleaving dry wood echoed as she worked methodically. Once she had enough fuel to last the night, Seneca returned to the campsite where the fire was burning low and hot. She fed it a few pieces of oak, then leaned back on a rock to watch it burn.

The night noises which had ceased while she chopped wood now returned as though there had been no pause. Seneca allowed herself to listen for a time before unholstering the Browning Hi-Power on her ribs. She deftly took it apart to clean.

After only a few minutes, she swapped the cleaned firearm for the compact Beretta she kept on her ankle. Having finished that, she snapped the Beretta Nano back into her ankle holster and packed her gun cleaning kit into its spot in her bag. Glancing up, she found the sun had sunk and that the stars were now distinct in the open sky.

Seneca retrieved her small, leather-bound journal and jotted down the date. She looked around before taking out her state map and recording her location coordinates as well as the name of the town and the little bar in which she'd eaten. After another pause, she wrote the names of the people she'd met thus far.

She packed her journal away as she retrieved her copy of *Leaves of Grass*. She withdrew the gum wrapper she'd been using as a bookmark and settled into Whitman. Seneca's sense of the night dissolved away. She'd read the volume before but did so again and again because she found comfort in the humanity of Whitman's poetry.

The moon had risen over the trees before she was ready to put the book aside. After banking the fire, she crawled through the flap of her simple tent. Seneca shucked her guns, boots, and jacket before snuggling into the sleeping bag. Her pistols she kept close by, but at a safe enough distance from any sort of midnight movement.

Setting her alarm, she knew dawn would come soon enough and with it the promise of work and a full belly. As her head hit the padded top of her bag, her eyes fluttered shut and her ears filled with the noises of the night woods. Drifting off, Seneca exhaled deeply and wondered how long she would stay in Butterbean Hollow before her itch to move returned.

Chapter Two

Monday morning, Robyn parked her car in front of a weathered building and let herself through the big doors. Years ago, the building had been used as a barn, but it had been remodeled. Now it served as an operational hub for the cowhands and maintenance people to receive their daily assignments, to secure equipment and supplies from storage, and to break for lunch. She knew she would find her father here, poring over some scheme he and JD had dreamed up. They both had offices—and a secretary—in her building, but often chose to commandeer the ranch from this spot in the middle of the action.

Her heels clicked on the stairs. She smelled coffee and heard low voices. Spurs clinked dully in the loft. Clearing the banister, she found her father and JD just as she had supposed, leaning over a drafting table and mumbling around their coffee cups.

Her footsteps alerted them to her presence, and they straightened as she cleared the top of the stairs. "Good morning." She smiled at them. "New project?"

"Just confirming some plans for the drive." Her father rolled up the paper they had been studying.

"Taking a different route this time?" She retrieved a mug from the mini-kitchen cabinet and poured a much-needed cup of coffee. She had worked late the previous evening to finalize the details of her own project.

"No, we just have a few hands that aren't experienced. We want to be clear on what we can before we update the crew and start preparations." JD took a sip of his brew.

She nodded. "Sounds reasonable." Robyn was not incredibly interested in her father's struggles with the cowhands. They were grown men, after all. She was more concerned about the event she had organized for the boys under their care. Her gaze found JD. "Are you ready to switch your spurs and hat for a tie and jacket tomorrow?"

"What?" He sputtered over his coffee.

"The job fair?"

"Oh, right." JD nodded. "I'll be there to rub elbows." After a moment, he grinned. "It's tough to be the boss." Robyn's father laughed.

Robyn turned to him. "I was wondering if you could lend me one of your cowboys to help."

He raised his brows. "Don't you have a secretary?"

"I do, but last year she was far more interested in getting a date than in helping me, so I didn't even ask her to help."

Both men looked at her in polite confusion.

"The farrier, the mechanic, the welder, and the plumber are all fairly attractive and single?"

They continued to scratch their heads and she huffed. "Never mind. I'm getting the tables and decorations set up this evening, but I need one of *your* cowboys to help with the event and cleanup, Dad."

"Yes, ma'am," he said with mock gravitas.

"Please don't forget." Robyn sighed. She wished she wasn't used to having to remind and cajole her father and their boss just to get things done at this time of the year. They both could be absent-minded on any given day, but with the cattle drive, they were more distracted than ever. Even so, she would not have her practice and programs suffer because of it.

Seneca arrived at the barn on Monday just as a shapely redhead was leaving. Her auburn hair was cut in a bob framing a slightly squared jaw. The wavy tresses were dark embers spun to silk. She wore a beautiful cobalt blue skirt suit with matching heels and a white blouse. Seneca could tell that even with the height of the heels, the woman stood a solid eight inches shorter than her. The other woman was engrossed with her phone and so did not notice Seneca. It wasn't until Seneca stopped to avoid the woman walking into her that the smartly dressed lady lifted her gaze. Seneca was immediately struck by how incredibly golden her eyes were. Like drops of amber.

"Oh, excuse me," she said with a slight frown.

"No problem," Seneca replied. "A couple of folks pointed me to this building. I'm looking for Mr. McCleere."

"He's in the loft of this building, yes." She paused. "Are you new?"

"Yes. I'm Seneca Twist."

She extended her hand. "Dr. Robyn Mason."

Seneca shook the small, delicate-looking hand and was surprised to feel slight calluses on Dr. Mason's palm. "It's nice to meet you, Dr. Mason."

"And you, Ms. Twist. Are you here to help with the drive?"

"I'm here to help in whatever capacity I can."

After another brief assessment of her, Dr. Mason said, "I see. Well, good luck." She smiled. "I have an appointment in a few minutes if you'll excuse me."

"Of course." Seneca smiled perfunctorily and stepped aside. Seneca watched as Dr. Mason entered a silver Prius and slowly backed away from the barn. She pondered her presence. Dr. Mason seemed out of place in her pencil skirt and heels. JD had mentioned that the ranch worked in conjunction with the state, but how often did that program coincide with what Seneca would be expected to do? Maybe the boys worked with the animals. Seneca had been hoping for some straightforward labor, but it seemed like there was more going on at the ranch than she realized. Hell. She didn't want to be responsible for the kids in any capacity. She'd just have to keep her head down and muck stalls until she earned enough to hike out of Idaho. Or find other work in this small town. Seneca sighed. Well, she was here now, wasn't she? Ignoring her reservations, she entered the big doors of the barn.

❖

"Who's that?" Win's distinctive voice sounded from above.

"Seneca Twist. We met yesterday at Jack's."

"Seneca Twist! Right." JD's head appeared over the loft banister. "Give me a minute and I'll be right there."

"Sure thing." She looked around while she waited. Her eyes cataloged worktables, tools, and an old Ford Ranger with the hood up. It seemed this barn, the smaller of the two she'd seen when she had arrived, was a catch-all garage and machine shop.

"I'm glad you're here. We'll get you to Paula for that form later. Ready to work?"

"Sure am."

JD looked her over. "Uh, before we go, there's a storage room round back," he said. "Put your pack in there and no one will bother it."

Seneca nodded, relieved to have a place to stow her possessions. When she returned, JD was at the door.

"Follow me." He led her a distance to another, more modern-looking barn with a shiny tin roof. "Now, we've got about thirty horses in all here and three hundred head of cattle, most of them at the summer pasture now, of course. You probably saw our chickens and a garden on the way in. There are larger plots of farmland beyond the pastures and main buildings. All these features help provide chores and experiences for the boys. The horses are roughly split into three groups. Some are used in our therapy program, others for trail rides to raise money, and of course, there are horses for the hands to use while working. As you can imagine, this barn is well-used. Something that needs doing before the drive is a bit of organizing. Think you can manage?"

"Sure." She looked over the fifteen rows of stalls. Her eyes traveled to a loft area which seemed half hay loft and half storage. The smell of horses, leather and sweat permeated the air. Again, Seneca was struck with a comfort she'd not experienced in a long time. "Anything in particular I should know?"

They both looked at the haphazard assortment of gear ranging from tools to tack to stacks of feed. JD shifted his stocky body from one booted foot to the other. "Well…I suppose you should consider this your interview? We want to see what you know about the equipment; how you organize related things together and store them. We will eventually be pulling together the wagon for the cattle drive, so it'll be important for us to know where things live. Do your best to get things into neat piles."

"Will do, Mr. McCleere."

"It's just JD."

"All right, JD."

"Okay, then. One of us will see you in a few hours." JD stepped out into the September air.

Seneca was glad for an easy task she could do solo but that would allow her to get familiar with the space. It'd only be better if it were outdoors. She got to work, trying to lose herself in the mundanity of sorting and cataloging, and trying not to think about Dr. Robyn Mason. She had *really* come to love the Idaho scenery, she considered with a grin. There had been a great number of scenic and inaccessible mountains on her hike, and Dr. Mason was just another beautiful vista.

As it neared noon, Seneca stepped back to survey her progress. Not bad. There was a crate of blueprints and maps that she assumed her new bosses would want in the barn loft. After wiping sweat on her sleeve, she lifted the crate and headed back to the older barn.

Inside, she nodded to a small group of cowboys chatting over sandwiches. One handsome man flashed a broad, charming smile which she conservatively returned before looking around for a place to stash the crate.

"Seneca," Win called. She looked to see his mustached face squinting at her from the loft. He beckoned and she mounted the stairs. Seneca could sense the smiling cowboy staring.

"Hello," she said with a smile.

"Hey." Win looked at the crate. "What's this?"

"Some papers that I guessed ought to be in here."

"Set it on the table and I'll go through it."

"Right," Seneca said.

"Uh, hey, did you happen to bring lunch?"

"I didn't, no." She dusted her hands on her denim. She'd had only enough time and money for a sausage biscuit that morning.

"Well, I keep loaf bread and cold cuts on hand if you're interested. There's water and soda, too."

"Sure, thank you." Win nodded to the fridge in the corner. Seneca washed her hands in a little sink by a coffee maker, then began to make a turkey sandwich as unobtrusively as possible.

"There are cups in the cabinet."

"Right. Thanks." Seneca rinsed a Mason jar and filled it with cold tap water.

There wasn't a table or chairs to sit in, and so she stood. Win leaned over the drawing table as she leaned a hip against a filing cabinet. After a few bites of his sandwich, Win looked over his shoulder. "What do you know about agriculture?"

That was an unexpected question. Seneca covered her surprise with a quick drink of water. "My grandparents grew hay."

"That counts," he said. "We've been thinking about planting a couple of lower acres with alfalfa next year." He tapped a finger on the map. "The issue is irrigation."

"Alfalfa doesn't need much irrigation. Do you have a creek?" She came forward to squint at the map.

"Sure do." Win leaned an elbow on the table. "Here." He traced it with a blunt finger.

"Can you just pump from it?"

"Could do that. It tends to dry up somewhat in the summer though."

She munched her sandwich as she leaned over. "Maybe you could build a water tank; pump into it like a reservoir, and then have it when you need it."

Win stroked his mustache. "We'd have to call the local branch of the EPA to make sure we don't need a license or anything, but…Yeah. That could work." He seemed to be appraising her; or at least, Seneca knew what it was to be measured. She leaned back and took a bite of her sandwich while Win decided what to make of her and her idea. "Well, finish that sandwich and let's get crackin', then." He stood tall.

Seneca frowned slightly. "Crackin'?"

"Sure, I've got some things to do before the end of the day. But first, we need to get to the lower forty and see how close that creek runs to the plot."

"Uh, right." Seneca shoved the last few bites of sandwich in her mouth and nearly choked; she took another sip of water to wash down her food. She quickly followed Win to the stairs as he fitted his hat on his head.

❖

"What do you think?" Win called over his shoulder as he led his blue roan, a Tennessee Walker, into a gully before leveling out onto the field.

"Not there yet." She'd be lucky to get there before the end of the day. She dug her heels into the sides of the slow paint mare. "C'mon, girl. I swear I'm not going to fall off." Lucy pricked her ears and picked up a bit of speed, only to slow again down the side of the gully.

When the mare finally reached the level field, Seneca glanced around. She then turned the horse to check the path they had just traversed into the gully. "Well, the incline should help with irrigation, but how are you going to get a tractor into this channel for harvest?"

"Oh, there's a long way 'round." Win pointed to a wider trail through the trees. "Runs along the creek, there."

"Ah." She prompted the mare and Lucy accelerated a bit quicker. "I see. And this is the creek you would use for pumping?"

"Yes. I'm thinking we could put the water tank at the top of the hill and then use gravity to irrigate when necessary."

"That's a fine idea." She surveyed the area. The tank might be fine outdoors year-round, but the equipment and hoses for the irrigation would be susceptible to damage in colder weather. "Do you have problems with ice?"

"Sure do. We would probably have to detach the whole pump and bring it in."

"Ah, I see." She grinned. "Alabama doesn't have much of that sort of weather."

He squinted at her out of the corner of his eye. "That's right. It's a long way off, isn't it? Alabama?" Win adjusted in the saddle and leaned on the horn.

Seneca nodded. "Ever been there?"

"Not a once."

"It's a pretty place. Not breathtaking and rugged like Idaho. It's more...domestic, I guess, but beautiful."

"Domestic?"

"Yeah, it's like..." She dropped her gaze. "Alabama is a solid, predictable horse. She's got some get-up-and-go and she's always ready to work, but she's not the shiniest. She just sort of *is*, and you love her for it."

Her boss looked at the mare she was riding, too, and nodded his understanding. "Okay, I get that some. But what sort of horse is Idaho?"

Seneca smiled. "I've only been here a few days," she said with a shrug.

Win grinned back. "That's enough time to have an opinion."

"All right." She looked at the snow glittering on the Rocky Mountains and felt the chilly breeze rush across the field by the water. "Idaho is like a temperamental mare. Cold and glistening and hard to win over. Predictable only in that she is unpredictable. She's amazing and unforgettable, and she can easily turn you aside, or break you. But earn her trust, and she'll love you true." She watched her companion for his reaction.

"Hmm." He looked to the mountains, and then turned back as though he was going to say something else but stopped.

Something in his expression impelled Seneca to prompt him. "Yes, sir?"

Win turned his horse on the trail cut through the trees. "It's Win, cowgirl. Let's head back. I've got something I want you to see."

"Another project?"

He shrugged. "Maybe. It's clear you know your way around a horse, but what sort of experience do you have, really?"

"I've ridden since I was old enough to climb the fence post to mount." She looked at him. "But it's been ten years or more since I've been routinely in the saddle."

"You've done fine so far." His mustache twitched.

Seneca tossed a tendril of hair from her face. "Lucy is a great horse, but she's not exactly a challenge."

"No, she's one of the horses we use for equine therapy. I would apologize, but I didn't know your level of experience."

"So, you were testing me?"

He smirked. "You'd be surprised how many people lie in an interview."

She mirrored his expression. "I didn't exactly interview, Win."

Win laughed heartily. "Fair enough, cowgirl. Well, so far, you've proven you have experience with a ranch and horse equipment, at least; you work hard, have a brain, and can be patient with an old horse. Now, I've got a task I need help with, and I need someone who isn't afraid of big animals or getting dirty."

"I'll do what I can, but recall JD only hired me for the week," she said. "I'm on my way to Washington, and it's going to take me at least four more days to get into Oregon before I can head north."

Win shrugged dismissively. "Yeah," he said. "It *is* only for this week. She'll probably throw you right away."

"Throw me?" No horse had thrown her in a long while. Seneca's pride rose to the challenge in his words. *That* hadn't happened in a long while, either. "You've got an unbroke horse?"

"Well, they said she's broke..." He raised his eyebrows in a show of disbelief. "But we're starting to think she might not be."

"I see." She patiently waited for more explanation.

"She does real good standing for the saddle. She will let you put the bit in her mouth no problem. And even for the first ten minutes or so, she's all good. After that, though, she starts stomping and tossing her head like she's ready to buck. It's the damnedest thing. I haven't got the time to work with an unpredictable horse. There are other things to do."

"And if you can't ride her, she's useless."

"Exactly. Just a mouth to feed."

"Pasture ornament."

"Yeah, that's it." Win nodded and his mustache twitched again. "We need working horses the same as we need working cowhands."

He led them around a bend and the major buildings of the ranch came into view in the distance. The sprawling nature of the old ranch was typical. The older barn was closest to them and sat west of three other buildings arranged like points on a compass around a grassy center. The front of the barn faced them and a graveled arena circle. The newer barn with its shiny tin roof stood north of the old barn and arena. She could just see a two-story farmhouse farthest away east and atop a small hill. Seneca reasoned at least one of the other buildings around the compass circle had to do with the young residents of the ranch. *They must live somewhere.*

"She's just for looks right now."

"That's a shame," Seneca murmured.

Win's tone turned serious. "If we don't have any luck with her, we'll have to sell her, and that would be a shame." He glanced at her with appraising eyes once more. "I know you've got your hands full organizing, but maybe tomorrow you can saddle her up and we'll see what happens?"

Seneca tried to tamp the excitement bubbling in her gut. She was grateful for the position, but she certainly had more to offer the ranch than barn organizing. She didn't want to seem overly eager for the experience, but she couldn't deny the thrill at the idea of being back in the saddle and on an inexperienced horse. "Sure, after morning feed?"

"I'll meet you in the tack room."

Chapter Three

Seneca fell into her hammock heavily. After meeting Paula and a discussion with JD about the best place to pitch her tent, he had suggested she take the loft in the new barn she'd spent so much time cleaning. This arrangement suited her fine because it meant a reprieve from the wind. It had been a good day. It had been a long time since she'd been so blissfully exhausted.

Only seconds passed before the sun came creeping through the dusty glass windowpanes of the loft. For a moment, she was confused as to where she was, but a rooster crowed commandingly and the soreness in her thighs and backside brought her to reality.

With a soft grunt, she rolled from her suspended bed. Her sock-clad feet thumped against the worn floorboards with a dull echo. Once she'd taken a moment to stretch, Seneca retrieved her leather toiletry bag and, grabbing clean underwear, made her way past the still-stabled horses to the small three-quarter bath on the barn's lower level.

Heading out thirty minutes later, Seneca noticed more vehicles coming and going than the day before. She even spied a few of the teenage residents in clean jeans and ties walking across the quad. After Win failed to show for their appointment, she went to the older barn to look for him.

Letting herself in and muttering a quick good morning to a small group of cowboys, she looked to the loft. Before she could reach the steps, however, Collin Shepherd blocked her progress. He smiled what she now knew was a smarmy grin while extending his hand. "I think we got off on the wrong foot yesterday."

Seneca looked at his hand, and then into his eyes. "Oh?"

"You see, I didn't realize you were in the building. If I had, I wouldn't have—"

"Been speaking so openly about my body?" She spoke calmly, but internally, Seneca retched. The only negative part of her first day had been the end of her shift. She had entered the stable barn to find Shep entertaining a couple of the other hands with a detailed narrative of his randy intentions with her. The scenario included a crass description of fucking her behind the stables accompanied by fake moaning.

Shep smirked while ducking his head. *Jerk.* "That's right. I didn't realize you were here to work like the rest of us." He nodded toward some cowboys who watched the interaction.

"Right." Those same cowboys had guffawed while Shep asininely illustrated the theoretical situation with hip thrusting. "Well, I do need to get to work, so I'll see you around." Seneca pushed past him to mount the steps.

At the top, Win stood with his coffee. "Seneca." He smiled and his mustache fluttered. His face fell quickly. "Oh, shit. We were supposed to saddle that troublesome mare."

"Yeah, but there is a lot going on—"

"Shit!" He sputtered and plonked his coffee. "Oh, she is going to kill me."

Nonplussed, Seneca watched Win pace a step while rubbing his mustache on both sides. "Who?"

"Robyn." He said the name as though it carried all the weight in the world. "Uh," he said, stepping forward, "I need you to get across the quad ASAP. Just follow the residents to the event going on."

"All right." She smoothed the front of her shirt on reflex. Whatever this was, it sounded serious. "What will I be doing?"

"Anything she tells you to do. Now get going!"

"You got it, Boss." Seneca hurried away, wondering what she'd gotten into.

❖

Robyn exhaled. The large conference room seemed rustic and comfortable yet looked professional and neat. Conversation chairs were set up in a couple of corners of the room and the tables were ready for their designated tradesmen to arrive. With any luck, she could get each tradesman to commit to a couple of new apprentices.

As she was standing there, the door opened and the newcomer, Seneca Twist, entered. Despite how busy Robyn had been the morning before, she'd had time to notice how attractive Seneca was. She was unusually tall, and her angular jaw and broad shoulders were handsome and spoke of obvious strength. Her rich mocha hair was the color of chocolate and pulled back with a folded handkerchief tied over it. As Seneca turned her head left and right, Robyn noticed Seneca's long hair was braided and trailed between her shoulder blades. Robyn watched Seneca find her and use those lanky legs to head in her direction. She could make out the lean muscle through her jeans. Robyn was surprisingly glad to see her again. She smiled inwardly. She might have more in common with her secretary than she wanted to admit. Then again, she did have a heartbeat, and Seneca did not need to know what she was thinking.

"Can I help you?" Robyn was careful to keep her tone professional.

"Win sent me." *That voice.*

"Sent you? For what reason?"

"I'm supposed to help with this." Seneca's long fingers caught Robyn's eye as she gestured to encompass the room. *Those hands look talented, too.* Robyn willed her attention back to business.

"Oh?!"

"Were you expecting someone else?"

"Honestly, I expected my father to forget."

"Your father?"

"Win Mason."

"Ah." Seneca smiled. It looked like a reluctant upward tug at the corner of her mouth. Robyn liked it. "He left that bit out."

"Did he?" Robyn laughed softly. "What happened? You were the first one at work today, and he suddenly remembered I needed help? Sent you over here in a hurry?"

"That's about right." Seneca's eyes crinkled at the corners when she laughed. "So, tell me, what's going on here?"

Robyn launched into an explanation partly to distract herself from how much she liked the throaty sound of Seneca's laughter, and partly because she was eager to discuss her favorite part of her job. "Well, every year I invite tradesmen to come and discuss with the boys what it is they do, and how they do it. They can even do an interview here if both parties agree. Usually, about a quarter of the boys finish an apprenticeship."

"And these are the state boys?"

"Yes."

"What happens to the rest of them?"

"We don't always know." Robyn sighed. "Once they leave our care we lose track of them, unfortunately."

"Sounds like a losing battle."

Robyn studied Seneca's profile. Her currently narrowed eyes and clenched jaw gave her the air of someone who guarded herself closely. Robyn was curious. She wondered briefly if Seneca's reserve guarded some secret, or if it indicated she was slow to trust new situations. She sighed. Either way, not her business—and not like her to be curious about someone she had just met. "It feels that way most days, then I have a kid call me to say how great he's doing, and that he owns a business. Makes it all worth it."

Seneca nodded. "I imagine that is a good feeling."

Before Robyn could reply, she spotted a broad-shouldered man. He sidled into the building carrying a box with horseshoes, rasps, and hoof nippers, amongst other basic tools of his trade. She greeted him, smiling. "Devon, how are you?"

He grinned slow and easy. "Doing just fine." His eyes slid from Robyn to Seneca.

"This is Seneca, my helper today. Your table is the second one on the right."

Seneca moved forward to greet Devon. He shuffled the box around so that he could grasp her hand. "Seneca Twist." She smiled and led him to the nearby table. "You're the farrier?"

"I am." He nodded confidently, but his demeanor seemed to quickly turn shy. Robyn understood. Seneca was confident and attractive. Poor Devon didn't stand a chance. "I've apprenticed a couple of boys from this program before."

"Is that right?"

"Oh, yeah. Great young farriers now." He nodded to Robyn. "That woman has gotten more of these young men jobs than the unemployment office ever could."

"With the career fair?"

"The career fair, certificate programs, GED classes. You name it, and Dr. Mason lines it up for these boys. They're lucky to have her here."

Robyn was slightly embarrassed as she eavesdropped, and so she stepped back to the door to greet the incoming tradesmen. For the next hour she had little time to dwell on Seneca but was busy running the event. When JD arrived, Robyn was able to relax briefly and let the boss rub elbows. She sensed someone at her side and turned to find Seneca.

"He looks good in a suit." Seneca nodded in the direction of JD.

Robyn smiled at him shaking hands and joking with the boys and tradesmen. "You wouldn't know he was uncomfortable, would you?"

"Not at all."

"He doesn't like the limelight. He'd rather be outdoors, but he can't ride and work in the fields all the time. He's enough cowboy to know how to ranch and enough businessman to know how to run things...When he first took the job, this place was on the verge of bankruptcy."

"Is that right?" Seneca raised her brows.

"Yes. The ranch itself has been here forever, but it changed hands and was opened as an orphanage for kids who lost their homes during the Great Depression. They lived here and helped work the farm and the animals. My father's father was one of those kids."

"So, you've always just been here, I guess?"

"Always." Robyn smiled. "Many of us in these parts have family affected by this ranch. When JD wanted to expand the social work department to include psychology, I jumped at the chance."

"Ah, *Dr.* Mason," Seneca said. "You're a shrink."

Robyn was suddenly wary. Seneca surveyed the crowd milling about and seemed to be avoiding her gaze. Robyn typically experienced one of two reactions when she shared what she did for a living. There were those who were a little too interested in her job and wanting to know inappropriate details about others or seeking help for themselves; and there were those made uncomfortable by it, wanting to avoid the topic altogether. Seneca seemed to fall into the latter category.

"Is that a problem?" Robyn tilted her head.

"That's a shrinky question." Seneca gave a slight smile.

Robyn wanted to dig deeper but held back. As increasingly intriguing as Robyn found Seneca, she was an unknown. Seemingly nothing more or less than a temporary cowhand. She was attractive, sure, but Robyn was undecided as to how much she *really* wanted to know about her.

"It's a habit, I suppose." Robyn replied with a smile to help ease the tension. She watched Seneca relax her shoulders slightly.

"No, it's not a problem. I guess I thought you were a social worker. You're quite involved for a psychologist, aren't you?"

Seneca had her there. It was hard to explain that the ranch was large, but small at the same time. To an outsider, it seemed massive. Cows, horses, chickens, and boys all over the place. Those who worked here, however, wore many hats. Paula was JD and Win's secretary, the human resources admin, *and* she managed the residence hall. JD was both the president and the trail boss, and her father was both operations manager and personnel supervisor. There was much to do, and a moderately sized staff to accomplish it all. Most employees had multiple roles to play.

"Well, you've only been here a couple of days, but stick around long enough and you'll find that everyone does everything here. We all have multiple jobs."

"I've noticed that already with JD, at least. And you." Seneca glanced at her with a slight frown.

Despite her recent resolution to *not* learn more about this handsome stranger, Robyn's stomach fluttered a bit at the idea that Seneca had been contemplating *her*. She rolled her eyes internally. She needed to get a grip. She willed herself to remain aloof.

"Today it's the job fair, tomorrow it's meeting with clients, and the next day I'll check in with Kevin and the equine therapy program." Robyn laughed. "That's the schedule this week, anyway. It's not a typical operation, but it works for us."

"That's what matters."

The beat of silence between them was interrupted with a crash. Both of them turned quickly to find two boys had knocked over the welder's display table and were trading blows.

"What the hell?" Robyn started forward, but Seneca was a blur.

She crossed the room in three great strides and calmly plucked one of the boys off the other. Seneca grasped her captive's wrists, crossed his arms over his chest, and then, pressing his back against her body, dragged him away from the bleeding boy on the ground. JD was only a step behind her. He crouched to inspect the injured Noah.

Robyn was disappointed to see Nathan red-faced and still struggling in Seneca's arms. She approached him first, though Seneca seemed to have it well in hand. Robyn couldn't tell what she said softly to the boy, but soon after, he slumped. Seneca sat him in a nearby chair and stepped back without a word. Robyn looked at her searchingly for a moment, impressed with her calm and stable presence.

"Nathan." Robyn crouched before the boy. "Look at me." The boy raised his blue eyes. There was a bruise already swelling below his left eye as tears coursed over his face. Robyn's heart broke for him. These young men had already experienced loss, and only wanted control, but they had so little of it in their lives. "We'll talk about this tomorrow, Nathan. Tonight, you will write about this event, so we can work through it together."

Nathan dropped his head. Seneca put a hand on his shoulder.

"Did you hear her, young man?"

Nathan looked up at Seneca, then back to Robyn. "Yes, ma'am."

Robyn turned to Seneca, who kept her hand on Nathan. "Could you stay with him a moment? I need to check on Noah." He would receive the same assignment.

"Sure. Do what you need to do. I'm here."

Robyn stood, dusted off her skirt, and turned to search for Noah and JD. She had experienced a warm rush of relief at Seneca's words. *I'm here,* she had said.

I am certainly glad for it, Ms. Twist.

Robyn was embarrassed. Never had such a thing happened in the years she'd organized the career fair. Neither Noah nor Nathan had any substantial injuries, but they would have restrictive consequences. They would also meet with Robyn twice a week so she could try again to understand the underlying reasons for their animosity toward one another. She was already exhausted just thinking of how to fit the necessary arrangements into her already overfull schedule. More than this, Robyn worried about the impression made on the tradesmen, and the possible negative impact on the opportunities for Nathan, Noah, and the other young men at the ranch.

The fair was ending. Despite the earlier chaos, Devon, the plumber, and miraculously, the welder had decided to take on a couple of boys each. Robyn was so relieved she could have cried. It wasn't until the last tradesman thanked her and departed that she allowed herself to sit.

Across the room, Seneca had already begun to collapse the tables and stack them by the door. Robyn idly watched her work, appreciating the grace of her movements. She then recalled the power with which Seneca had lifted Nathan, and the gentleness of her murmurs as she had defused his anger and brought him back to reality. There was more to Seneca Twist than met the eye. Deciding that she wanted to know more, Robyn stood to make her way over to Seneca.

She paused when a pair of large men ambled in. At first, Robyn assumed a couple of the tradesmen had forgotten something. When she saw the swagger of the leader, however, she stiffened.

"I heard your career fair was a riot." Collin Shepherd drawled with his typical cocky grin.

Robyn nodded perfunctorily and internally rolled her eyes at the limp attempt at humor. All Shep's jokes were in poor taste. She tried to seem busy. She did not want to talk about any aspect of the job fair with him.

"Exhausting, the amount of preparation that went into this thing." Shep spotted Seneca, who continued her task. "So consuming, in fact, Win needed one of my cowhands to help you."

"One of *your* cowhands?" Robyn raised a brow, irritated at the notion that Shep was an authority on anything having to do with this ranch. She wouldn't let the arrogance in his tone go unanswered. "I didn't realize you paid their salaries, Shep."

He grinned. "I don't, but that doesn't mean they don't know who runs the show."

Robyn huffed and turned away to clear pens and sign-in sheets from the nearest table. Maybe if she ignored him, he would leave.

"But if I *were* the boss," Shep said, following her, "I wouldn't be wasting resources on things like this."

"Oh?" She didn't bother to hide her disdain. A reasonable person would be a touch more tactful, especially with the person who organized the fair. But Collin Shepherd had never been much for diplomacy, nor spared an ounce of compassion for anyone.

"It's not going to matter anyway. This is a ranch, not an orphanage. These kids don't need connections, they need hard work and discipline. That's what got me into shape at that age."

Robyn's ire burned. "Yes, you are the model of—"

"Dr. Mason, someone dropped money over here."

"What?" Robyn turned toward Seneca with her back to Shep.

"Looks like a twenty." Seneca handed the bill to Robyn. "That's a good chunk to go missing, especially if it belongs to one of the boys." She acknowledged the cowhands in turn. "Shep. Tommy."

"Seneca Twist." Shep's drawl was obnoxious. "What did you think about the fair? Find your new profession?"

Tommy guffawed as Shep re-addressed Robyn. "Seneca is our temporary help. She breezed into town with nothing but a pack. Your father and JD felt sorry for her." He motioned to Seneca. "Isn't that right?"

Seneca merely shrugged with a look of indifference. Robyn was angry on Seneca's behalf. Seneca should say something and not allow Shep to speak to her that way. Robyn tried to catch her eye to communicate this silently, but Seneca watched Shep with a flat expression.

Looking annoyed, Shep continued. "But it turns out she's a pretty good worker. So far, she's organized the supplies real nice, and cleaned all the stock tanks. We haven't seen her on a horse yet, but I reckon we can make her into a real cowgirl." He hooted, Tommy chuckled, and both Robyn and Seneca stared.

"Right." Seneca nodded. "Dr. Mason and I are going to finish here and then I'll be 'round for afternoon check with the horses."

"Yeah, I've got plenty of work to be getting on with, too. Win stuck me and Tommy with that kid, Cliff. Barely knows his ass from his elbow. I've got him mucking stalls right now, but I should make sure he hasn't made a mess of it." He tipped his hat. "Dr. Robyn."

Robyn reluctantly nodded back a cordial farewell. Some childish part of her would rather have kicked him in the shin. She huffed, and then took a soothing breath as Shep exited with Tommy on his heels like a faithful dog. Robyn regarded Seneca, who watched the door swing shut behind them. "That man is by far, the most insufferable asshole I've ever met."

"Agreed."

Robyn considered Seneca's stoic demeanor. "How you could stand there and let him insult you, I cannot fathom."

"I've met a lot of men like him. Guys who needed to belittle me to make themselves feel important. I don't let it get to me."

Beautiful, mature, wise. Robyn was more intrigued by the second. "Was all that true? About you hiking into town?"

"Yeah, that was true." Seneca stuffed her hands in her pockets and shifted her stance. "It's true he hasn't seen me in the saddle, too."

"But you can ride." Robyn watched her closely.

"Better than him, probably." Seneca's mouth twisted into a wry half grin.

Robyn suspected as much. The best didn't need to boast about it. "I thought so."

"Oh? And how is that?" Seneca seemed amused. "You don't know me."

"No, but I do know that real cowhands clean the stock tank, feed the animals, and take care of their tack. Ranching isn't all about riding. It takes caretaking and patience."

"That's true." Seneca suddenly seemed somber. "I'm sorry the fair didn't go as planned today. What you are doing here is important."

"It is important." Robyn sighed. "I'm certainly disappointed that fight happened, but I remind myself of the small victories. Some apprenticeships did still come through."

"True. And—" Seneca bit her lip.

It was the first time she'd appeared less than confident. "Yes?"

"I hope I did not overstep today when I grabbed that kid."

"Oh!" Robyn pressed a hand to Seneca's forearm in reassurance. "No, you did *not* overstep! I'm glad you were here. You did everything just right, Ms. Twist."

"Please, it's just Seneca." She held Robyn's gaze briefly in the now dim light of the building.

Warmth seeped through Robyn's system right to the pit of her stomach. Her fingertips tingled with the sensation of Seneca's firm muscles beneath them. Regaining her composure, Robyn pulled her hand away. "Of course, Seneca. I appreciate all your help today. You certainly rose to the challenge."

"I get suspicious when things are easy."

"Suspicious?" Robyn softly chuckled, tilting her head at the curious word choice.

"Uh, vigilant?"

"Vigilant." Robyn quietly echoed, almost to herself. Another interesting word, and perspective, given the circumstances. This was a ranch, not a battlefield. Not usually anyway. Seneca certainly sounded guarded against trouble.

Seneca eased backward in seemingly renewed discomfort just as Robyn's father stuck his head in.

"I'm here with the truck, Seneca. I figured it would be easier to load the tables in the bed rather than carry them back to storage one by one."

"Right! Thank you." Seneca turned from Robyn. She grabbed a couple of folded tables to take outside. Robyn stood gazing after her. Not only was Seneca leaving, but it seemed she couldn't get away fast enough. Robyn pushed away a surge of disappointment. She wasn't sure what she had expected. She and Seneca had only just met and were not likely to cross paths often. With Robyn's responsibilities, she wouldn't have time to puzzle Seneca out anyway. Still, she did not want to see Seneca leave.

Her father interrupted her thoughts. "So, how did it go?"

"Haven't you heard?"

He stroked his mustache. "Devon was pleased with the boys he chose, but he mentioned there was a scuffle."

"There was. Noah and Nathan."

"Again?"

She sighed. "Again." Robyn glanced where Seneca still worked. "I'm glad you sent her."

"Yeah?" He looked surprised.

"She was great. Jumped right into the fray and pulled those kids apart. Kept her cool and calmed Nathan."

"Did she, now?" His gaze briefly followed Seneca's movements before returning to her. "I saw Shep and Tommy leaving here. They weren't bothering you, were they?"

"Shep is a general nuisance."

"Say the word and I'll get rid of him."

Her father was sincere. He would fire Shep if she said the word. That would make her cowboy interactions much less difficult, but Robyn considered what Seneca had said. Robyn could certainly control her reaction to Shep, too. She shook her head. "No. He's an ass, but I know how hard it is for you to find experienced cowhands, and Shep is definitely that."

"That's only because he grew up here." Robyn heard frustration in his voice.

"Isn't that another reason to keep him? As a success story? He's the poster child of a boy who grew up in state care at the ranch."

"He is, but lately he's getting too big for his britches. If he gives you any more trouble, you let me know."

"I can handle him myself, Dad."

"I know, but I'd like to be there when it happens." He winked at her before joining Seneca to finish moving the stack of tables.

Robyn watched them work for a few moments, caught again by Seneca's strength and the fluid way her body moved. But when Seneca glanced her way, Robyn quickly turned aside, hiding her interest. How unlike her, staring like that. She supposed she should be thankful they wouldn't be seeing a lot of each other.

Chapter Four

I have missed this. The thought hit Seneca right in the chest. Monday had been busy and Tuesday morning had wrong-footed her, but by Tuesday afternoon the pace had slowed. She'd met some of the other cowhands and shared a sandwich in what it seemed everyone called the Old Barn.

Sitting around socializing at least seemed familiar. The fight earlier in the day and her interaction with Dr. Mason had left her head buzzing. Robyn was certainly more than Seneca had initially supposed. She had erroneously judged her out of place. After the bit of history Robyn had shared and watching JD schmoozing with the tradesmen, Seneca was forming a picture of the way things worked here. It seemed an oddity, but she supposed nonprofits could be unusual in the way they functioned.

Even more unusual was Dr. Mason herself, or, more specifically, Seneca's reaction to her. She could still feel her soft fingertips pressed into the flesh of her arm. Glancing down, she almost expected to see an imprint of fingers. Such a small thing, an unconscious thing for Robyn, surely, that had caused an explosion of sensation in Seneca's body. Seneca shook her head. She was overreacting. Dr. Mason had barely touched her. She didn't want to dwell on the lovely psychologist or her body's involuntary reaction to her. And she did not want to dwell on what that reaction might mean.

Looking about, she was reminded of the camaraderie she'd shared with the other soldiers in her troop. She fondly recalled sitting around on base, jawing as they stitched buttons or repaired equipment. Carly would have been reading a novel or poetry collection. She had given Seneca *Leaves of Grass*. Garrett would have been telling a whopper of a story about a fish he caught once, and Hunter—

Hunter.

The desert heat burned. She heard artillery and smelled diesel fuel. She realized she kneaded both forearms with the opposite hand, experiencing the ghosts of her pain. *Damn.* Remembering the past was more difficult than processing her feelings about Robyn. She fought her way back to the present.

Grabbing her soda in one fist, Seneca swiped at the cold sweat on her forehead with the opposite forearm. She took shaky breaths, focusing on the cool breeze fluttering through the open doors of the barn and the familiar smell of hay and horses. Just as she had unobtrusively regained her composure, Win called from the loft.

"Seneca!"

She shielded her eyes from the afternoon sun coming through the glass gabled ends of the old roof. "Yes, sir?"

"You ever driven a wagon?"

"Yes, sir."

"Come on up here a minute."

Seneca attempted to shake off the remnants of the flashback as she climbed the exposed stairs. The loft space was exceptionally peaceful given her state of mind. The afternoon sun slanted in from the glass high above them and Seneca's attention was captured by the mountains in the distance.

"That's a great view."

Win followed her gaze and smiled. "Wait until the first hard frost. The pastures look like glazed gingerbread."

"That would be something to see." *Careful, now.* Chances are she would not be around that long.

"It sure is." He studied her. "So, you've driven a wagon? How far?"

"Not far. My grandparents had a team of mules that pulled the wagon 'round the property carrying supplies and such. They only had about forty acres."

"Can you hitch a team?"

"So long as they've got four legs and a mouth, I can hitch them."

"All right then." Grinning, he pointed to a topographic map on the drafting table. "We've got to drive the cattle from the mountains to the winter pasture here at the ranch, and we need to take a supply wagon. The cowboy that drove it for the last few years just moved to Boise. Now, I've got a young gun I'm pretty sure could do the work if he had some instruction."

"That's where I come in?"

"Right."

"Who is it?" She studied the map.

"Cliff. He rides that red roan Appaloosa."

She thought a minute. "Cliff." She nodded. "I remember meeting him. Nice guy."

"He is. And he works hard. I'm hoping he's a long-term addition. He's eager to learn how that wagon drives, especially in steep terrain. You could help pack it proper, too, or at least help him identify what all needs to go on it."

"Right, I'll set to it, then." Seneca had already started a mental checklist of the information she needed to share.

"And about that horse…how about tomorrow after morning feed?"

"Yeah?"

"I promise I won't stand you up this time." He grinned sheepishly.

"That's all right, I had a good time at the career fair today."

"Hmm…I hope you didn't feel as though I was throwing you to the wolves."

"I would hardly call Dr. Mason a wolf." She grinned, then teased Win. "But you could have told me she was your daughter."

"Would you believe me if I told you I just forgot?"

"I might." Seneca chortled and indeed, did believe it. She recalled Robyn's accurate theory on how Seneca had come to help at the fair.

"Got more than you bargained for, I heard."

"Well, I wasn't expecting to bust up a fight, but I'm no worse for wear."

"Robyn said you saved the day." Win seemed to be watching her closely.

Seneca experienced a little jolt of pleasure, but didn't want to analyze it, and especially not in front of Win Mason. Robyn's opinion of her did not matter. "I'm just here to help." *Not be a hero.* "Just doing my job."

"Right." He straightened up a bit. "Tomorrow morning, cowgirl."

❖

That evening, Seneca was in the tack room, stooped over a dusty saddle with a brush, cloth, bucket, and a tin of saddle soap.

"What are you up to, Twist?"

Seneca found JD peering in from the door. "Trying to whip this saddle into shape." She gestured toward her project.

JD stepped into the room. "Damn, that thing is old. Where did it come from?"

"Shep brought it from storage."

"Is that so?" He tapped his stubbled chin. "Mind if I take a look?"

"Of course," Seneca said. She stepped back.

He ran his hands over it, checking the stitching and underneath the seat. "Everything seems all right."

"Don't trust Shep?" She asked the question instinctively. Seneca's impression of Shep had been solidified in less than two days. For all his swagger, he knew his way around a horse, and several of the other cowhands seemed to get along with him. But what she'd experienced of his disrespectful attitude toward women made her want to keep a wide berth. She wasn't afraid of him, but Seneca had known too many men like him to ever trust Collin Shepherd. Still, she may have overstepped to ask the boss his sentiment.

Seneca furtively met JD's gaze before she resumed her cleaning. He finally answered in a measured tone. "What Shep thinks is funny, and what I do, might be different things."

"Fair enough." She was glad to know JD had his eyes open, but she needed to change the subject. "How is Noah?"

"I'd like to say he learned his lesson, but I doubt it." JD sighed. "Those boys go at each other constantly. Like two bulls that can't help but to lock horns."

"I'm glad it didn't derail the fair too badly. It seemed like Dr. Mason worked hard on it."

"She did." JD gazed toward Seneca's hammock swaying in the storage loft. "How was last night? You didn't get too cold, I hope?"

"No, sir. A hammock in the loft is better than a tent on the prairie."

"Don't I know it?" He chuckled. "It's just going to get colder."

Seneca paused her polishing of the dark leather. It was already the third time someone had expressed as much to her two days on the ranch. She resumed her work. "That's what I hear."

"Well…I just wanted to make sure you were settling in."

Seneca squinted at JD. What she knew of her new boss wouldn't fill a thimble, but, in her gut, he was a hardworking, true-blue cowboy. Whatever it was he was doing, he was not *just* checking on her. "I'm good, Boss. Is there something else I can help you with?"

"No, no…I was just wondering if you were still planning on leaving at the end of this week."

"I hadn't thought much about it." She became uneasy. She usually did whenever anyone began asking about her plans. It made her itch. What she wasn't sure of, she couldn't communicate to anyone else.

"Well, the winter drive is coming up fast, and we could sure use the help. If you don't have anywhere else to be, of course."

She smiled. "I've got no big plans." Seneca could tell it wasn't the definitive *yes* he wanted, but that he didn't want to press. She had no plans at all, but she wasn't quite ready to commit to staying in Butterbean Hollow.

"All right, I just wanted you to know it's a big project. Plenty more wages to earn."

Now, that was something to consider. "A real-life cattle-drive then."

"Ever been?"

"No, sir."

"It's an experience worth having. Sitting in with the cattle, cooking sausages on the fire, enjoying the men around you—" He looked at her apologetically. "And the women."

Seneca acknowledged his amendment and accepted his amends with one grin. "Sounds like a fun challenge."

"Well then. Let us know if you're sticking around." He rapped on the saddle with his knuckles. "Get to shinin'!"

"Yes, sir, Boss!" She laughed while she dipped her rag in the saddle soap.

He winked and made to leave but hesitated once more. "And keep an eye open for Shep. He's a good cowboy, but he's also trouble."

"So am I." She responded with a smile, and then resumed her scrubbing and buffing. JD laughed as he stepped into the night.

An explosion rocked her body and sent her sprawling to the rock-strewn ground. Seneca tumbled, disoriented. Acrid smoke cloaked her surroundings, blinding her. Her ears rang so shrilly she wanted to scream. Choking on the fumes and sand in her mouth and nose, she tried to rise, but pain lanced through her back and side. Groaning, she clutched her ribs. Blood seeped through the thick material of her fatigues.

"Not like this." She gritted her teeth and stood before dropping at once to her knees. The pain was incredible. With another groan, she found her footing and began looking about for human shapes. There was one body ten feet to her left. She crouched over while she tried to put aside her stabbing pain. Recognizing the bloodied face she whispered, "Valestro."

Valestro slowly opened his hazel eyes. He groaned loudly. He then tried to rise, but Seneca stayed his movement as she surveyed the damage to his lower body.

"Goddamned IED," she muttered. "I'm dragging you behind that wall." She jerked her head toward a crumbling wall twenty yards back.

"Twist—" He groaned again in pain.

"Shut up, Valestro…and watch the sky."

Behind the wall, another of her troop was already hunkered down.

"Twist," said the panting soldier with sweat streaming his face. He took in Valestro's condition. "Oh, shit—"

"Get a tourniquet on his leg, Hicks. Call for support." She slapped his dusty helmet to reassure herself as much as him, then headed out again into the black smoke.

She was moving slowly, but still stumbled over the soldier clutching a piece of metal protruding from her chest.

"Farris." Seneca dropped to her knees and grabbed Farris's hand. "Don't touch it." Farris took a rattling breath. It sounded as if the projectile had pierced her lung. "Leave it be. I'm carrying you back, and it's gonna hurt like hell." Seneca sat Farris up and reached under her knees. "Ready?"

The injured woman nodded and took another unnatural sounding breath, shorter this time. Seneca surged upward. Added to the pain in her right side, her right forearm and thigh burned. Pushing aside her torment, she tucked Farris against her bloody chest and moved as smoothly as possible back to the wall. After depositing Farris, she found several more soldiers hunkering behind the rubble. They tended to the wounded as best they could.

In the distance, through the hazy heat lying on the sand, a cloud of dust rose, kicked up by large vehicles. Their distress call was being answered, but the trucks were still several minutes out. Seneca was painfully aware that a lot could happen in a few seconds in the desert.

"Twist, we're missing three," Hicks said, calling her attention back to her troop.

She quickly looked around. Her stomach plummeted. "Hunter?" Hicks shook his head, and she took a deep breath. Hunter had been right beside her before the explosion. With any luck, he was just sprawled in the dirt somewhere, unconscious.

Another soldier spoke. "I came across Stephens and Ito on my way back, but…" She shook her head.

"I see." Seneca had never seen so clearly in all her life.

"You're bleeding bad," Hicks said. He reached for her, but she backed away.

"It's a scratch." Hurrying away again, she scrambled among the ruins of the small village as she sought other survivors. The dark heat pressed thick against her like a living thing. She wondered if there were guns pointed at her on the other side of the black banner of smoke.

❖

Seneca startled awake and leapt from her hammock, crouching low, ready for the attack. As she caught her breath and became aware of her surroundings, she registered the thunderstorm raging against the barn's tin roof.

Wiping away cold sweat from her face, she drew her shirt to her shoulders and stuffed her socked feet into her boots. She clomped to the hay loft door and cracked it open. The tops of the trees whipped back and forth as the rain lashed at the building. It was a hell of a storm. Seneca reasoned that a boom of thunder or the sound of rain on tin had triggered the nightmare. She grabbed her pack on the other side of the hammock.

Full of nervous energy, she retrieved her weapons. Sitting on the top step of the stairs leading below, she thoroughly cleaned the already clean guns and replaced them. After this ritual, Seneca got her hatchet and her knife and sharpened them both with her whetstone and oil. When they had been wiped clean and re-sheathed, she glanced about once more. She shouldn't disturb the horses, though she could hear several of them moving about while the storm continued; she was stuck upstairs. She sighed. Her mind's war would not allow Whitman, and her journaling was already complete. In a last-ditch effort to get some peaceful rest, she dug around in her bag for her emergency liquor.

She unscrewed the bottle's lid. Taking a swig of whisky, she sat again on the steps descending into the darkness. Flashes of lightning illuminated the building's interior; the organized equipment she had hung on the walls loomed like monsters in the night. Seneca preferred these monsters to those occupying her head and dreams.

She slugged another mouthful of alcohol and let the liquor burn a path to her belly as she replayed the day's events. The night was still young, might as well pass the time until the liquor did its work. Taking one last swallow before replacing the top, Seneca mused on the feisty Robyn Mason. She smiled as she remembered watching Dr. Mason work the room at the career fair, and the multiple facets of her demeanor, all represented with the same soft voice. *Huh.* Dr. Mason intrigued her. It had been a long while since she had really looked at a woman; was genuinely attracted. Experiencing that flash of heat for Robyn had certainly been a surprise.

Seneca shook her head as the liquor began to take hold. She wasn't planning on sticking around. Leaving Butterbean Hollow was inevitable. It was her pattern. Getting involved with anyone, least of all the boss's daughter, was a bad idea. An incredibly bad idea. She wanted to stay if she wanted, not be run from town. This place and most of the folks she'd met thus far suited her just fine. Despite her nightmares, she was content, for now. Seneca took a deep breath in and exhaled. She hadn't experienced contentment in a long time, either.

So, she wasn't ready to leave just yet, and there was the drive coming up. From her conversation with JD, he and Win needed all the help they could get. She needed the money, and she had her ambitions, too. She wanted to break in that horse. Win's challenge still inspired her pride. She wanted to break in that saddle. She'd spent long enough whipping it into shape. It had been an awful mess when Shep had pulled it from storage.

At the memory of Shep's smirking face, she frowned. Cowboys were known as a rough sort, but Shep was maybe a bit too much *cowboy trouble* for his own good. The way he had harassed Robyn rubbed her all the wrong way. *I don't like him, and I don't trust him.* She didn't let his comments about her get under her skin, but his disdain and dismissal of Robyn's work irritated her.

The rain had relented. Seneca pushed up from the stairs and traversed the creaking boards. She tucked her bottle back into her pack, and she shucked her boots to climb into her swaying bed once again. Robyn was not her problem. Robyn surely did not need her or anyone else to fight her battles. Or to protect her. Besides, she was done with all that. Closing her eyes, Seneca willed herself not to see Robyn's face—or any of the others.

Chapter Five

The next morning, Win helped Seneca bring the necessary tack into the round pen, then handed her a halter and lead rope. "I'll bang on the food can a few times. This mare never misses a meal."

"All right." Seneca shielded her eyes from the sun. There were several horses dotted here and there along the ridges and flats of the land; a few turned to her curiously. They seemed to sense she was new and were trying to judge her intent. Behind her came the sound of metal striking the bucket. Seneca smiled as she noted the previously disinterested horses now looked in her direction.

She stood solid as quarter horses of all colors and in various states of cleanliness made their way toward her. A few passed by without even acknowledging her; others stopped to sniff her for treats. Disappointed, they moved on. As the larger crowd dispersed, stragglers arrived. A tall mare with a black mane stood directly in Seneca's line of sight.

Seneca tilted her head at the horse and extended a hand. The mare sniffed and then bumped it gently with her nose as if in greeting. Seneca flecked freshly caked mud away from the horse's neck. Underneath was a pale cream color.

"That's her." Win's called affirmation sounded surprised. "How did you pick her out?"

"She picked me." Seneca walked around the mare's side, petting her as she slipped the lead rope over her neck and guided the halter over her face. The horse stood silent.

"What's her name?"

"Phoebe. And she rarely stands this still."

"We'll see how she is when I mount up." She clipped the rope to the loop beneath the halter and led the mare to the hitching post.

"Here." Win handed her one of her organized buckets of grooming tools. "I thought you might like to brush her first. She loves to roll in the mud and last night's weather made her happier than a pig in shit."

Seneca snickered. "She *is* awful dirty." Seneca tied a slip knot in the ring of the post before she pulled a curry comb from the bucket. She shook it at Phoebe. "I'm going to brush you. Don't get any ideas."

Win chuckled. "I need to step back to the barn for a minute. You good?"

"Yeah, I'm just going to work her over a bit," she murmured without looking up.

❖

Robyn closed her office door with a sigh. Her first appointment for the day had just left, and she somehow had an hour before the next one. Lucky for her, there was a mountain of paperwork to tend to. Movement outside her second story window caught her attention. The building afforded a commanding view of the rest of the ranch. Robyn frowned. Seneca had Phoebe in a halter and seemed set to start a training session. Surely someone had warned her...Robyn stopped and took a deep breath. It was not her business. She had plenty of work without worrying over what a cowhand—a temporary cowhand—was doing. Turning her back firmly on the window, Robyn began updating her notes and client treatment plans.

She worked steadily for five entire minutes before voices in the hallway interrupted her concentration. She generally kept her door open except when she had a client. Unfortunately, some days she found it difficult to focus, and today was one of those days. With a soft huff, Robyn crossed the room to shut the door smartly. When she turned back, her eyes were drawn again to the image of Seneca with Phoebe. Her father stood nearby next to a dark brown saddle.

"Nope," she said to the empty room. She was not going to get involved.

Seconds later, her weirdly sourced anxiety was a hard knot in her gut. *Damn it all.* She sighed heavily, then placed a call to her father only to reach his voice mail. She watched as Seneca finished brushing Phoebe. Seneca simply could not get on that mare. The beast was as unpredictable as they came. She called JD.

He had scarcely answered when Robyn spoke.

"Did you know your new hire has Phoebe tied to a hitching post?"

There was a tick of silence on the line. "No, but I'm sure she's only doing what Win told her to do. Did you call him?"

"He's not answering." Robyn tried to keep any accusation from her voice. She knew her father relied heavily on his instincts, as did JD, but the latter had a better understanding of what *liability* meant. Robyn could practically hear JD thinking.

"I'll go check it out. Don't need her getting hurt now, do we?"

"Absolutely not." Robyn realized she sounded as though she was personally invested in Seneca's well-being and changed her tone. "You might need her for the big drive."

"You bet," he said. "I'm going."

"Thanks, JD."

Robyn turned back to the window. Her father leaned on the fence, watching Seneca fit the bit into Phoebe's mouth. Why was she so concerned about Seneca? What did it matter if Phoebe threw her? Robyn tried to objectively analyze her motivations.

She'd been acquainted with Seneca Twist for a short amount of time. Sure, Seneca was capable and attractive and interesting— Interesting. That had to be it. Robyn watched the cowhand closely. The town was small, and though Robyn wouldn't characterize her life as dull, it certainly lacked a great deal of luster.

Her family and her work were her everything. Especially since she'd moved from Boise five years ago. Most of her days were spent with people she'd known for years. A newcomer, an attractive newcomer at that, was bound to catch her attention. That had to be the root of it. There was nothing else it could possibly be.

Robyn stood abruptly as JD approached her father and Seneca. She watched them talk a short time before Seneca took a blanket and settled it onto Phoebe's back. It looked like Seneca Twist still planned to ride. *Damn.*

❖

"What are you doing?" Robyn's voice rang across the yard as she strode toward the trio standing around Phoebe. All of them turned in her direction, even the mare.

"Seneca is going—"

Robyn spoke over her father. "Ms. Twist, I—"

"It's Seneca, please." Seneca's husky alto was calm while she continued her preparations.

"Seneca, I must insist you do not mount that horse."

At this, Seneca raised her brows. She turned to her bosses, but Robyn quickly cast them a glare, willing them to steer clear of the discussion.

"Hmm…Why not?" Seneca's tone was conversational.

"Because her last rider had a cast on his arm for weeks." Robyn came abreast of the fence, trying to hide she was a bit winded. "JD and my father may be willing to gamble with your safety, but I am not."

"Seneca is an experienced rider," her father said. "She's got no expectations for this horse. This could be our best chance to know if Phoebe can be worked."

"Robyn," JD said as Seneca adjusted the stirrups, "Twist knows what she's doing."

Regardless of their assurances and Seneca's confidence, Robyn was uneasy. "So did Tommy."

"Tommy was too eager. He's a good cowboy, but impatient."

"And can you attest to *her* patience?"

"She rode Lucy for a mile and a half. If that doesn't require patience, I don't know what does. Lucy's the slowest damned horse we've got."

"I'm still not convinced." Robyn turned to Seneca, searching her face for any evidence she would heed her argument. "Ms. Twist—Seneca, please. Can't you see this is foolhardy?"

"I can."

Shocked, Robyn froze. That quirky little smile was on Seneca's face. "What?"

"I agree with you. It is a bit foolhardy. Being 'round horses takes a certain tolerance for danger. Even the most experienced horse can spook or have a bad day. That's the nature of the business." Seneca gave the saddle a good tug. Phoebe chuffed.

"But Phoebe—"

"Is worth the risk," Seneca said. She deftly clipped the reins onto the bridle to pull them over the buckskin's head.

Damn this woman's cool rationale and sexy smile. Why will she not see reason?

"I don't see how."

Seneca put her left foot in the stirrup and hoisted herself astride the mare. The animal shifted and Seneca gave the reins a small tug and leaned back. "And that's why I'm the one in the saddle." Seneca nodded to Robyn before prompting the mare forward and away from the fence.

She does have a point. Seneca watched JD cross the wire. He met her at the gate. She looped the mare around as she waited for him to open it. When Seneca was a kid, she would jump on any damned horse. Just grab its mane and go. She knew now that the ground was hard and could do damage if anything went awry. She didn't blame Robyn for her concern. She smirked under the guise of checking her stirrups again. She certainly did tear across the ranch intending to keep her from harm. It was kind of cute, actually—and understandable. Only Win had seen her in a saddle, and what he'd seen hardly counted. They didn't know she wouldn't sue them if she was injured.

But she was here now. Seneca resolved to not fall and to not get injured. Hell, Dr. Mason might try to hurt her worse if she did.

JD opened the gate. "If she gets to stomping or you get nervous, just get off. You don't have anything to prove."

She smiled. Glancing back to see Robyn's alluring figure striding toward the arena, she nodded in Robyn's direction. JD followed her eyes. "I think I do."

In the arena, Seneca had Phoebe walk slowly around the oval. While Win and Robyn approached the wooden stands, JD had opted to stand just outside the gate.

"Take it slow," Win called, and she nodded. Seneca returned her attention to Phoebe, who plodded along.

"Here's the deal, Phoebe." The horse's ears quirked backward to the sound of her voice. "If you don't learn how to get with the program, they're going to sell you off. Now, I don't know these people well, but I can tell they're good folk. You have plenty of land to graze and good feed. You can't ask for better. Sure, it's a ranch and you've got to work, but hell, it's not like you're pulling a cart or ponying children." Phoebe tossed her head and the wind snatched at her dark mane.

"Just show them you can act civilly is all I'm asking. After that, you might get to do some trail riding, and see some places outside the pasture. Idaho has so many lovely sights and smells and sounds, and you're missing out because you can't behave. Seems a damned shame to me."

Seneca pulled the mare to a stop. She leaned forward in the saddle to praise Phoebe.

"Very nice, ma'am." Seneca stroked Phoebe's neck. The horse smacked her lips in response.

"Great, I've got your attention. Now, let's see what else you can do. How about a nice trot?" Seneca squeezed Phoebe back into a walk, then into a trot. "Good." She began posting along with the mare's gait. "Nice rhythm." Slowing her again, Seneca praised Phoebe more. "You're such a lovely girl."

Seneca continued in this manner for several more minutes. She tried hard to focus solely on Phoebe, but knowing Robyn watched from the stands made it difficult. She had to get it together for Phoebe's sake.

After about ten minutes, Phoebe began to show signs of impatience.

"Attitude," JD commented as they passed, but Seneca disagreed.

"I think it's restlessness!" she called to JD from the other side of the ring.

"Let's fix that, Phoebe."

Seneca urged her into a canter; the familiar sound of the three beats thrummed against her ear drums. After several laps, Seneca reined her back to a trot, and then into a walk. Seneca could swear Phoebe was happy to be exercised. She huffed and her great sides heaved with her breath.

Seneca spared a glance to the stands to find Robyn's eyes on her even as she conversed with Win. JD met her at the gate with a smile.

"That's the longest Phoebe has gone without giving the rider too much trouble." He stroked Phoebe's pale nose. "We might make use of her after all."

"She'd make a decent trail horse for an experienced rider." Seneca swung from the saddle as Win and Robyn made their way to the arena wall. Seneca couldn't resist calling to Robyn. "What did you think, Dr. Mason?"

"You can call me Robyn when there are no clients around, Seneca." Robyn studied her. "And it's good to see Phoebe in better form. But I still think you're foolish for mounting her."

"No doubt." Seneca smiled. *Stubborn woman.* "But I hope that you can see it was worth it."

Robyn tilted her head. She wasn't quite smiling, but her demeanor seemed playful. "I suppose we never know that which we never try." Robyn held her gaze longer than seemed proper. Robyn's soft voice and those bright amber eyes lit a familiar burn within Seneca's core.

Phoebe stamped her feet.

Seneca did not have an intelligent reply to Robyn's cryptic statement, and so was glad when JD drew her into conversation about the mare's history, and the future he now planned for her. She agreed to work with Phoebe a little each day she remained at the ranch.

Hopefully, she could quickly get the horse into riding shape. After turning Phoebe out, Seneca walked to Cliff's wagon lesson.

Seneca could not push away the image of Robyn watching her. The way the golden eyes had sunk into her had caused the sort of stir in her body that Seneca had forgotten. Her blood thrummed, and her pulse quickened. In that moment, she'd wanted to kiss Robyn, and to be kissed by her. She'd wanted more. She still wanted more. Whoa. Just last night she was content. *No kiss is going to happen.* Even if she wanted to welcome the attraction, which she decidedly did *not*, Seneca couldn't. Someday soon she would leave Butterbean Hollow the same as she had left every other town. Putting away her longing for Robyn's kisses, Seneca refocused on the young man in front of her and asked him, again, to repeat his question.

Chapter Six

Early Friday, Seneca descended the loft in a foul mood. She'd had *the dream* again but had not been able to get back to sleep, even with Whitman and whisky. At dawn, she'd finally given up and risen for her last day at the ranch. *Maybe.* Getting dressed, she discovered the jeans she wanted to wear had a hole in the backside. She hadn't provisioned much for her trek, and so was forced to reach deep into her bag for her rarely worn skinny jeans. She did a couple of squats, and bent side to side trying to loosen them up a little. Great for a bar, maybe, but not what she'd choose to wear to work.

Everything seemed harder today. As she hefted a bag of feed pellets onto her shoulder, it ripped, and she received an alfalfa baptism. Pellets washed the front of her flannel and hung in her pockets and sports bra. She gritted her teeth. Now she was a walking feed trough. She retrieved the broom to sweep the mess and put the food in a pail. Small favor, there was no ten-second rule for horse feed.

When Seneca started to clean the stock tank, every horse in the pasture predictably raised its head and gave her a hopeful sniff.

"Don't even think about it!" She removed the large aluminum tank's plug.

Despite the warning, one mare plodded up. She stood and looked Seneca square in the eye. Seneca ignored her, using a cloth to wipe inside the tank as the water drained. In Seneca's periphery the horse took a single step forward and looked hard at her again. Seneca couldn't figure out what she wanted.

"What's your problem?"

Seneca wiped the last bit of green scum away. Righting herself, she hung the cloth over the fence, re-plugged the tank, and started the water. Still the mare watched her.

As the tank filled and the horse stood its ground, Seneca stared back. She was a dapple-gray Appaloosa. Her coat gleamed almost silver in the morning sunlight and her charcoal socks were visible through the mud caked about her ankles. Her mane and tail, too, were charcoal and one lock of it fell into intelligent eyes. Seneca looked her over more critically. She was on the smaller side; Seneca guessed she was fourteen hands at the most. But the beautiful horse was sturdily built. Her powerful hindquarters were evidence of her stock horse breeding.

Seneca shut the water off and stepped to the horse. "Can I help you?"

The mare seemed to think the question less than rhetorical because she began sniffing and nibbling at Seneca's jacket and face. "I know I smell like food," Seneca said.

She brought her hands up to stroke the mare's face, and the horse stilled. *Now, that's odd behavior for this breed.*

"How do you feel about cows, ma'am?"

Seneca had been thinking about the upcoming drive. She knew the ranch was pressed for help, so she had considered sticking around for it. Unfortunately, she did not have a stock horse to ride consistently. Neither Lucy nor Phoebe was an option, though Phoebe might make it into the remuda if she kept improving. Added, most of the horses that belonged to the ranch were therapy horses, which weren't quite so bold, and trail-riding horses, a bit longer in the tooth. This mare didn't seem to be in either category.

Seneca backed away, and the horse came forward a half-step to close the distance. She repeated the action to the left and right and watched the horse's reaction. Having partially proven her theory of the mare's herding instinct, she patted the horse on the neck. The mare's breed qualified her as a trail horse, but her age and reactions indicated she could be more.

"I like you." The animal nudged her, and Seneca leaned in contentedly, so they touched foreheads.

"Seneca?" Win called from the fence. "What's going on?"

"Just finished cleaning the tank, but this one won't leave me alone. Who is she?"

"Annie Oakley." He stroked his mustache. "She been following you around and staring at you?"

Seneca grinned. "Yeah, it's a little unnerving, truth be told."

"I don't know why she does that. She's supposed to be from herding stock. Kevin has worked with her some, but no one rides her consistently."

"Cliff is all good with the cart." Seneca tried to sound casual, but she was eager to get on the back of this horse. "I've got a few things to do this afternoon, but I started early and have an hour or so to spare. Can I take her 'round the ring? I might ride her during the drive if it works out. If that's all right with you, of course."

Win smiled broadly. "Glad to hear you might be staying. Kevin uses a Hackamore bit with her."

"I'll grab my gear." Seneca patted Annie Oakley on her way to the tack room.

"I'll be right back, girl."

That morning, Robyn arrived to work early. Both the successes and challenges that transpired at the career fair created extra work for her. Beyond the impact of the fight for Noah and Nathan, the apprenticeships meant there were slots opening at the ranch. Robyn had to start the process to fill them. And she could not stay late today. The family was throwing a party at Jack's to celebrate JD's birthday, and she was on set-up duty.

She unlocked the building and let herself in. The ranch was quiet save for the sound of the wind whipping around the corners of the structure. Her heels clicked rhythmically on the stairs. Robyn hoped to find her father at the barn to discuss a few party details, but he wasn't around. She left a note on the drafting table asking him to call. He would check there.

As she turned to leave, Robyn heard a faint voice. She listened more closely as the wind died. It was singing. She winced. Awful singing. She approached the loft window scanning the back pasture to find the source. Beautiful Seneca with a pretty horse graced her sight.

Robyn watched as Seneca brushed the horse, patting the animal with the opposite hand on each pass. Robyn thought she recognized a Don Williams tune. Seneca's voice was not outstanding, but on closer hearing, it was clear and soothing with a fair pitch. The horse certainly didn't seem to mind. Robyn stepped closer to the scene.

Seneca's posture was relaxed as her hands moved fluidly over the horse's body. Robyn wondered what it would be like to have those hands roam her body. A flash of heat seared her and somehow her view wasn't close enough. Robyn headed downstairs to exit the back door.

Robyn knew Seneca could not see her from her position and so she crept forward to get a better vantage point. By this time, Seneca was adjusting the blanket and saddle pad. She then took hold of her ancient, but well-shined saddle and placed it across the Appaloosa's back. Seneca shifted it around a bit, but like all experienced horse people, she seemed to have plopped it down in just the right place the first time. The horse's silvery-gray color shone brightly in the morning sun and Robyn noticed the mare had a charcoal forelock waving in the middle of her eyes. As Seneca went about her preparations, she talked and sang to the horse, working with steady and patient hands.

Robyn was mesmerized. Both horse and human seemed to communicate on a higher plane while Seneca led the mare around the pen and worked on her stopping and turning. Robyn had been around horses and cowboys her entire life, but there was something in the way that Seneca Twist handled the animals that was unlike anything she'd ever experienced.

After a few minutes of leading, Seneca mounted easily. The mare quirked her ears around. As Robyn watched, Seneca began a process like the one she had used with Phoebe.

After several minutes, Seneca was smoothly posting along with the gait of the horse's canter. Robyn was again struck by the fluidity of Seneca's movements. Her desire flared as she watched Seneca's thighs and hips flexing rhythmically beneath her form-fitting denim.

Tearing her eyes away and trying to settle the flutter in her stomach, Robyn checked the time. *Shit.* She'd spent a full half hour watching Seneca work with the horse, burning through precious time. Robyn could not work late today. She turned to leave just as JD rounded the corner.

"Well, good morning." He smiled. "What are you up to?"

"Um…I needed to drop something off for Dad…And I watched Seneca with a pretty Appaloosa."

"Is that so? What did you think?"

Robyn wasn't certain if he was referring to her impressions of Seneca or the horse. Robyn responded to the less treacherous query. "Seneca clearly has a way with the horses. But I don't think I've seen anyone on this mare before."

"An Appaloosa, you said?" She nodded. "Could be Annie Oakley. She's supposed to be a stock horse, but Kevin's the only one that's worked with her. The other cowboys are partial to their geldings. Less temperamental, they believe."

"Seneca doesn't seem deterred by a mare. You saw how she was with Phoebe." *Wait, when did I become an advocate for the mystifying Ms. Twist?*

"Good point." He rubbed his hands together absently. "Well, I didn't think we'd be able to use Annie so soon, but if Seneca's taken a shine to her, maybe we can see her in action. I'd like to know what she can do with a herd."

"Especially with the big drive coming."

"And we've got that twenty head of heifers that just got donated. I was planning to ask Shep to pen them for branding, but I might ask Twist instead."

"Why not ask them both?"

JD frowned. "I don't think Shep would be too pleased to work with Twist."

"I didn't mean to have them work together."

JD's expression cleared. "Oh, you mean, make it a competition?" He rubbed his chin. "Could be fun."

"Like a small exhibition," she said as the idea took form. "See who can get ten penned in the least amount of time."

JD's eyes twinkled with mischief. "That's a right good idea, Robyn."

"Hey, I don't have a doctorate for nothing." She winked and JD hooted while clapping her on the shoulder.

"Well, I didn't know you had it in you." She laughed with him while he teased. "I'll set the *exhibition* for this afternoon. Bring your gang by around three, yeah?"

"Sure." She smiled as he headed into the barn whistling.

"A penning exhibition?" Seneca regarded Win. "What for?"

"Just to have a bit of fun and see what that horse you were working with this morning can do."

"So, who will I be working with?"

"We'll pick teams when we get ready to do the comp—when we get ready."

Seneca laughed and Win looked at her quizzically. "No one will work with me. They haven't seen me ride."

"Hmm." He stroked his mustache. "You might be surprised, cowgirl, you might be surprised."

"Just a bit of fun?" Seneca questioned quietly when Win arrived at the corral. There were at least thirty people milling about, ready for a show.

"Exhibitions are rare here. Word gets 'round." He sounded reassuring, but Seneca thought she saw his mustache twitch a bit. She ducked her head, irritated at the situation, but not willing to offend her boss.

"Very well, it would seem." Seneca caught Robyn staring at her from across the corral. She disliked being the center of attention and would rather not do this. Her hold tightened on Annie's lead rope for a moment, but the horse bumped into her gently. She loosened her grip.

"You're right, Annie. I don't have anything to prove." Seneca exhaled while reaching to softly stroke Annie on her nose. "You and I ought to do well enough."

Then, Collin Shepherd swaggered up and sneered. "You ready for some healthy competition, Twist?"

"I reckon. I don't care so much for this event, but I'd like Annie Oakley to have the chance to prove herself."

"Annie Oakley has hardly been outside the pasture, and you think she's going to pen cows?"

"Stranger things have happened."

Shep laughed and walked away, mumbling something about women and their fantasies. *Asshole.*

JD walked up. "So, this is your girl?"

She smiled against the knot of anxiety in her stomach and stroked Annie's nose again. "Yeah, this is my girl."

"It looks like Shep has picked his team." He nodded over to the three cowboys who stood around jawing.

Seneca squinted at the other cowboys milling about. A lean man taller than her and with freckled skin raised his hand in greeting. Surprised, she smiled as Kevin made his way over. "Picked your two yet, Twist?"

"No, I haven't."

"Well, I'd like to be one of them."

"Sure." She was relieved; Kevin was an experienced cowboy. "Know anyone else?"

"All right, let's see." Kevin looked through the cowboys assembled. "How about Cliff? He's not been here long, but he's a hard worker and he takes real good care of his horse."

"Yeah, I know Cliff. We're working together on the wagon. That sounds good to me." Smiling, the fear she wouldn't be able to scrounge up teammates dissipated. Kevin and Cliff were both respectable, hardworking cowboys. She could hardly do better.

"All right, we'll get ready. Annie is a decent horse in my experience. She already seems raring to go." He shook her hand.

"Thanks, Kevin."

"Don't thank me yet." He smiled. "Shep and his team are going to be good."

"It wouldn't be a *competition* if they weren't," she replied evenly. Then, mustering confidence she wasn't sure of, she winked. He grinned back and headed toward Cliff.

Shep's team was good. They were better than good. It took them just under four minutes to pen ten cows. They worked together well, trusting Shep to direct them. Seneca admitted that Shep, asshole or not, did seem to have it well in hand. As she, Kevin, and Cliff lined up at the gate and the other ten cows were let in, Win approached.

"Just trust your horse. She'll know what to do."

Seneca figured she must look as nervous as she was.

"Right." She wiped her sweaty palms on her jeans and mounted Annie.

He looked at her team. "Communicate."

"Yes, sir," Kevin and Cliff replied.

Win patted the mare. "Do your job, Annie Oakley."

Seneca looked at him. "Thanks, Win," she said, and meant it. Whether he intended to or not, Seneca appreciated Win giving her a moment to regain her composure.

The three of them went to work when the gate opened. Within seconds, Seneca confirmed Annie Oakley was a true cow horse. She was quick, agile, and aware of the animals she was herding. Seneca lightly guided the horse while communicating to Kevin and Cliff, who worked on her flanks. Together, they had half the herd in the pen in about forty seconds. Seneca wordlessly signaled Kevin, who broke off from the team. The other cows were scattered; Seneca and Cliff alternated passes against the backs of two cows to head them toward the gate where Kevin stood guard. When they were close, Seneca signaled Cliff, who switched to work with Kevin on the final pen in. There couldn't be much time left. Seneca gritted her teeth. "Annie, push!" She urged the horse into the last three cows, slapping her thigh and whooping at them.

The animals ran from her in a blind panic. Just as they reached the pen gates, one broke off. She groaned, not liking but accepting the fair defeat. Then, Kevin appeared and flanked the small group. Both of them forced the cows to change direction and scamper into the pen. When the gate closed, the audience erupted. Yes! It felt faster than Shep's team, anyway. She found Win and JD clapping. Seneca slapped Kevin's back, then Cliff's shoulder. "Good work, team! Thank you."

"Damn, woman," Cliff said. "You're better than Shep."

"Don't let him catch you saying that." Kevin's eyes scanned the crowd. "He and Tommy are definitely pissed they got beat by a couple of gays and a new guy."

"Let them be pissed." Cliff's eyes flashed as he dismissed Shep and Tommy.

JD came toward them with his stopwatch. "Three forty-one. You won by eleven seconds." There was another round of celebration among the trio before Seneca slid from Annie Oakley's back. As soon as her boots hit the arena's packed earth, Shep strode forward. Seneca glanced around at the crowd. Whatever scene the cowboy was about to make would be public. She steeled herself for the confrontation.

"I would like a rematch." His request sounded more like a demand. "Kevin guarded the gate the whole time. That was a cheap trick."

"That's a strategy some teams use in penning." Seneca stood her ground. "Not a trick."

"It's lazy at the very least. *Me* and *my* crew worked harder. We didn't cut corners."

"There is a difference between cutting corners and being smart." Seneca tried to let the insult roll off, but she did not appreciate being called lazy. It was one of the few things that truly set her off. "This wasn't about style points, and it's not a Wild West show here, Shep." Seneca couldn't keep a bite of derision from her voice.

"I still want a rematch."

Seneca looked at JD. "I'm good for whatever, Boss. Annie can always use the practice."

JD shook his head. "We've got the heifers in the pen where I want them. No sense getting them all riled up again." His look seemed to will Shep to stand down. "No rematch, son. Your team lost. Next time we have new cattle, we can—"

But Shep's face flushed dark red. He turned about and strode away.

"Asshole."

"So right, Cliff." Kevin's voice was a soft mumble, too, as Seneca turned again to JD.

"I'm sorry to cause you trouble, Boss."

"Don't apologize." JD clenched his jaw. "It's about time I set him straight on a few things, anyway." He shook his head.

She changed the subject. "Well, what do you think of Annie?"

JD grinned at the horse. "She's a fine animal. Probably one of the three quickest horses we have on the ranch. I'd like to see her work with Cash; none is quicker than him."

"That's your Morgan gelding, right?"

"Yup. Best damn horse I've ever had. All-around sort of fella."

"Well, I'm sure after the drive they'll get to do some work." *Until then, Annie Oakley, you are my ride.*

Seneca led the mare from the arena. She was happy to be staying in Butterbean Hollow a little longer, and she'd enjoyed winning with her team, but she wanted out of the spotlight. Seneca tied Annie Oakley to the hitching post and removed her tack to brush her.

Robyn expected Shep to be sore about the loss, but the tantrum was a bit much. The way he stormed off from JD in front of the entire crowd would mean trouble in the future, she was certain. There were a few loyal to the young cowboy. They followed Shep because he looked good in the saddle and had a charismatic air. But most of the men knew JD was to be respected and would disapprove of Shep's behavior.

Robyn watched Seneca's gorgeous form disappear around the structure with Annie Oakley walking calmly behind her. She had perched on the edge of her seat as Seneca had led the trio to victory. She'd never seen a more exceptional penning team. Seneca was an exceptional leader, and she was an exceptional woman. More than eye candy. She wanted to know more about the lovely stranger.

Robyn made her way to the hitching posts beside the barn and found Seneca brushing the mare. "You were right." Seneca turned.

"About what?"

"You *can* ride better than Shep." She came to stand near Annie. "And Annie Oakley's a better cow horse than most we've got here. But we didn't know that until *you* rode her. You and Annie are a good pair."

"Well, she did most of the work." Seneca demurred as Robyn scratched between the horse's ears. Annie Oakley closed her eyes.

Robyn wondered at Seneca's humility and studied her. There were a few tendrils of dark hair coming loose from her braid and it did nothing but make her more attractive.

"Shep seemed pretty put out."

Seneca's face flitted into a brief smile. "Yeah, he wanted a rematch."

"For what reason?" Robyn laughed.

"Seemed to think our strategy was cheating. Leaving a guard at the gate didn't occur to him."

"I'm sure it didn't."

"That's the way I've always penned. You try to nab half the herd in the first go, and then leave a guard at the gate. All I did was point, and Kevin knew what I meant for him to do. It doesn't make sense to use everyone and leave the cows free to leave the pen."

"No, it doesn't," Robyn murmured. She was entranced by the low, husky quality of Seneca's voice.

"They may be dumb, but they're instinctual and they *will* get loose." Seneca continued working Annie over while speaking. "The trick is keeping them in there while not getting in the way of the others coming in. Guarding the gate is a hell of a lot harder than Kevin made it look. He's a fine cowboy; he and Cliff both."

"That they are." Robyn wanted to keep Seneca's attention. This was the most she'd heard her speak. Seneca's voice was sweet and salty, sticky—like salted caramel. Robyn was mesmerized by the passion wrapped in that slow, husky drawl. "And they had a great leader."

Seneca paused her work and met Robyn's gaze. "Are you surprised?"

Robyn smiled. "Not surprised. I guess you seem so…" She searched for the right word. "Phlegmatic about everything. You're calm, stoic—you go with the flow, mostly. To see you on that horse animated and totally in charge was…" She trailed off, attempted to control her arousal, and exhaled. *Hot.* "Unexpected."

Seneca seemed uncomfortable but resumed grooming Annie as she untangled a lock of her mane. "I like this work and being in charge is something I'm familiar with."

"I'm sure it is." After a moment, Robyn wondered why Seneca had stopped grooming Annie again to look at her with a half-smile and brows raised.

"Oh, um…" Realizing her gaffe, Robyn bowed her head as blood rushed to her face. There was no taking back the unintentionally suggestive comment. *Well, maybe unintentionally said aloud.* She exhaled softly and braved a look into Seneca's eyes, preparing to make a dismissive joke. But the sunlight hit them just right, and Robyn realized they were a deep, mossy green color. She'd somehow mistaken them for brown in the dim light the other day. Her breath hitched in her throat. This woman just kept surprising her.

Seneca tilted her head. "What?"

"Nothing, I just noticed something."

"What?" Seneca seemed suspicious.

"It's not important." Robyn went back to scratching Annie. "You should come by Jack's tonight. We're throwing JD a surprise birthday party."

Seneca chuckled. "He knows."

"What? No!" She fake-pouted. "What makes you say that?"

"He just knows. You can't get the jump on a man like him."

"We're not trying to *jump* him." Robyn put her hands on her hips. "We're trying to surprise him."

Seneca looked at Robyn's stance and then laughed outright. "It's the same thing."

"Well, anyway, you should come. Most of the cowhands will be there, and his friends and family, of course..." *And I'll be there.*

"Oh?"

"There'll be free food."

"Sure, I'll stop by then."

"Good." Robyn nodded as the wind kicked up. The cold was sharper than it had been earlier. Seneca quickly turned her collar up against it. Robyn wondered if Seneca had a thick work jacket. Probably not. "Well, I've got to be going. Congratulations on your win."

"Thanks."

"See you tonight."

"Sure." Seneca gave a brief nod before turning back to Annie.

Robyn glanced at Seneca and Annie Oakley again as she backed away. Seneca would need better boots, a work jacket, and thermals for the cold months. Robyn headed back to the corral, looking forward to the evening for at least one added reason.

CHAPTER SEVEN

A fter a quick shower, Seneca selected her best clothing for JD's party. She had immediately washed and dried the denim she had been wearing that afternoon so she could wear them again. The snug jeans were a better choice for the evening. Pulling on a flannel shirt, Seneca replayed the day's events.

The exhibition had been more than she had bargained for, but she was pleased with the outcome. She wasn't looking for a fight with Shep, but if Win told her to pen cattle, she'd be damned if she didn't do her best to get the job done. It wasn't in her nature to slack off for the sake of other people's egos, least of all for a character like Shep. What was he thinking, disrespecting the boss? Seneca shook her head. Well, at least Annie had proven herself a gem of a horse. Her closer camaraderie with Kevin and Cliff was a great result of all the excitement, too.

It was the conversation with Robyn that had been the most interesting, however. Seneca straightened her gold-toe socks as she ruminated. Seneca was a little rusty, but something in Robyn's voice had been teasing. It was as though Robyn had been...flirting. She couldn't decide if it had been intentional. That shade of red in her face almost matched her hair, so probably not entirely. Either way, Robyn's words had certainly sent a warm jolt through her system.

The real question wasn't if Robyn had been flirting. It was what she was going to do about it. *Absolutely nothing, remember?* Flirting back was an option and incredibly appealing but would probably give Robyn the wrong idea. The sort of idea that could end badly for everyone involved.

Seneca shook her head. She would not pursue Robyn. There was no room for that in her life. Seneca wanted—no, *needed simple,* and Robyn Mason had *complicated* written all over her.

Seneca stood to contemplate her weapons. She might as well be naked without a firearm, but she surely didn't need to be fully strapped at a party. Deciding to leave the Hi-Power in the bag, she put on her ankle strap, then pulled on her boots and strapped the Nano in. Seneca smoothed the front of her flannel and descended the loft stairs.

Just as she reached the bottom step, the sound of tires on gravel alerted her to Win's arrival. He had offered to pick her up for the party. A woman was riding shotgun, so Seneca climbed into the back.

"Hi," the woman said even before Seneca closed herself in. "I'm Joan Mason."

"Nice to meet you." Joan seemed kind.

"I heard you won the team penning competition this afternoon." She cut her eyes to Win. "Did you take out an ad in the paper?"

Win and Joan laughed. "I considered it." Win winked over his shoulder. "But I decided against it."

"I'm glad." Seneca sat back to buckle her seat belt. "I don't think Shep would take too kindly to it."

When her father and his wife got there, Robyn raised a hand in greeting while continuing to help prepare for JD's arrival. She was glad to see her father was on time. She was even happier to see that he'd brought Seneca with him. When Seneca stepped through the door, Robyn paused, and drank her in. Heat crept up her neck. Something primal had the rest of her blood rushing south.

A surge of arousal engulfed Robyn as she sized Seneca up fully. Seneca had a strong jaw and high cheekbones that seemed a bit reddened by the wind and sun she'd been working in that week. The dark jeans she wore encased lean, muscular legs that Robyn knew could rise and fall in mesmerizing rhythm as she rode and wrangled.

The way she smiled softly as her father offered to take her coat was genuine and honest.

Seneca was gorgeous, capable, and hardworking. Robyn respected this. For all her father's flaws, he had instilled in her an appreciation for individuals who humbly did their work well. Seneca struck her as this sort of woman, and it made her doubly attractive.

Robyn watched as Cliff greeted Seneca and pulled her into conversation. She was certain Seneca knew she'd been flirting with her earlier that afternoon. As much as she was convinced she would like to pursue the attraction between them, Seneca had to want that as well. Robyn wasn't certain she did. The not knowing frustrated her to the extreme. She would get to the bottom of it tonight. She needed to *know*.

Seneca glanced around the bar and found an amber gaze scanning her. Unless she was much mistaken, Robyn Mason was giving her a hungry once-over. The flirtatious tone Robyn had used earlier echoed in her head. She dismissed the thought; she'd obviously been on the road too long to think this amazing woman could be interested in her. Robyn was the ranch psychologist, and she was—at best—a wandering cowhand. She revisited her ruminations of not even an hour before. No matter her attraction to Robyn, and no matter the betrayal of her body, long looks across a room were about as far as this would go. Even if Robyn was interested in her, it couldn't go further. The idea of drawing close to Robyn, of being open with her... that sort of vulnerability panicked her, anyway. There were truths she would prefer not to be known and if she kept her distance, Robyn need never know them. Never mind that Robyn looked delicious in her plum business slacks and matching blazer.

Earl greeted Seneca at the bar with a tumbler of Maker's Mark. "I heard you put Shep in his place today."

She brought the glass to her mouth to hide the proud grin. "Our team beat his by eleven seconds."

"That's a solid win. Who was on your team?"

"Kevin and Cliff."

"Really, now? Did they do well?" He absently wiped the bar.

"Yes, indeed. Kevin is quick. He anticipates things." She savored a sip of whisky on her tongue. "Cliff has more to learn, but he has a great instinct and a great connection with his horse. He was certainly a fine teammate."

"I like Kevin," Earl said.

"And Cliff?"

"Cliff is my nephew."

Seneca lifted her brows in surprise, but after further study, noticed they had similar features. She considered the Masons and their ties to the ranch and town. "Family runs deep around here, doesn't it?"

"You have no idea." Earl moved away to answer the call of another patron.

Seneca turned when an older woman took the barstool beside her. She met a pair of keen blue eyes that sparkled like spring water. "Hi, I'm Sarah."

"Hello." Seneca quietly studied her new bar mate. Sarah had a willowy frame and a warm smile. Her thick, graying hair was barely restrained by a few bobby pins, and this gave Seneca the sense that Sarah was comfortable in her own skin.

"I heard you're quite the horsewoman."

Seneca chuckled. "You and everyone else."

Sarah motioned to Earl, who retrieved the Hendricks and poured a generous serving in a glass before topping it with lime and tonic water. Impressed, Seneca simply sipped.

Sarah took a small swallow of her libation. She continued the conversation. "Well, you see, you're a bit of an oddment here." Sarah motioned over the room. "You're a woman, and you outrode a man—and Shep specifically. That hasn't happened much in this small town."

Seneca shrugged. "My team won. Shep will get on with his life, and everyone else will forget it."

"I think you overestimate Collin." She sipped her gin and tonic. "For the record, I'm glad you beat him. He needed a dose of humility, but I doubt it will do him any lasting good."

It seemed best to not comment.

"So, tell me about the horse that everyone is talking about."

Seneca grinned into her whisky. "She's a fine animal. Strong, quick, athletic. You couldn't ask for a better horse. Annie Oakley is her name."

"Oh, I like that." Sarah smiled approvingly. "That's the perfect name for a stock horse."

"She's not your typical mare. She's calm, but when she gets the scent of those cows, she transforms."

"Well, Win was impressed."

"He's the one who told you, too?" Seneca sighed. "Win has been telling everyone within earshot."

"He's never been one for keeping quiet, at least not about other people's business. Even when we were kids, he was the first bird to sing."

"You grew up together?"

"We're siblings."

"Wow." Chuckling, she looked about. "So, you're Robyn's aunt?" Small-town communities could be a double-edged sword. People would give you their last dollar but expect you to do the same. It was the expectations that often made her uneasy.

"And Jack's wife."

"What?"

"Surprised?"

"Well, I…" Seneca was at a loss for words. Jack seemed gruff, and Sarah's energy was so welcoming.

"It's okay." Sarah raised her drink in a toast. "We are a bit of an oddment, too."

Seneca backpedaled. "I didn't mean to be rude—"

"You weren't, dear." Sarah laughed. "Odd fits just fine with me and this family."

Seneca didn't know what to say so she swallowed the last bit of her whisky and put the glass on the bar. "Well, it was nice meeting you. If you'll excuse me, though, I'm going to find Win and ask him to tone it down a bit."

She started toward Win, who watched at the window. She passed Robyn chatting with friends and tried to ignore the blaze of heat in her core. Just as she reached Win, he called over the crowd. "All right, everyone, hide! JD is here!"

There was a great kerfuffle as everyone scrambled for a hiding spot. In seconds, it was Win, Robyn, Earl, and Seneca standing in an empty bar. Earl wiped the counter while Robyn seemed frozen in the middle of the room.

"Oh—" Robyn looked around.

"Get her!" Win grumbled to Seneca, who grabbed Robyn and pulled her underneath the nearest table, hastily covering them with the red and black gingham tablecloth.

"Seneca," Robyn began whispering, but Seneca gently hushed her and pulled her closer.

Robyn was nearly sitting in her lap under the table. Seneca wasn't sure where she ended, and Robyn began. She could only process how good it felt to have Robyn's amazing backside pressed into her center. She fought hard not to fidget as arousal again thrummed through her.

Robyn put a hand on Seneca's forearm, and then frowned. When she opened her mouth again, Seneca whispered close to her ear.

"You're going to give us away."

Seneca's breath stirred the auburn hairs along Robyn's neck, and Robyn shuddered. Seneca experienced the hard tremor in the center of her being. Her stomach clenched tight in reaction. Her heart sped up. Robyn squirmed in her lap, and the friction nearly broke her self-control. It was all Seneca could do to keep the rumble of a groan locked in her throat. With an enormous amount of willpower, Seneca redirected her focus to JD's party.

The door opened. She could picture the scene clearly based on the sound of boots on floorboards. The guest of honor had arrived.

"Wow, not many folks here tonight." JD sounded genuinely surprised.

"I guess the wind is keeping them at home," Win said. "I invited the winning team, so I suppose they'll be along anytime now. Ready for your beer?"

This was the designated phrase. At these words, everyone was to jump from their hiding places and shout—

"Surprise!" Seneca and Robyn burst from under the table near the same time as most of the other partygoers. Overall, the effect was good; there were only a few late bloomers. Looking at JD's face, Seneca could tell he had not been expecting a surprise of this magnitude.

JD looked at his wife, Rosemary, who grinned at his dumbfounded expression. "Well, I'll be damned." JD shook Win's hand and backslapped others as Jack presented a rare smile and a massive meatloaf topped with a dangerous number of candles. "Thank you so much," JD said. Rosemary kissed him lovingly on the cheek as he wiped at his eyes. He took a deep breath. "This is too much."

Jack leaned on the bar. "Quit your sputtering, old man, and blow out the damned candles before they start a fire. We're all hungry!"

Everyone laughed, and JD got to his task. It took several tries, but he managed it in the end. The bar was laden with potatoes, greens, and macaroni and cheese, and everyone served themselves buffet style. Seneca was eager to try the huckleberry pie.

After dinner, Win unearthed a karaoke machine and several of the partygoers were in front singing badly. Seneca, who had her fill of the revelry for the moment, escaped to the empty back porch. After having spent so much time alone on the road, the crowded bar was suffocating. She was all for a good time, but the air was a bit too thick, and the backslaps were getting old. Uncomfortable with the big to-do everyone was making over the exhibition, Seneca was glad for the quiet.

Leaning on the pitted, wooden railing, Seneca looked over a small courtyard. She couldn't see the water in the darkness, but she could hear its unmistakable gurgling. The creek beyond must be the same one she'd camped beside the first night in town, and at least connected to the creek running on the ranch's lower forty.

With a deep breath, she tilted her face to the sky. The smell of rain was on the air. The stars were obscured from view by the clouds. It wasn't quite cold enough to snow, but she was not warm. The chill prickled on her exposed skin and her exhaled breath hung in the air in frosty puffs.

Still, the cold was a welcome change from the heat inside. There had been too many bodies, too much movement. Seneca enjoyed the people in Butterbean Hollow and had even had the pleasure of getting to know Kevin and Cliff better over a couple of drinks, but she was a true introvert and needed the quiet to recalibrate. More than that, she was rusty at socializing. She'd forgotten what it was to have so many people call her name or smile at her familiarly. There was a part of her that enjoyed the experience, and a part of her that rejected the notion of being accepted and settled in.

As she mused, she heard the door open behind her and turned to see Robyn exit the bar. "Hey," Robyn said.

"Hey." Seneca leaned back on the rail. All was quiet for a beat. "Look, I'm sorry for manhandling you," Seneca said.

Robyn waved her off. "Don't worry about it. I froze up."

"Yeah, well, I just wanted to make sure I didn't unnerve you or anything."

Robyn seemed confused. "Unnerve? Why would I be unnerved?"

"I mean, I wasn't gentle…"

Robyn's features smoothed, and a small smile played across her lips. "What makes you think you would have to be gentle?"

Seneca's pulse quickened at the suggestive tone in Robyn's voice. Again, Seneca wondered if she was flirting intentionally. It was hard to believe a woman like Robyn would do anything accidentally.

At a loss, Seneca said the first thing that came to mind. "Well, I just mean because you're so small—"

"Small?"

"Well, yeah."

"I'm not small."

"You are in comparison to me."

Robyn bristled and folded her arms. "Just because I'm not built like an Amazon doesn't mean I'm weak."

"Weak?" Seneca shook her head. "That's not what I said. I just wanted to make sure you didn't get the wrong idea."

"Oh? And what sort of idea would that be?"

Seneca felt a flush rise in her neck and face. She must be doing a poor job explaining given the tension between them. *What sort of idea* might *that be?* "Well, that I would take advantage of you in some way."

"Oh." Robyn's arms unfolded and her demeanor softened. "I don't think that. You're a good person."

A wry chuckle bubbled from Seneca's throat. "You don't know me."

"I suppose I don't know your history or quirks or any of that, but I am getting to know the measure of you by your interactions at the ranch."

The wind whispered around them, and Seneca shoved her hands in her pockets. She was exposed. Robyn Mason seemed to see straight through her. The unfamiliar sensation put Seneca on edge. "That's just like a psychologist to analyze."

Robyn smiled. "Yes, I suppose it is. But I've always enjoyed puzzles. I've always analyzed people, they're so—"

"Confusing."

"Fascinating."

Seneca shook her head. "Maybe some people are fascinating, but I think most are pretty simple."

"You mean you think of *yourself* as simple."

Robyn's statement hit her in the gut. Seneca worried that Robyn could know her mind. Trying to recover a bit of distance, Seneca turned to sarcasm. "Is that your professional opinion, Doctor?" She absently rubbed the scars on her forearm. When she realized what she was doing, she stopped.

"It's from shrapnel, isn't it?"

Robyn wore an odd expression that Seneca couldn't quite place. There was a long pause as she decided what to divulge before she nodded. "Yeah."

"Iraq?"

"Afghanistan."

"Ah." She looked at her again. "You were an officer or something?"

Seneca swallowed her surprise. Robyn must be a hell of a shrink to be able to guess so much. "Yeah. After the IED that did this, I trained soldiers. I came home six months ago and started walking about three months ago."

"I could tell that you were used to leadership from the way you worked with the cowboys today. I also felt the gun on your ankle and noticed the scars when we were under the table tonight."

"You're very perceptive." Seneca glanced to the door. "I appreciate you not telling anyone. I'm proud of serving my country, but I don't like to answer questions about it."

"I respect that."

"You do?"

Robyn smiled. "I'm not a shrink all the time. And even if I was, all good psychologists know when to pry and when to back off."

"I don't need a psychologist."

"Good, I'm not taking any new patients right now."

Seneca grinned playfully. "Don't think you could handle me?"

Robyn paused, and her eyes roamed over Seneca's face and body slowly. She smirked. "I'm sure I'm capable, but my time slots are reserved for teenage boys, and you're certainly not an adolescent." She smiled broadly and raised a brow. "Nor a boy, thank goodness."

Now, there was no denying Robyn was flirting. It was clear to Seneca that Robyn would gladly demonstrate her abilities if provided the opportunity. Seneca was agitated. Robyn was sexy as hell, but Seneca could not allow them to take the attraction any further than friendly banter.

This time, Seneca crossed her arms over her chest. "No, I'm definitely a fully grown woman."

"And we couldn't be friends if I was your therapist."

"And you want to be my *friend*?"

"Of course."

"I'm afraid, Dr. Mason, that I won't be here all that long. I'm not sure a *friendship* is a great idea."

Robyn looked her over. "It's Robyn. And how about we just see what develops?"

Seneca found no fault in the logic, especially given her firm resolve to not get involved with Robyn Mason. "All right." She grinned. She crossed the porch and held open the door for Robyn. "Back to the party?"

Robyn smiled and passed through. However, once inside, Robyn stopped dead in her tracks; Seneca nearly stepped on her. "What's wrong?"

"Shit." Robyn's eyes seemed to be trained across the room where a short, older woman was in conversation with Sarah.

"Are you okay?" Seneca was concerned. Robyn usually seemed so confident and was now nervous.

"Yeah, it's just that my mother is here." Robyn took a breath. "She can be dramatic."

"I see."

Robyn grimaced. "No, you don't, but I think you're about to."

Robyn should have predicted her mother's presence. Though her parents were divorced, her mother was still a part of the community and attended events from time to time. Her party crashing often caused Robyn anxiety because her mother lived in the past.

As she crossed the room, Robyn noticed the bar was subdued in contrast to the earlier antics. There was a sourness in her stomach as Robyn crossed to where her mother stood with Sarah. Robyn's eyes locked on her mother's, and her chest constricted, as expected. Her mother's unpredictable behavior always set her on edge. She had to force herself to breathe slowly through her nose.

Seneca had been stopped by other partygoers on the way inside. She saw her mother's gaze slide to where Seneca was standing. Her mother frowned. Robyn now understood why her mother was there. She wanted to check out the new ranch hand.

"This is a good turnout. It looks like all the cowhands are here." Robyn heard a sneer in her mother's voice.

Robyn glanced to Sarah, whose gaze was inscrutable. "Yeah, JD was surprised. I think he's over there by the bar if—"

"I have eyes, Robyn, I can see him standing there with your father and his *new* wife." Robyn internally rolled her eyes. Her parents had been divorced for more than a decade. Robyn waited for the next of her mother's antics. Her mother turned her gaze back to Seneca. "That must be the new girl. The one everyone's been going on about."

"That's Seneca, yes."

"I'm sure poor Collin was humiliated today."

Poor Collin humiliated himself today. "It was a good showing. Seneca's team won fair."

"Did I say they didn't, Robyn? Why are you so defensive?" Her mother scrutinized her, and then looked back at Seneca. "Is it because that new girl is attractive?"

Sarah shuffled uncomfortably, but Robyn managed not to react. She'd come out in college and since then, her mother had treated her like a lust-filled predator.

Concentrating her efforts on a neutral reply, she responded. "She is attractive. She's also a good cowhand and will be a great help to JD and Dad during the drive."

"What about Collin?"

Not this again. Robyn sighed. Vallie had watched Shep grow up at the ranch and had a soft spot for the troubled boy he had been. "What about him, Mom?"

"*He's* attractive and good at his job."

He's also a complete douchebag. "I'm not interested in Collin Shepherd."

"But you are interested in that woman."

"I didn't say that."

"Again, so defensive." Her mother smiled widely at Sarah as though including her in on a joke. She was clearly pleased to see that she had gotten under Robyn's skin. "You must *really* like her."

"Seneca is very likable, Vallie." Sarah could be counted on to try to help divert her mother's negative energy. "Would you like to meet her?"

Her mother sniffed. "No, thank you. I came to wish JD a happy birthday and then I need to be going."

So soon? Robyn's internal sarcasm was her only outlet, and so she happily bade her mother good-bye and turned away. She sought Seneca in the crowd. She found her being beckoned by Jack and headed toward the kitchen. Curious as to what her uncle wanted, Robyn traveled in the same direction.

She had just reached the still swinging kitchen door when her father caught up with her. "Robyn," he said.

"Yes?" She was too interested in what Seneca and Jack were doing in the kitchen to fully note the concern in his voice.

"Are you okay?"

Robyn looked at him. "Um, yeah." He raised his eyebrows. "Yes, Dad, I'm fine."

They both glanced to where her mother was now in conversation with JD and Rosemary.

"Mom was just, you know, being herself." Robyn sighed. "It's only been fifteen years," she said wryly. "One day she will adjust to how things *are.*"

He still wore a troubled expression. Robyn forced herself to brighten. "It's okay, Dad. I'm used to it."

"I know you are." He grimaced. "You're tougher than you should have to be."

"Tougher than you." She grinned at him.

"No doubt."

Robyn patted his hand reassuringly. "It's all right, Dad. Let's just get back to the party."

CHAPTER EIGHT

Monday brought Seneca the experience of a disconcertingly friendly Collin Shepherd. "Good morning, Twist." He took off his hat to greet her.

She kept her face neutral. "Shep."

"I wanted to apologize for last week. I'm not used to losing and certainly not to a..." He paused. "A newcomer."

They both knew he had been about to say *woman*, but Seneca let it pass. "Well, we all win some and lose some." It sounded cliché, but she was at a loss for anything more gracious to say.

"Right, anyway, I hope there are no hard feelings." Shep extended his hand, and she took it firmly. He squeezed a bit too tight. Not enough to be painful, but it sure wasn't comfortable. Seneca merely smiled, unflinching.

"No hard feelings."

He put his hat back on and strode away.

"What the hell was that all about?"

"Shep apologizing," Seneca answered JD, who had walked up behind her, as she tracked Shep walking away. *Shep pretending to apologize, more like it.*

"Huh." *JD doesn't sound like he's sure of Shep's sincerity either.*

"Yeah." She turned to JD and found he had a big bag in his hands. "What's all that?"

"Clothes." He looked at her. "There was frost on the ground this morning, Twist. You need some real winter gear to keep warm while you're working."

"I'm fine with—"

"Take the damned clothes." He thrust them into her belly, and she wrapped an arm around the garbage bag. "That's me being the boss. You're one of the best cowboys—cowhands—I've got now. If you get sick, that puts me out. I'm not doing this for you. I'm doing this for me."

"All right." She peered into the bag. "Mind me asking where—"

"They're nothing fancy, Twist," JD said. "Just some banged-up and weathered odds and ends. You might want to take a gander before working today."

"Well...." She looked into his eyes as he waited. She smiled. "Thanks, JD. I'll put them to use."

Seneca carried the bag to the loft to peruse. She was grateful for the extra layers. The chill in the air had become more pronounced and she hadn't relished the idea of riding into the mountains in her current wardrobe.

As she riffled through the flannel and thermals, she pondered Shep's behavior. At the party, Jack had invited her into the kitchen to show her his *meatloaf recipe*. This had been a ruse for him to share with her his personal brand of moonshine. As they had sipped a shot, and had shot the shit, he had also shared a bit of history about Win and Vallie—and Shep and Robyn.

Learning Shep had grown up at the ranch in state care had not surprised Seneca. The way he swaggered around like a king now made perfect sense. It also made sense Shep had relentlessly pursued Robyn since they were teenagers. Seneca almost felt bad for Shep because it was clear Robyn was utterly uninterested in him.

After changing quickly to include a thermal shirt beneath her flannel, Seneca pulled on her new work jacket and fiddled with the zipper. Everything fit perfectly and she would be much more comfortable than before. She left the rest of the clothes in the bag and hurried to the Old Barn where she was supposed to find a checklist of more supplies to ready for the drive.

She found Win sipping coffee. "Morning," he said with something strange in his voice. Seneca pretended not to notice as she approached the drafting table and retrieved a list in JD's handwriting.

"Morning." She tucked the list into her breast pocket. Seneca went to the cabinet and grabbed a cup as she tried to remember where she'd seen or put everything on the list.

Win cleared his throat. "So, you saw Vallie, then." She poured herself coffee.

"Yeah, I guess I did." She waited.

"We divorced when Robyn was in high school and pretty soon after I married Joan."

"Oh."

He looked hard at her a moment. "Me and Joan were involved... before I divorced Vallie."

"Okay." She had no idea why Win was telling her this, but it seemed important to him. So, she sipped her coffee and let him talk.

"It was a pretty messy divorce."

"I hear divorces can be." Seneca was uncomfortable. It still wasn't clear why Win felt the need to bring her into the loop.

He sipped his coffee. "I guess that's more than you want to know, but I owed you an explanation in case she said anything off-color to you."

"You don't owe me anything, Win," Seneca said flatly. "I didn't have the pleasure of making her acquaintance, but even if I had, there's no reason you should be apologizing to me."

"Good. I..." He wrestled with the words. "Well, you always feel responsible when..." Win struggled to explain, but he didn't need to. Seneca had seen the way both he and Robyn had been embarrassed. It was as if they felt the need to apologize for Vallie's actions.

"No one holds you accountable for Vallie, Win. You or Robyn. She made some people uncomfortable, but no one expected either one of you to do anything about it."

"Right." He looked at her and grinned. "That's exactly what Joan said, but it's hard. My choices impacted Robyn negatively, and I worry about her, every time. I still feel that burden for how everyone else is impacted, too. Some things are conditioned into you, you know?"

Seneca felt the weight of the Beretta on her ankle. She certainly did. She nodded. "Yeah, that's true. But don't apologize to me about it."

"All right, yeah. Good." Win nodded at the list in her hand with a grin. "You better get started. It usually takes most of the day to find that stuff."

"We'll see about that."

❖

Seneca was enjoying lunch with Cliff, Kevin, and a few others when Win hailed her from the loft. "Hey, cowgirl!"

Knowing that could only be her, Seneca stood from her straddled position on the bench, gulped the last of her soda, and wiped her mouth with the back of her hand. "Be right there, Boss!" With a last nod to her friends, she mounted the steps wondering what task Win would set before her this time.

"How are your carpentry skills?" he asked before her feet touched the top stair.

"Decent. I can make anything square. What do you need?"

"Bookshelves." His mustache seemed to bristle with the disgruntled tone of his voice. "I told Robyn I would build some bookshelves for her office a couple of weeks ago, and I haven't gotten around to it. I've been busy."

Seneca tried not to grin. "Very busy."

"Right. Well, my daughter is the impatient sort, I'm sure you've noticed. She is claiming she's hired a carpenter to build her shelves since I won't do it."

"I see." From what she knew of Robyn, she did not find it hard to believe she would do exactly as she had threatened. "I'll need the bench and power tools, and that stack of lumber behind the chicken coop. Can I borrow the truck?"

"Sure, the keys are hanging there by the gun rack. If it doesn't start right away, pump the gas a few times. That should get her going."

Seneca took the keys and set about gathering supplies. It seemed she was endlessly fated to interact with Robyn. She was of two minds about it. Robyn's presence seemed to stoke an unquenchable fire in her belly. The smell of her skin and the rich glitter of her eyes were etched into Seneca's memory. Robyn challenged her and made her laugh. Her passion for and commitment to her work impressed her. However, it was the thrill of all these things that made her wary. Seneca was afraid Robyn could look into her eyes and lay her bare; know every secret of her heart. Robyn was the boss's daughter. And she was not staying here in the Hollow. Seneca was determined to avoid Robyn and the reality of *friendship*—or something more—that she was not ready for. At war with herself, Seneca loaded the truck and set off for Robyn's building.

❖

"Well, Nathan," Robyn said to the young man across from her, "I'm pleased with how you handled the most recent situation with Noah." She reviewed her notes. "You got along well and managed your temper during your added, and joint, ranch chores. You will be starting to work with the horses this week, correct?"

"Yes, ma'am." Nathan spoke quietly.

"Is that something you are looking forward to?"

He shrugged.

She pressed gently. "I know you said you've never been around such big animals. It's hard to believe *they* are often afraid of *us*."

He nodded. Robyn waited.

"All the other guys like working with the horses. They say they're like big dogs."

"How so?"

"Just that they're smart and have their own personalities. Every guy has his favorite."

"Well, that's your homework then." Robyn smiled encouragingly. "When we meet next week, I want you to tell me which horse you like best."

"I can do that." He looked relieved to have something simple to do. Robyn knew his last homework had been a challenge for him. It often was when her clients had to be introspective and self-aware.

"I know." She stood to end the session. "I'll see you next week, Nate."

"Sure, Dr. Mason."

The young man shuffled out and Robyn retreated to her desk to copy her handwritten notes into computer files. Nathan was a tricky client. He was quiet and unassuming but had a great capacity for rage with the right trigger, as evidenced by the fiasco at the career fair. Before Robyn had time to get well and truly into her post-session analysis, there was a knock on her door frame.

"Come in." She spoke without lifting her head.

"Good afternoon, Dr. Mason."

Robyn's mind went momentarily blank. She stood abruptly. "Seneca?"

Seneca's tall frame filled the door. She had a tape measure clipped to her belt and a pad and pencil in her hand. Robyn couldn't fathom why Seneca was there, but she wasn't sorry to see her. "Can I help you?"

"I'm here to measure your walls."

Robyn was confused. "My walls?"

"For the shelves."

"The shelves." She echoed Seneca again, and then felt her blush when Seneca smirked. Clearing her throat, she stepped around the desk. "What shelves?"

Lifted eyebrows joined Seneca's smirk. "The bookcases that Win promised you?"

This jogged her memory. "Well, it's about time. I was going to hire a carpenter."

"I believe the carpenter you *already hired* is why he sent me over." Seneca folded her arms and caught Robyn's gaze.

Robyn was hardly chagrined being caught in the small lie. She would do what she needed to get him moving on all the projects promised. Besides, he delegated well. Exceedingly well this time around. Dad placed a lot of faith in Seneca Twist. She seemed worth more than all the other cowhands combined. Excited at the prospect of watching Seneca work, Robyn prodded her.

"And you are equal to this task?"

"Excuse me?" Seneca dropped her arms and frowned. Robyn was satisfied to know she had regained the upper hand.

"I can be rather *demanding*. Are you sure you can satisfy my needs?"

Seneca's reaction to the innuendo was slight, but Robyn could read it all the same. Perhaps the gorgeous woman was not so unaffected as she had first thought. *That's right, Ms. Twist, let me unravel you.*

"I'm certain I can. So long as you tell me the *expectations*."

Robyn was amused as Seneca gazed at her with a glint of challenge in her narrowed mossy eyes. "I'd like two bookcases, please." She pointed to the wall. "Floor to ceiling."

"Simple enough." Seneca withdrew her tape measure and began making notes on her small pad of paper. "And do you want the shelves all the same?"

"I'm not sure what you mean."

Seneca snapped the tape measure back onto her belt. "Do you want all the shelves the same height and width or would you like some small cubbies or shorter shelves?" Seneca sketched on the pad. "Like this?" Robyn took the paper Seneca passed her and assessed the crude sketch.

"You could do this?" Customization like what was drawn would take more time and attention to complete. She was surprised at Seneca's investment in the project.

"Sure, it's just wood."

"Most people wouldn't know what to do with *just wood*, Seneca." Robyn returned the sketch. "Is there anything you can't do?"

Seneca considered the question for a long while. "I'm a terrible cook," she finally said.

At this, Robyn laughed heartily. The admission was so genuine and offered so purely that she couldn't help but to smile. "Well, I can. What would you like me to make you upon completion of this project?"

Seneca physically backed away. "Nothing, it's my job to build the bookcases."

"Yes, but a job well done deserves a reward."

"My reward is room and board."

"That's part of your *pay*, not your reward." Robyn wondered at Seneca's sudden unease. Seneca seemed itching to run from the office.

"My reward is knowing the shelves will be put to use."

"If you insist." Robyn resolved to bake her something anyway—and try to understand what that abstruse reaction to the offer of a simple treat was about. "When can you start?"

"Today. I should be done within two days, at most."

"That fast?" Robyn was surprised.

"Sure." Seneca tucked the pad of paper in her back pocket. "I like to get things done."

"Yes, I can see that." Robyn smiled broadly.

Seneca stood for a moment in the middle of the room as though at a loss for what to say next. Robyn let the silence stretch and took note of the way Seneca rocked slightly back and forth on her heels. She then watched as Seneca smoothed the front of her shirt. "Well, I'll get to work. Let me know if there's anything else you need, Doctor, er, Robyn."

Soon, the unmistakable whine of a saw met Robyn's ears and she spun in her desk chair to watch from her office window. Seneca measured and cut methodically. Her dark hair was braided back loosely under her handkerchief and a toolbelt was slung low around her lean hips. She had shucked her heavy jacket and rolled up her yellow flannel shirt sleeves so that her tanned forearms showed, corded with muscle, and covered in sawdust. *Hot damn.*

Robyn experienced that low tug in her belly that she was coming to associate with Seneca. She was mesmerized by Seneca's movements and the ease and confidence with which she went about her work. As uncomfortable as she had seemed in the office, Seneca carpentering outdoors was now as in her element as she had been with the horses and cattle. Robyn wanted to get to the bottom of what drove Seneca Twist. What had perhaps begun as professional curiosity had turned into something much more personal, and slightly more lascivious. But she knew herself well enough to know there was an even more significant emotion growing within her. She wanted to *know* Seneca, and she wanted Seneca to know her.

Robyn tore her eyes away and returned to her work. She had to push the enigma of Seneca from her mind.

❖

Somehow, Robyn accomplished the difficult task of focusing on her work. Despite Seneca being near, several productive hours went by. Around three o'clock, Robyn heard steps in the hall outside her office. She looked up at the same time Seneca made it to her door.

Seneca stepped in smelling like prairie wind and lumber. She had flecks of sawdust on the handkerchief atop her head and in the dark hair left at her shoulders. Her cheeks were flushed a cheery pink with exertion and the cold. Robyn was overwhelmed by how tantalizing the true southern belle was and must have been staring because Seneca raised her eyebrows.

"Robyn?"

"Um, yes? How is it going?"

"See for yourself." Seneca grinned and gestured to the window. Robyn stood to see the results of Seneca's labor. One new bookshelf was fully assembled and the other lay in organized piles of boards.

"Wow."

"I built the first one but wanted to make sure it looked all right before I assembled the other. Would you like to change anything about the design?"

"Yes," Robyn said. "I mean, no."

Seneca frowned.

"I mean to say…it looks perfect. Job well done, Seneca." Robyn turned to Seneca and realized she was standing close, closer than she usually would. Seneca seemed to realize this, too, because she suddenly looked uncomfortable and tried to shift back. Lucky for Robyn, the desk denied Seneca a convenient escape.

"I'm glad you're satisfied," Seneca said.

Robyn grinned as she watched Seneca redden. "I am *very* satisfied," she said with a smirk. "You exceeded my every expectation."

Seneca now tried to sidle around the desk, never taking her eyes from Robyn. "Uh, I'll be back first thing to finish the second shelf and then I can get one of the guys to help me haul them in here."

"I'm usually here by eight."

"Great, I'll be by around then."

"See you in the morning!" Robyn called airily to Seneca's back as she left the office. Robyn smirked at the curiously increased pace of Seneca's steps through the building. She then turned back to the window. She watched as Seneca gathered her tools and loaded them into the bed of the battered, teal truck. Robyn looked forward to putting the shelves to use, but more than that, she looked forward to more interactions with Seneca. She could think of only a few developments that would satisfy her more.

CHAPTER NINE

Midweek, Seneca mended fences with JD. He'd found several holes in the fencing of the wintering pasture and enlisted her help to patch them before the drive. Seneca had watched a beautiful sunrise from the fields and was happy to be out in the sunshine and the wind. She and Cliff had finally wrangled all the provisions and supplies needed for the drive and had repaired and packed the cart. Add Robyn's shelving build and install and it had been a productive week thus far. But beyond a couple of short rides with Phoebe, Seneca had not been in the Idaho countryside. She had missed it.

JD pulled the truck close to the last hole in the fence. A large copse of aspen trees was growing nearby, and one had fallen across the fence. The damage must have happened recently because the tree's foliage was still a cheery shade of yellow. She climbed out of the truck and pulled on her rough work gloves. She then retrieved the chainsaw from the bed and set to clearing the tree.

Seneca stacked the surprisingly light wood to the side before joining JD in cutting through the ruined wire. With this task completed, they straightened the posts and stretched new wire between them. Barbed wire was added to the top of the fence line to discourage the cattle from anything foolish. Seneca stepped back to admire the way the metal gleamed in the sun. Satisfied with the day's job, she took the spool in her gloved hands and loaded it back into the truck. When she dropped the coil onto the bed, the end came loose and sprung up to strike her in the face like an angry rattlesnake.

"Shit." Her curse was soft as she touched her cheek where the wire had struck. The leather glove came away with a line of crimson.

"What happened?" JD called absentmindedly as he gathered the remaining tools.

"Nothing, just this barbed wire." She pulled her handkerchief off her head to press it to her face. "Wasn't paying attention and it got me."

"Yeah, I always come away from mending fences with my arms all scratched."

"No, not my arm…" She trailed off as she removed the cloth and found another line of blood.

JD came around to the back of the truck. "What do you mean?" He hurried forward after looking at her face. "Damn, Twist," he said in a scolding tone. Seneca grinned.

"Am I in trouble?"

He blinked and dropped the hand he had reached toward her face. "No, of course not." He stepped back, still frowning at her.

"Well, let's finish packing." She smiled as broadly as she could. She desperately wanted to downplay the injury. It was nothing to fret over.

"There's a bandage in the truck's first—"

Seneca chuckled dryly. "I've had worse."

"Worse than barbed wire to your face?"

"Four ounces of shrapnel worse." The words were out of her mouth before she could take them back. She watched JD's face transition from mild concern to alarm.

"What's that?"

She shook her head. "I'm sorry, that was supposed to be funny or something, I think…"

"Four ounces?"

Seneca huffed. She had not planned to share her military experience—or any experience—with anyone. She was getting far too comfortable here. "Yeah, IED. I was lucky, they got it all. Four in my unit died. I only spent time in the hospital."

Concern was etched into the weathered lines of JD's face. "Well, at least put a bandage on it, because if you don't, Rosemary will kick my butt."

She laughed. "All right." She daubed the slice. "Just for the sake of your butt, and not because I really need it."

❖

Robyn was happy Seneca was making use of her new thermals, clothes, and boots. Robyn had put the bug in JD's ear about Seneca's need for suitable winter clothes, and he'd bought all new clothing for her. Well, he'd given Rosemary money to buy all new clothing; Robyn had helped with the sizes. Something in her knew that Seneca would never accept such a gift. So, she'd worked with Rosemary and Joan to distress all of it so it looked as if it'd been donated or gotten from a thrift store. They had had a lot of fun completing the task in and of itself, but Robyn smiled recollecting how the conversation amongst the three of them had revolved around Seneca and her fit to the ranch and town.

The old timers were predicting snow within the month. Seneca could take care of herself, but she lacked experience with a northwestern winter. It was only wise to consider better living arrangements for Seneca should she have to shelter in Butterbean Hollow for the cold season.

Of course, Robyn liked the idea of Seneca's continued presence at the ranch. She had certainly made Butterbean Hollow much more stimulating. Robyn cared for Seneca. And then there was the undeniable sexual tension between them. Robyn was eager to explore that attraction before Seneca left town. Luckily enough, she knew just the place for Seneca to stay and weather the winter. She just needed to discuss it with her father.

Her father was sitting at a worktable, a carburetor half-assembled before him, when Robyn reached the Old Barn. "Hey, there."

"Hey." He acknowledged her with a smile and wiped his grease-blackened hands on a stained rag. "What are you up to?"

"I wanted to run something by you." She glanced around at the mostly empty barn, not wanting to be overheard.

"Shoot." He straightened to give her his undivided attention.

"Well, I've been thinking about everyone's favorite new cowhand, and how winter is coming fast this year. I don't think she ought to be walking any further until spring."

"Yeah." He nodded. "I've been thinking about that, too."

"You have?" She was surprised. JD was usually the one with the schemes. Her father was typically the executor of the plan. It made them a great team. This insight meant Seneca had been on her father's mind, too. Curious.

"Yeah, she's been a great help, and we can use her beyond the drive." He tilted his head to the side. "So, you have a plan."

"She obviously can't stay in the barn all winter. She'll freeze." Robyn paced away and then back. "I was thinking about that old caretaker's cottage in the orchard. No one has lived there for a while."

He stroked his mustache. "Now, there's an idea."

"It's basic, but it's still structurally sound, right?"

"It's brick," he said flatly. "And we put a tin roof on it several years back. There's no heat or air, but there's plenty of wood to be had for the fireplace. Should do well enough for a winter." He stood from the bench seat and motioned for her to follow him into the loft. "I've got the key up here. I can ride out and look things over unless you want to do it."

"I would appreciate it if you would do it. You know more about what to check for, anyway," she said as she followed him up the stairs.

He crossed the loft to open a cabinet door where keys hung for every ranch lock and vehicle. "I can take a look now and if anything needs doing, we will have time to get it done before she would need to move in." He somehow selected the one correct set of keys from the dozens stored there. He flipped them over in his hands to scrutinize them, and then looked back up at Robyn. "I know a place we can get some cheap furniture—"

Robyn quickly motioned for him to hold his thoughts as the barn door opened.

She heard JD and Seneca enter, laughing. They moseyed up the steps. Seneca nodded her hello while on a direct route to the coffee machine.

"Hey, Robyn," JD said in greeting. "What brings you this way?"

Luckily, she was quick on her feet. "The equine therapy program. I wanted to make my rounds today. It starts at ten, right?"

"It sure does. I wish I could walk that way myself, but I've still got a few things to take care of before we're gone this weekend." JD turned to Seneca, who had her back turned as she poured a cup of coffee. "But I'm sure Seneca wouldn't mind walking you over."

At the mention of her name, Seneca turned around and Robyn's eyes lit on the bandage. "What happened?" Robyn was unable to contain her disquiet.

"What?" Seneca leaned on the counter with a frown.

Robyn took a step toward her. "What happened to your face?"

"Oh." Seneca touched the bandage and grinned. "Barbed wire."

Her father looked at her deadpan. "I told you to cut that from your diet, cowgirl."

"I just can't help myself."

Robyn, however, didn't see what was funny. She closed the few steps between them and reached for Seneca's face. Seneca caught her wrist. "Seneca—"

"I'm fine," Seneca said. "Honestly. I've had worse, you know." Seneca's green gaze met her own, and Robyn was briefly lost in the silent message that passed between them.

She recovered to say, "I know, but—"

Her father chuckled. "What's worse than barbed wire on your face?"

Seneca exchanged a look with JD. She shrugged.

"Four ounces of shrapnel, apparently," JD said. Robyn's blood turned cold.

"What?!" She immediately regretted her reaction when Seneca seemed to recoil at her alarm.

"You've seen the scars on my arms. You knew—"

"But—"

"You served in the Armed Forces?"

Seneca answered Robyn's father. "Army. Afghanistan."

"Vietnam. Corporal Mason, Twenty-fifth Infantry Division."

"Sergeant Twist, First Cavalry Division."

"Sergeant." He saluted first, signifying his lower rank.

Seneca seemed reluctant to return the gesture even as she did so. "At ease, Corporal." Seneca laughed, but the sound was odd to Robyn's ears. "We're not on base, Win."

As the moment passed between Seneca and her father, Robyn tried again to check Seneca's face. "Robyn." Seneca's tone was one of exasperation. "Please don't."

"It's bleeding," Robyn said. "Let me at least clean it properly."

"I can do that later—"

"Better let her tend to it, Seneca," her father said. "She won't let it go." He glanced between Seneca and Robyn with a half-smile on his face. Robyn nodded at him.

❖

Seneca sat on an old wooden chair as Robyn retrieved the first-aid kit. Robyn's father and JD officially left to check the packed supplies, but Robyn suspected they were escaping the tension. She slowly peeled back the lopsided bandage.

"It's not deep, but it doesn't look like you cleaned it."

"JD just spit on it."

Robyn drew back to look her in the eye and Seneca raised her brows.

"That's not funny." Robyn huffed. She opened an antiseptic wipe as she tried to ignore how much she enjoyed their proximity despite the circumstances.

Robyn took Seneca's strong jaw in one hand and began cleaning the scratch gently. She couldn't tell if the flesh beneath her fingers was still flushed from the wind outside or if something else was making it warm. The laceration ran diagonally over Seneca's right cheekbone and toward her mouth. A beautiful mouth that Robyn was finding difficult to ignore. She leaned in closer.

Seneca broke the silence.

"So, Win, uh, enlightened me the other day. About your mother… and his affair."

Robyn was surprised her father had mentioned either topic to Seneca and was surprised Seneca was sharing the conversation with her. "Really?" She drew back to retrieve the antibiotic ointment. She began daubing it on Seneca's tanned face.

"Yeah, I think he felt responsible. Like he owed me an explanation or something."

"What did you say?"

"I mostly just listened, and I told him that neither of you were responsible for Vallie. That he didn't owe me anything."

"That was nice of you to say."

"Nice had nothing—"

Robyn shushed her so that she could place the bandage carefully. She needed a minute more to adjust to the shift in her focus.

"Nice had nothing to do with it. It was the simple truth."

Robyn drew back. "You're finished now. You can go back to gallivanting around with horses and barbed wire."

Seneca stood and shoved her hands in her pockets. "I'm sorry, Robyn. I shouldn't have said anything. It's not my business—"

"No, it isn't." Robyn paused and then took a deep, soothing breath. She turned her back to put away the first aid kit. Robyn was irrationally upset with Seneca, even as she realized it wasn't Seneca's fault that she felt vulnerable. Robyn looked back at Seneca and found nothing but understanding in her eyes. "But I suppose my father made it your business. It is his story to tell as much as it is mine."

"You don't like that he told me."

"As I said, he has a right to share it. I was just surprised."

"That he told a lowly cowhand?"

"No. It's just that, with that situation anyway, he's usually very private." Robyn nodded. "Like you."

Seneca looked beyond her for several moments as silence fell in the barn. Robyn was drawn to Seneca by the sheer intensity of her rumination. "I am private." She rubbed a hand over her face and touched the bandage on her cheek. "For good reason."

"Four ounces of good reasons?" Robyn joked, attempting to ease the tension in the air. She was rewarded with a small, sad smile.

"I don't know why I said that. It just came out. I wasn't trying to cause a fuss."

"I know."

"And then having Win salute me." Seneca shook her head. "It makes my skin crawl."

"He is proud of his service," Robyn said. Something in the strength of the emotion in Seneca's voice softened her own.

"As am I, but…" Seneca rubbed where Robyn knew her physical scars lay under her flannel and jacket. "To have a man twice my age salute me is hard to bear. It's wrong. I don't deserve that sort of respect." After these words, a change seemed to come over her. She grinned at Robyn and changed the subject. "But you don't care about all that. Let's go see those kids with the horses."

Seneca turned to descend the steps. Robyn followed. They were both quiet as they walked. Her heart ached over the chagrin and disgust Robyn had seen on Seneca's face. Clinically, Robyn knew the sort of trauma that soldiers experienced, but she had little experience with it in her own practice. The idea of Seneca not feeling like she deserved respect from a fellow veteran seemed ludicrous though, regardless of the circumstances. Then, there was the practiced ease with which Seneca seemed to shove tough emotion away. Altogether, perhaps these were the reasons for Seneca's nomadic behavior. After a few minutes of contemplation, Robyn pushed the thoughts away—wryly recognizing the similarity of her response to Seneca's and noting the irony of it. *But I'm just keeping my word to Seneca.* She had specifically told Seneca she was not interested in counseling her.

They arrived at the small arena where there was a group of five residents. Seneca leaned forward on the railing rather than take to the stands. "That's Noah, right?" She nodded to a blond teenager brushing a large sorrel horse.

"Yes, it is." Robyn stood beside her and watched the boy with the horse. "It's amazing the change that comes over these young men when you put them in the ring with an animal."

Robyn and Seneca both watched for a time. Robyn noted Lucy in the ring and was glad to see her again.

"I haven't had much interaction with the boys." Seneca spoke so softly Robyn almost missed it.

"Is that something you're interested in?"

"Me? No." Seneca laughed. "I don't know how to interact with them."

"You did just fine with Nathan."

"That was different." Seneca dismissed the comparison. "I can handle a crisis, but I'm awkward around kids in general."

"I'm sure you would find yourself equal to the task."

"Nah, I won't be here much longer anyway. I don't want to get attached and then leave."

"Is that the plan? Leaving after the drive?"

"I don't have a specific date in mind. It's just the pattern. It's what I do."

"I see," Robyn said. Beside her, Seneca shifted.

"I'm just here to work, you know? To earn enough money to move on."

Robyn wondered if Seneca meant that. She'd not been in town long but had already made friends and earned a good reputation. "Unfortunately, I think you should abandon the idea of leaving here anytime soon."

"And why is that?" Her husky voice sounded harsh with suspicion. Robyn was pinned by Seneca's mossy-eyed look.

"Because it's already too cold for you to camp at night. You're not from here so you don't know this, but your window for foot travel has closed and won't open again until spring." Robyn watched the effect of her words on Seneca. She went stiff and turned back to the arena. She seemed to be contemplating this new information.

"Spring. Are you sure?"

Robyn spoke softly. "I know it's not what you want, but it would not be a good idea to continue on foot."

Seneca sighed deeply. "I think I already knew that. Last night, I put an extra blanket over my hammock in the barn. I'll need to make better arrangements."

"JD and Dad can help you there, I'm sure." Robyn tried to hide how pleased she was that Seneca had not struggled too hard against the idea of staying. Perhaps she wasn't quite so desperate to get away.

"Right. Well, I should get going. There's still plenty to do before we head up the mountain."

"Right," Robyn echoed. She watched as Seneca crossed the yard with her head bowed.

❖

Back in the loft, Seneca retrieved her last to-do list and tried to focus on the few tasks she had left before the drive. Robyn's words echoed in her mind. She shook her head. A nagging bit of doubt crept in. It couldn't possibly be too late for her to keep moving. But Robyn wouldn't lie about this. And she *didn't* know Northwest winters.

She heard Win and JD come back in. She tried to wipe her face of all emotion. As they ascended the stairs, she was tidying the loft space and barely acknowledged them.

"Well, did Robyn doctor you up?" Win asked with a smile in his voice.

She rounded her shoulders. "I guess so." Seneca glanced out the window where a cold wind was blowing through the colorful trees. She cleared her throat. "So, uh, how long do you think I have until the weather keeps me from marching onward?" she asked as casually as she could manage.

They looked at one another. "Well…" JD said.

Win stroked his mustache. "Uh…"

"It's too late, isn't it?" She sighed.

"It probably is," Win said. "You may have another week of some decent weather, but there's usually snow sticking on the ground by the beginning of October."

"I see." She fully accepted the reality of her situation. Robyn was right. Seneca abhorred the idea of being stuck, but there was an unfamiliar relief in the situation, too. Finally, she had to stop wandering, if only for a season. "And when would I be able to hike again?"

"Probably May?" JD looked at Win.

"Yeah, that's about right. May," Win confirmed. "I know it's not what you want, cowgirl, but to keep trekking could be dangerous and that's the truth of it."

"I appreciate your honesty." She nodded then grinned. "Well, if I'm going to be here awhile, I'll need somewhere other than the barn to sleep."

"Right, you will."

"There's that old caretaker's cottage, Boss." Win looked to JD, and JD nodded. Win turned to Seneca. "It needs some work. There's only a fireplace and a wood burning stove."

Seneca considered this. "It sounds great for the winter. How would rent and utilities work?"

"We'll just work out a flat rate and take it from your check?" JD lifted his brows. "Would that suffice?"

"Yes. Sure." She nodded.

"Good. Win can take you to see it after the drive. We'll help you get it in tip-top shape then, too. Keep you snug all winter."

"I appreciate that and…" She struggled to communicate what she was feeling. "I don't want you to think I'm just dying to get away from y'all. I just…I don't usually stay put for long and I'm not great at…" She fought with herself. "I don't know what I'm trying to say."

"That's all right, cowgirl." Win smiled kindly. "I think we understand." He looked at JD. "I'm going to do a last check on Cliff to make sure he's ready to handle that wagon."

"Great," JD said. "I've got to go be the boss for a while. I'd rather be riding broken fences, but duty calls. See you tomorrow."

"Right." She nodded as they left. When they had exited, Seneca leaned against the counter heavily.

What was her problem? It had been months since she'd experienced this jumble of emotions. Walking had been easy. It had taken little in the way of intellectual power or emotional exertion. Walking had been straightforward and simple. *And boring.* It hadn't afforded her much in the way of a challenge, or anything else for that matter.

At Butterbean Hollow, she'd met people she genuinely liked and had work that she genuinely liked. Win and JD seemed to depend on her more each day and of course, there was Dr. Robyn Mason. Slowing down at the ranch had afforded her some good things, but a few things had also caught up with her. With blinding clarity, she remembered the conversation she'd had with her mother before she had walked away from Alabama.

"You can't outrun this, Seneca."

Seneca looked up from the bag she was packing and into the tired face of her mother. "I'm not trying to outrun anything, Mom. I just can't stay here. I can't stay here when—" She stopped. "Where he—" She stopped again.

She put her hands on her shoulders. "I know you blame yourself—"

"Don't you? Don't you blame me? You should."

Her mother looked at her for a moment. "I did for a time. Right after you two ran off, I blamed you." She sat on the bed. "I knew the Army was your idea. Hunter would have followed you to hell and back."

"He did. Except I'm the only one who made it home." Seneca continued to pack.

"I don't blame you for that. He followed you in there, but you didn't kill him."

"But I put him in that place." Her voice cracked. "If it hadn't been for me, he would be making headlines in Alabama right now. He wouldn't be another name on a list of dead soldiers."

"Don't you dare minimize him like that." Her mother's voice was stern. "Hunter was a son to me. He is much more than a dead soldier."

Seneca looked at her hands. "I can't stay here, Mom. I thought training soldiers would help me make peace with all of this. And I think it did for a while. I thought I was rectifying what I did to Hunter, but the truth is that I never can."

"And you think wandering around will give you peace?"

"I don't know." She lifted her shoulders. "But I know if I stay here, I'll go crazy."

Her mother pulled her into a fierce hug. "And I know you'll wander until you find a place you belong."

"I don't plan on staying anywhere long-term, Mama."

"I know, but when you find a place you like, give it a chance, okay?"

"Okay."

"I'm serious." Her mother pulled back and frowned at her. "If you find peace, stay there. No matter where that place is."

"All right."

"But remember that peace and pain are not mutually exclusive. Sometimes they exist in the same place."

"Okay, Mom," Seneca said. She shouldered her pack before kissing her mother on the cheek. "I love you. I'll miss you."

At the time, she had not understood what her mother meant even as she placated her. Now, she was beginning to. As desperately as she did not want to get involved, Butterbean Hollow was sucking her in. On the one hand, getting attached made leaving more painful. On the other, getting attached was human nature, and she craved the intimacy of belonging.

CHAPTER TEN

Thursday brought a weirdly warm breeze that made the last-minute drive preparations more pleasant but put Seneca on edge. She couldn't explain why, but she was certainly uncomfortable with the strange mild air. She wasn't the only one. Cliff, too, was distracted in his work that day. He was constantly checking the clear sky with shrewd eyes.

"I don't like this warm wind," he finally said.

"Neither do I." They were packing extra leather ties, duct tape, and other small necessities.

"Did you see the sunrise this morning?"

"I did." Seneca remembered the scarlet hue of the morning sky. "Blood red."

"It's a bad sign."

"Couple of superstitious women." Shep's voice sounded from where he had obviously stopped to listen to them talk.

Cliff looked at him but did not comment. She nodded to him. "Shep."

"You don't believe all that nonsense, do you?" He laughed. "I'd expect it from *him*, but I thought you were smarter than that."

She measured her words carefully. "In my experience, I've found that it's never a good idea to ignore what's right in front of you. Sometimes the universe is simply trying to communicate."

He squinted at her. "Through sunrises and wind?"

"Worked well enough for our ancestors."

"But we don't need all of that now. We have weather technology to tell us what to expect."

"True…Still, I'd rather learn to read the signs for myself."

"Whatever you say, Twist." He laughed at her. "You and Cliff go burn some herbs or sacrifice a goat or whatever and I'll stick to my radar app."

He walked away and Cliff turned to Seneca. "He's such an ignorant asshole," Cliff said.

"I know." Seneca shook her head. "Everyone knows you sacrifice a young steer for a weather forecast. Goats are only for a good harvest."

Cliff looked at her for a moment and they both burst into chuckles. It felt good to laugh at Shep. He was such a tool.

Just as they were getting back to work, Robyn appeared around the corner of the tack room.

"Do I even want to know what is so funny?"

"We might have had a laugh at Shep's expense," Seneca said.

"He probably deserved it."

"Ahem!" Cliff cleared his throat as the object of their discussion swaggered back up.

"Well, hey there, Dr. Robyn." Seneca wondered what the hell Shep did all day to be lollygagging around.

"Shep." Robyn nodded.

"Were these two telling you their theory about the weather?"

"No, I was just passing by on my way to—"

"They're under the impression this warm wind and the red sunrise are bad signs."

"Well, the old men at the pharmacy were talking about snow this week." Robyn met Seneca's eyes briefly.

Shep cocked his hip and put his hands on his belt. "So, you agree with them?" He laughed. "I suppose I'm the only one 'round here with any sense at all." His voice was so incredibly patronizing that Seneca briefly fantasized punching him in the throat. Fortunately for him, that was not who she was.

"Is that so?"

Shep drew a little closer to Robyn, as though trying to block Seneca and Cliff from the conversation. Seneca shifted uneasily.

"But sense doesn't matter when you're talking romance."

"Romance?"

"Like taking a pretty lady out on the town."

"I wouldn't call that romance, exactly—" The jerk cut her off again.

"Call it what you like when I pick you up at eight."

There was a tick of awkward silence as Robyn's eyes flicked to Seneca who stood motionless but watched intensely. Shep was being incredibly obtuse and making everyone uncomfortable. Seneca was almost embarrassed for him. Almost.

"Um, no thank you," Robyn said.

He grinned. "Come on, Robyn, we've been doing this dance for years now. Me flirting, you playing hard to get. I think it's time to put that aside."

"I haven't been playing hard to get, Shep. I've been turning you down. I'm not interested in dating you. I have never been interested in dating you, Shep."

The smile slid from his face.

"Well, why not? What do you mean?"

Robyn glanced to Seneca and Cliff. It was clear she was glad she was not alone. Beside Seneca, Cliff scuffed his boots in the dirt. He was amused. Seneca watched Robyn and Shep closely. She knew Shep was not the sort of man to take rejection with any amount of grace.

"It means I won't be going out with you tonight or any other night. I'm not interested in a relationship with you, Shep. Ever."

"Are you sure about that?"

Seneca had heard enough. "She didn't stutter, Shep."

He rounded on her. "You can butt the hell out, Twist! I'm talking to Robyn."

"No, you're talking *at* her. You're not listening. She said no. Now would be the time to walk away and save face."

Shep stepped away from Robyn to crowd Seneca. Seneca stood completely at ease. They were nearly the same height and though he was broad, Seneca had thrown men his size onto their asses.

"Save face? If you weren't a woman, I'd hit you."

"We all have our excuses."

Shep's face turned a nasty shade of purplish red. "Excuses? You think I couldn't kick your ass?"

"I didn't say that." She was calm as she replied. "But it's not wise to threaten just anybody, cowboy. You don't know me." She stared hard into his blue eyes.

"Seneca." Robyn spoke her name. It wasn't a warning or a scold, but hearing her name assuaged her growing temper and brought her back to the present. She purposefully looked around the fuming man to meet Robyn's lovely eyes.

Looking back at Shep, Seneca exhaled a breath and spoke softly. "Besides, you start a fight and you'd probably be looking for another job." She offered an easy out.

He took it. "Yeah, unlike you, I've got a truck payment and rent. I don't need this bullshit." Shep stepped back and looked Robyn over. "We could have had a lot of fun."

"I don't think so." Shep visibly clenched his teeth and walked away.

Cliff looked at Seneca. "You better sleep with one eye open on the trail."

"What's he going to do? Put shaving cream in my hand and tickle my nose?"

"Cliff is right, Seneca." Robyn looked concerned.

"I'm not afraid of Collin Shepherd," Seneca said.

"We're not saying you should be afraid of him, Seneca," Cliff said. The concern was evident in his soft voice. "But a little caution might be nice."

"Things happen even to the cautious." She shook her head. "Look, I'm sorry y'all are worried, but I'm not. Of course, I don't trust Shep—but I won't be pandering to him either. We both have jobs to do. Let it go."

Later that afternoon, Seneca found JD and Win in their usual spot. She'd been looking for Win. She wanted to report that everything was in top shape, and they were ready to leave the following morning. She found them reviewing a full map of the ranch's territory. She leaned in to study the document. "So, this is the whole thing?"

"Yes." Win traced a jagged circumference with one blunt finger. "These are our borders and these"—he traced a smaller area within it—"are the summer pastures."

"Nice chunk of land."

"This ranch has been here since before Idaho was a state." Win's mustache quivered. "Staked the claim a long time ago."

"Have any trouble with rustling?" Seneca surveyed the area and noted the waters that crossed the borders.

"Not all that often." JD paused. "All our cattle are branded, and it takes someone who knows the area to get away with more than a few. Still, maybe a decade ago, we came up about fifty head short."

"Ouch."

"Yeah, we didn't know it until we got there in October and were counting." JD sighed. "Was a time that we sent cowhands up into the summer lands every few weeks to get a head count, but we're not able to employ that many anymore."

Win looked at his boss then back at Seneca. "It's been a while since we've had any big number go missing, though."

"That's good." She traced a ridgeline near the summer pastures that ran around the western border of the property. "I guess the terrain is a deterrent."

"It is." JD nodded. "But there's also the fact that if we caught anyone trying to steal what's ours, there'd be hell to pay." He glanced to the gun cabinet mounted to the wall.

"I see." She surveyed the rifles through the glass. "Hopefully, it won't come to that this time."

"I doubt we will have any problems." Win sounded confident. "You just worry about getting a good night's sleep." He winked.

"Right." She turned for the door before JD called her back.

"Uh, Twist." He reached under the drawing table and placed a slightly worn, Montana-style cowboy hat on top of it. "We figured you might need something to keep the sun and wind off you."

She returned to the table to take the tan felt hat from JD. It had a moss green, leather strap around the crown and soft, braided stampede strings of the same color. She smiled softly at the notion her bosses would pick a hat that matched her eyes. Her smile grew a bit more. It was pretty, and real nice. She plopped the hat on her head and adjusted it forward. It fit like a glove. "Where did this come from?" She only half expected them to admit Robyn's involvement.

"It's an old one we had refurbished."

She began to remove it. "I can't accept—"

"You can and you will," Win said. "We need you in peak condition, and that hat is part of it. Everyone chipped in for it."

"Everyone?" Seneca asked in bemusement.

"You've done good work, Seneca. What we're paying you is a pittance for all you have accomplished. We appreciate you. Take the hat and use it on the drive."

"Well, all right." She smiled sheepishly and put the hat back on before tipping it back to be caught by the strings. "Thank you, kindly."

"Of course." Win shot JD a grin.

CHAPTER ELEVEN

Seneca woke before dawn and dressed. She grabbed her saddlebags and her new hat and traveled to the Old Barn to start the coffeemaker. By the time the thick aroma of the earthy mixture was in the air, a slight, silver line was on the eastern horizon.

Seneca had just poured herself a steaming cup when she heard the barn door creak. She peered over the banister to find Robyn climbing the stairs. It was the first time she'd seen her in anything other than business attire. She was just as enticing in jeans and a sweatshirt.

"Where are your saddlebags?" Seneca teased Robyn when she reached the top step.

Robyn smiled. "I did this drive once and it was enough for me."

"You've driven cattle?"

With a pitying glance, Robyn placed a bag on the table. "You didn't think you were the first female hand here?"

"Well, I just…" Seneca frowned. "I've never seen you ride."

"I used to ride all the time. I did this drive when I was about seventeen. It was so damned cold. Much like today." She glanced out the window where the silver light was gleaming on the frosted pastures. "I never cared to repeat the experience."

There was a tick of silence. "What's all this?" Seneca gestured at the bag.

"I brought biscuits. Dad and JD usually forget to eat, and I figured you for the same."

"You figured well."

"Then sit and eat."

Seneca didn't need telling twice. She promptly sat and drew the bag toward herself.

"Now, before you get started, I want to talk to you about something."

Seneca focused on Robyn warily with a biscuit halfway to her mouth. She narrowed her eyes slightly at the timing of the interruption. "All right…"

"Each year, my dad comes back from the drive with some sort of injury," Robyn said. "He does something reckless and has a new scar to show for it."

"So?" Seneca was dying to dive into her breakfast and knew that Robyn was purposefully delaying her meal.

"So, he's not as young as he once was. I want you to keep an eye on him and do not allow him to do anything that seems too risky."

Seneca hesitated, but finally shook her head. "I can't do that."

Silence rang cold and hard in the loft. "Why not?"

"I respect Win too much to make a bargain like that behind his back."

"It's not behind his back, you can tell him if you want—" Robyn stopped talking, however, because Seneca was laughing. "Stop grinning like a fool."

"I'm sorry, but there's no way I'm going to tell your dad that he cannot do something. That's not my place." She took a bite of biscuit and chewed slowly before reaching for a packet of jam to slather on the bread.

Robyn watched with a frown. "I don't want you to boss him around, I just want you to persuade him from anything foolhardy."

Seneca took another bite and shook her head. She swallowed, then spoke. "Win knows what he's doing. I'm not going to assume that I know better than him. He's been at this a long time—" She raised her hand because Robyn looked ready to interrupt. "But, if a dangerous task needs doing, I'll volunteer before he gets a chance to."

"That's not what I meant." Robyn tapped her fingers on the table. "You're not to put yourself in harm's way either."

Seneca laughed. "You can't have your cake and eat it too, Robyn."

"We're talking about my father's safety and yours."

"Look, I'll keep an eye on things. You know I will," Seneca said and took another bite of her biscuit. Robyn now wore an odd expression on her face.

"Yes, I do know and trust that about you," Robyn said.

Seneca realized too late that her comment had perhaps been too familiar. She was supposed to be keeping her distance. *Hell.* "I'm sorry for stepping in with Shep the other day..."

"Don't apologize. I am glad you and Cliff were there."

"I just don't want to cross any boundaries. I know you can take care of yourself. You don't need me."

"No, I suppose I don't," Robyn said. Seneca paused in her breakfast. "But, as I said, I'm glad you were there. Just as I'm glad you'll be on the trail this week."

A tense moment passed between them as Seneca was at a loss. Her heart was hammering weirdly in her chest as though she were on the ledge of some great precipice, steps from falling. She wanted to be there for Robyn, for Win and JD. She cared deeply for them now, but it wouldn't stop her from eventually letting them down. She disappointed everyone eventually and didn't want to be depended on. She was uncomfortable with the amount of faith Robyn placed in her. The sound of the barn door creaking open broke the spell. Win mounted the steps to the loft and his head appeared over the floorboards.

"Biscuits!" He grinned. "And coffee!" He happily went to the cabinet to retrieve a mug. "You girls are the best."

By seven o'clock, the posse was ready to leave. Robyn was clearing away the mess of breakfast when Seneca came back into the loft and lifted her saddlebags from where they hung over the banister. Robyn came to take the bags over her own shoulder and tuck the leftover biscuits in one of the pockets of the oiled leather.

Seneca raised her brows and Robyn decided to explain. "For later. You'll get hungry."

"Give them to Win. I'll forget to eat anyway."

"That's why I'm giving them to you," Robyn said wryly, then stepped back a hair. "Did you pack toilet paper?"

"Yes, ma'am."

"And a first aid kit?"

"Right beside my mani-pedi kit."

Robyn frowned. "Don't be a smartass."

Seneca grinned. "The first aid kit is on the wagon, but I have a miniature one in my bags. Did you forget I was a soldier?"

"How could I?" There was a weight on Robyn's chest, a worry in her heart that something would go wrong. She trusted Seneca would do as she said she would, though. She looked Seneca over as though to memorize her face.

"So, what are you going to do 'round here while we're away?"

"My job." Robyn sighed. "You don't suppose I'll drop everything because you're gone?"

Seneca shrugged. "No, I just figured the ranch will seem empty without the men swaggering 'round."

Seneca was partly right. "It's not so bad the first couple of days, I get a lot done. But by day three or so, I'm ready to see everyone riding back into town."

"Do a lot of people show for that?"

"Most of the spouses and office workers. It's sort of a big deal here. Jack opens the bar for chili and beer."

"That late at night?"

"It's just always been tradition." Robyn smiled. "It's been a thing since long before I was born, even. Driving the cattle used to be something the whole town got involved in. Celebrating afterward is natural."

"Makes sense." Seneca gazed at the frosted prairie-grass outdoors. "JD said it's going to be cold. I suppose I'll have my first real experience with Idaho snow."

"I truly hope not." Robyn shivered slightly. "That will make everything harder." She looked Seneca over and noticed a red scarf hung about her shoulders. She recognized it from the clothing bag. "Have you given more thought to pausing your forward progress?"

"I don't have a choice but to stay until spring. Apparently, there is an old cottage in the orchard where I can weather the winter. I'll be working on that next week."

"That and chopping wood." Robyn smiled. "If I remember correctly, there's not a furnace."

"No, it has a fireplace and wood burning stove, but that's all a body needs."

"Is it?" Robyn drew nearer to her, and she noticed Seneca's gaze drop to rove over her lips.

"Isn't it?" Seneca sounded a bit breathless. The sound of the cart clattering to a stop outside the barn drew their attention. Seneca glanced to the door and then back to Robyn. "I've got to be going."

Robyn smiled. "They won't leave without you," she said. "Rest assured, you're the best hand they've got."

"It's all Annie."

"Your humility is so genuine it's obnoxious."

"Would you rather I swagger 'round like Shep?"

Robyn's response was to narrow her eyes.

"I need to get going."

"Then why don't you?" Robyn couldn't resist teasing her.

Seneca grinned and shook her head. "I'll keep an eye on Win for you." She turned to leave, but Robyn put a hand on her arm.

"No good-bye kiss?"

Seneca froze as Robyn stepped close and rose on her tiptoes. Their lips were a breath apart. Robyn pressed her lips softly to Seneca's philtrum, to her chin, and then to the right and left corners of her mouth. Seneca groaned softly. As Robyn was about to go in for a real kiss, the door opened, and someone shouted, "Twist! Let's go!"

Seneca jumped back. "Coming!" She looked at Robyn one last time before scrambling hastily away. Robyn snickered.

"Seneca!" Robyn called. Seneca looked to her from the ground floor. Robyn held the saddlebags over the loft's banister and dropped them. Seneca caught them and met Robyn's eyes once more. "Stay out of trouble."

Chapter Twelve

Seneca couldn't remember the last time she'd had such fun. They had reached the cattle in a half-day's ride and would camp among them that night. Sitting around the fire with JD and Win and the other cowboys was relaxing and peaceful, despite the many riotous stories they had to tell.

"…So then, we see flashing lights…" Win recounted a tale about himself as a teenager which ended with him being hit with birdshot. "That was probably the lowest point in my life, having my mother dig metal pellets out of my ass."

The group around the campfire erupted in laughter as Noah turned to her. "What about you, Ms. Twist? Ever been shot?"

JD leapt into the conversation. "Seneca, you don't have to share."

"It's okay, Boss." She smiled at the young man who was watching her closely. "I've been shot at, but no, I've never been hit with a bullet. The closest I've gotten is being hit with shrapnel from an IED in Afghanistan."

The campsite went silent. Noah, looking stricken, apologized. "Oh, man, I'm sorry. I—"

"Had no idea. I know. It's okay. They dug it all out and patched me up."

"Did they let you keep it?" Nathan asked. "The shrapnel?"

"No, unfortunately, they did not." She laughed and this broke the tension. "I was in and out of consciousness for about two days, so I didn't get to ask about it."

"Where was the IED?"

"It was in a truck. Pretty common there." She shrugged. "Now, I'd like to hear more trail stories. War stories suck."

With this, the talk of Afghanistan was over, and Seneca was relieved to find the conversation flowed once again around her until the moon was high and everyone unrolled a sleeping bag to lie near the fire.

❖

The next morning, an angry yell woke Seneca, and she flew from her sleeping bag reaching for her Nano.

"Rustlers!" JD's outrage boomed off the wall of the ridgeline. Seneca grabbed her jacket before shoving on her boots and rushing to stand beside him. Half their group watched a band of about a dozen men trying to steal their cattle. "Where's my rifle?!" He ran to the wagon to retrieve it and fired the gun into the air. The sound brought the rest of the gritty-eyed cowboys to their feet quickly and caused Seneca's chest to constrict. The report rang in her ears, hard and metallic. She could smell the gunpowder and fought a shiver.

The rustlers below looked toward them, and Seneca saw a glint of steel in the morning light. "Get down!" She dragged JD to the dirt as a report rang and the wood on the wagon next to them splintered. There were a couple of cowhands that had risen to their feet and as the second shot rang, one of them collapsed with a scream of agony.

"Shit!" another man yelled and scampered behind the wagon. Seneca's adrenaline kicked in. "Corporal! There's a field kit in the wagon."

"Yes, ma'am!" Win army-crawled to the wounded cowhand to drag him back toward the wagon. "C'mon, son."

"The rest of you crawl back to the—"

A third round was fired, and she clenched her teeth against the sound—

"—to the wagon. JD, get to the ridge and fire only at those who are armed."

She looked about for Noah and Nathan to find that Cliff already had them hunkered beneath the wagon. She nodded to him and then crawled toward the wagon. She reached for a rifle just as Shep's hand closed on the same weapon.

"I've got this," he said.

"Drop it, Shep."

"I'm a dead shot, and this isn't your troop." He sneered at her. She released the rifle and crawled to the ledge.

"We just need to scare them off taking our cattle. Land some shots close to their horses. Spook them."

"I've got it." He squirmed to the edge of the ridge on his belly to take aim. Everyone in the camp seemed to hold their breath. When Shep pulled the trigger, nothing happened save for a faint click.

Seneca wrenched the gun from his hand. "You left the safety on, dumbass." She raised the rifle where she knelt, intending to find her shot. Before she could disengage the safety, Shep's fist made contact from nowhere.

Her head whipped back, and her teeth clacked together. Seneca rolled to a three-point stance and crouched low.

Everyone stared at Shep in disbelief.

"Shep," Tommy said from where he hid behind the wagon, "what the hell?"

"She provoked me!"

JD started forward with anger in his eyes, but another shot rang out, and he staggered in pain. Red blossomed on his shoulder.

"Boss!" Kevin rushed forward to drag JD back behind the wagon.

Seneca filled with a sense of calm. She flicked the rifle's safety, aimed, and fired. One rustler fell yelling, but she didn't wait to see it.

"Guard the boys and shoot only if rustlers come over the rise," she said. Seneca then ran to the rise's edge to slide into the tree line.

She took aim again, then pulled the trigger evenly. She incapacitated another rustler before jumping up as before and sprinting through the trees.

Seneca slid to a stop, took a knee, and brought the scope to her eye once again. Most of the rustlers were bailing after seeing two of their men down. They drove their horses away from fire. Another two rustlers remained in the area reeling about looking for her. One leaned over and spoke to the other, pointing to the tree line some twenty yards from where she had last fired. Both started forward again, wading through shrubs and bushes cautiously.

Seneca moved silently to collect a stick. She tossed it and they turned sharply. She shot one man in the shoulder. He shouted and fell after she'd already begun moving again. Making as much noise as possible, she ran to a towering western hemlock and ducked behind it.

As the rustler ran past her, she tripped him, and he dropped his shotgun on the way to the hard ground. He rolled over, spat dirt from his mouth, and reached for his weapon.

"Oh, please," she said, "please do."

He smartly remained still on the ground.

Seneca heard Kevin calling her name. "Over here, guys!" Her eyes and the business end of her weapon never left the man on the ground. When Kevin arrived, she nodded to the man's gun. "There's another one back there."

"We've already got him." He showed her the duct tape. "Tommy and Cliff are securing the others."

"JD?"

"Win thinks he's going to be okay."

"Shep?"

Kevin grimaced and presented the duct tape again. "The boys didn't seem to trust him after he cold-cocked you." He looked at her face and grinned. "Speaking of which…I love your purple eyeshadow. Very eighties."

"Get gone or you and I will match."

They satellite phoned MedFlight, and several helicopters came and went. JD was the last to load. "I'm sorry I won't be with you on the way back."

"Well, I'm pretty sure you're faking that gunshot wound so I'm upset." She rolled her eyes; JD and Win laughed. "Go and let them fix you up, Boss. You'll be back to work soon enough."

The medics pushed them out and they cleared the landing zone before watching the chopper take off. Win clapped Seneca on the shoulder, before turning her face gently so he could see her blackened eye and cheek. "Damn, girl."

"Yeah, I didn't see that coming."

"None of us did." He looked to where Shep was sitting on the wagon and being given a wide berth. There were glares, but no one spoke to him. Not even Tommy. "I don't know what he was thinking."

"He wasn't." She shook her head. "He wanted to prove himself and he goofed. He attacked me because he was embarrassed."

Win shook his head. "Still..." Then, he chuckled. "Robyn is going to kick my ass."

"What?" Seneca frowned, but it hurt her face, so she smoothed her features.

"She made me promise I'd keep an eye on you." He laughed again. "Look at you!"

At this, she carefully smiled. "Well, she made me promise the same thing. To look after you."

"What?"

"Yeah, so I think I definitely did better." Seneca couldn't help but be proud.

He clapped her on the back again as his laugh grew into a shout. "She's going to be so pissed your face is banged up." Win's mustache fluttered with his guffaw.

"Why is that?"

"Because she likes it so much."

"What?" Seneca wasn't laughing anymore. She was mortified Win might mean what she thought he meant. "What do you mean?"

"Your face!" *That's helpful, Win.* He laughed even harder. "She can't keep her eyes off you. She's going to be so mad!"

Well, shit. He knows something. "I don't think—" Cliff was at her side.

"I think we need to get a move on," he said. He looked at the sky. "The quicker we get back, the better."

"What did the young steer say?"

"That there is snow coming."

❖

That night was savagely cold. The snow started that evening and fell thick and fast so that they took turns awake to keep the fire going. They were glad when morning came. They had a full day's ride ahead and it would now be much slower going with the inclement weather. Seneca just hoped they stayed on schedule enough to get back to the ranch by Sunday night.

❖

Robyn sat frozen between Sarah and Joan. They were all bundled against the temperature outside and sitting on the bench seat of Sarah's old truck. She checked the time and strained her eyes in the hazy semi-darkness; the binoculars were of little use. Any minute now. The crew was several hours late and what with all the excitement with the rustlers, the waiting families were beside themselves with worry.

Joan grabbed her arm. "Listen."

A sound like distant thunder met her ears. "Here they come." Sarah put an arm around her niece as the first few cows came around the bend and into view less than a quarter mile away.

Her father, as the only point man with JD missing, came into the glow of the pasture floodlights, slapping his thigh and waving his hat in the cold air. Robyn was relieved and clutched at Joan's hand on her arm. Swing rider Kevin came forward with another cowboy and helped her father corral the cattle through the gate. The waiting families drove closer to the gates as the cattle continued through them to the field. The sea of black cows surged past in the falling snow, a seemingly endless horde. Then, Annie Oakley pranced into view.

When Robyn finally saw Seneca working as the drag rider, she exhaled through the emotions filling her chest and throat. Seneca and Annie Oakley traveled back and forth alongside the back of the herd. Seneca's faded scarlet scarf hung half-loose from her jacket and streamed behind her in the whipping wind. She was all business until the last of the cows entered the holding pasture. Finally, the gate was closed, and everyone sighed a breath of relief.

The cowboys dismounted and their loved ones rushed forward. Joan went to her father, Robyn hot on her heels. He clasped both Joan and Robyn in his arms.

"I'm glad you're okay," Robyn said. Her voice was muffled against his coat. She pulled back and kissed his cheek. "JD and Stephen are okay, too," she said before he asked.

"Good." He sighed in relief and looked at Joan once again. "I'm getting too old for this." They all laughed and the tension broke. Satisfied that her father was well, Robyn turned away and began scanning the crowd for Seneca.

After watching Win envelop Robyn in his arms, Seneca rode Annie to the barn. She removed the saddle with her frozen fingers and brushed her wonderful steed. She paid extra attention to all Annie's favorite spots as her just reward for the hard journey home. Seneca then led Annie to her stall and offered her a generous amount of feed and her favorite alfalfa cubes. As she stowed the saddlebags on a hook, the door to the tack room creaked open. Seneca turned to find Robyn.

"I'm sorry we're late," she said. *I am so damn tired.* "I was working the men as hard as possible to get back on time."

"Don't apologize, Seneca." Robyn's reply was gentle. "From the sparse details I got from Dad, you're the reason they got back at all."

Seneca turned away. She was pleased Robyn thought of her as brave and heroic. But there was pain knowing she possessed neither of those qualities. She didn't have long to dwell on the contradiction, however, because Robyn closed the distance between them, and all the air seemed to evaporate.

Robyn traced the swollen contusion as her golden eyes seemed to scan every inch of Seneca's face. Robyn's thumb caressed the space under Seneca's bottom lip and Seneca fought a shiver up her back. Robyn was so close, now. The soft touch on Seneca's face became insistent as Robyn drew Seneca's face to her own. Seneca let herself be guided despite her trepidation. What would her weakness for Robyn mean for their relationship?

Their lips met. Tenderly at first. Robyn sighed softly against her, and Seneca did not resist the urge to draw her closer by pressing one hand on the small of Robyn's back. Robyn deepened the kiss, raising on her toes to lean solidly into Seneca's body. Robyn's warmth crushed against her as she opened her mouth and let Robyn's tongue glide inside.

Suddenly, the door to the tack room was opened again and a cold gust of wind blew in. Seneca and Robyn broke apart to blink at the intrusion.

"Oh, excuse me." Sarah cleared her throat. "Still on for chili at Jack's?"

"Um." Robyn's voice was thick, and she wore a dazed expression. Seneca was sure her face looked much the same. "Yes." She slipped away from Seneca's arms.

"And you, Seneca?"

Seneca cleared her throat. "Sure."

"Good." Sarah smiled before she closed the door again, leaving an awkward silence in her wake.

Seneca met Robyn's gaze. "How much did you hear of what happened?"

"I heard Stephen and JD were shot and Shep punched you. Your poor face."

Robyn looked ready to touch her again, but Seneca was glad she didn't. She didn't know if she could handle it right now. She was fragile. How was it that this woman could lay her bare so quickly? Her need for Robyn's approval and attention frightened her.

Pushing these emotions away for now, Seneca slapped on a grin. "Win told me that you asked him to look after me."

Robyn looked at her for a long while. Seneca knew Robyn was deciding whether to let her get away with the emotional avoidance and topic change. Finally, Robyn nodded. "I did. I knew if he was looking after you, and you were looking after him, at least one of you would come away from the trip okay." Robyn gently cupped the bruised cheek again and looked at the still healing barbed wire scar on the other side. She sighed. "I must say you did a far better job than he did. At least you'll heal in a week or less. We'll get you an ice pack once we get to Jack's."

Seneca shook her head. "No, thank you. I've had enough ice for a while."

"Well, let's get you a drink, at least. I think you've earned that."

"I should hope so."

❖

They arrived at Jack's to find honky-tonk music blaring and chili with all sorts of fixings lining the bar. Most of the cowhands were there with their families. Win had obviously shouted the story about what had happened to the rooftops, because as Seneca stepped in, applause broke out. Seneca ducked her head and landed on a sheepish smile and half wave in response before hanging her jacket and scarf and then skirting along the wall and toward the bar where Earl was already pouring her a drink.

"You get five free drinks tonight." He pushed the glass forward.

"Five?"

"One for each man you apprehended and one for that shiner." He pointed to her left eye. He leaned forward. "Did you really shoot three people?"

"They shot JD. When he went down..." She trailed off as flashes of another lifeless body surfaced in her mind.

"It's only a flesh wound," a voice behind her said. She turned to find her stocky employer sporting a sling on his left arm. "Through and through. Clean as a whistle." JD grinned.

Relieved, she shook JD's hand. "Earl, I'd like one of my free drinks to go to Boss."

Earl looked at her shrewdly for a moment, and then poured JD a drink. "Anyone else?"

"Win, of course, even though he can't keep his mouth shut." She raised her voice so he heard her. Turning back to Earl, she grinned. "And one each for Kevin and Cliff because they are fearless."

Jack growled behind her. "What sort of idiot gives away free whisky?" He looked at her with a soft expression despite his gruff tone.

"The sort who puts herself in harm's way to protect her friends," Sarah answered before Seneca could open her mouth. "Now, do go check on the sour cream. I think we're running low." She squinted to the end of the bar where there was a plethora of chili toppings. Jack nodded to his wife and patted Seneca on the shoulder. "Well done."

CHAPTER THIRTEEN

S eneca felt Robyn's eyes on her all night, like a tickle on the back of her neck. The attraction between them was undeniable. Seneca could still feel Robyn's lips against hers, and Robyn's back beneath her hand. The heat of that moment rose to her face again. It felt amazing to have her hands and mouth on Robyn. To express her longing and desire and relief. It had been a hell of a few days and having Robyn in her arms had felt *so good*. It felt like the most natural thing in the world. Excusing herself, Seneca took her jacket and scarf from the coat rack and slipped through the back door.

The cold air and the relative quiet were fortifying, but not undisturbed for long. Seneca turned her head when she heard the door. "Ah. I thought someone was watching me."

Robyn came into view and intimated innocence with an arched brow. "What do you mean? I needed some fresh air." She came to stand beside her, and they both gazed toward the unseen creek's occasional burble as it flowed around ice in the darkness, oblivious to the turmoil of its spectators. "Kevin told me what all happened."

"I'm sure he embellished a great deal."

"So, you're saying you didn't shoot three people and wrestle a bear?"

She chuckled. "It was a mountain lion, not a bear."

"Oh, sorry. My mistake." Robyn's voice softened. "How do you feel?"

Seneca hesitated, then grimaced. "My face hurts." There was a short silence between them.

"I think you might know that's not all I meant," Robyn said. Her voice contained its typical gentleness, but something in Robyn's delivery or in the moment encouraged Seneca to dig a bit deeper for a real reply.

She leaned on the rail heavily. "Shooting was easy." Seneca sighed. "Too easy. Combat was always easy for me." She swirled her liquor.

"That's a good quality in a soldier."

"But I'm not a soldier anymore."

Robyn nodded. "True."

Seneca looked at her hands. "Everything happened quickly. I didn't want to shoot anyone. That's why when Shep took charge in the first place, I didn't fight him too hard. I didn't want that rifle."

"Then the petty bastard punched you."

"Yeah, dumbass tried to fire without disengaging the safety." Seneca rolled her eyes. After a pause, she continued, speaking softly.

"Even when I took the gun from him, I didn't plan to injure anyone. I just wanted to spook them, stop *them* shooting *at us*. But when JD got shot, I—" Her voice caught and the emotion she'd held at bay while on the drive surfaced. She bit her lip hard and turned to watch soft flakes of snow fall into the drink sitting on the railing.

"You were scared. Scared that he was hurt," Robyn said. The soft voice cradled a firm note of fact and steeled Seneca's nerves. It helped her continue.

"Yes. I was terrified for him, and I flashed back to the desert. I was there in the hot sand. There weren't cattle rustlers and cowboys; there were insurgents and my troop, and I'd already lost two men and I wasn't going to lose any more. I aimed the rifle and—" She held an imaginary gun in her hands and stopped. Dropping her arms, she leaned again on the rail. She would not face Robyn.

"I'm sorry you had to use violence, Seneca," Robyn said. "But I'm glad someone with your skills and leadership was there. If not for you, there could have been a lot more of our guys hurt."

She shook her head. "I keep telling myself that, but it doesn't make me feel better. One of those men I shot is still in a coma. One will walk with a limp for the rest of his life. I did lasting damage, Robyn."

"At least none of them are dead. And none of ours are dead." She put a hand on her forearm. "Doesn't that balance the scales?"

Seneca looked into Robyn's eyes and nearly told her *No*. No, it would never be enough because the blood she had on her hands could not be balanced. The blood on her hands was Hunter's, and there was no amount of good in this world that could erase the sin she'd committed by leading him to his death. There was no redemption. The violence she'd taken part in on that ridge was another example of the trail of blood she left behind her.

Instead, she simply turned away. "I don't know."

"What you were doing was protecting your people. It was justified—"

"Was it?" She eased away from Robyn's physical contact. She couldn't allow herself the comfort she wanted so badly.

"I think it was. Everyone thinks it was," Robyn said firmly. After a beat, she added, "I'm sorry. I didn't mean to upset you."

"I'm not upset." Seneca lied irritably. She stopped, took a deep breath, and continued in a gravelly voice. "I think I'm just tired. A lot has happened." With a sidelong look, she continued. "And don't apologize to me again. You haven't done anything wrong."

The night pressed upon them. Soft snowflakes fell again, thick and lovely in the back courtyard. Robyn finally turned away and the quiet simmered between them. When she spoke again, it was with so soft a tone that Seneca had to lean in to hear her.

"I can't imagine what you've been through. I can't imagine what it was like to have a weapon in your hands again. I can't imagine what you must be feeling, but..." Robyn turned to her, small lines wrinkling her forehead. "You were in the right place at the right time."

Seneca frowned. "What?"

Robyn stared at her a moment before turning to watch the falling snow. "All the events in your life, good or bad, culminated in you being on that ridge, on that morning. Every scene in your life up until that morning put you in that position. A position from which you did *good*."

Seneca shook her head. "I can't say that I believe everything happens for a reason—"

"That's not what I said." Robyn turned back to her. "I believe we make our own destiny. That our choices and mistakes shape our journey." She took a breath as Seneca absorbed this. "What I'm saying is that your journey led you to that ridge at that time; to the perfect position from which to protect the people I love. I'm sorry you're hurting, but I'm not sorry you were there. It's selfish, I—"

"It's not selfish." Seneca cleared her throat and tugged on her scarf self-consciously. "I mean, wanting people you care about to be safe is not selfish."

"Even if it's at the expense of someone else's comfort?"

Seneca considered this. She wouldn't be walking if Hunter were alive. Would he be dead if she had gone into the Army alone? Would she have gone into the Army if she hadn't been so scared of failing and jealous of his success in the first place? The questions made her head hurt. Made her heart hurt.

"I don't know," she said finally. "There are things—mistakes," she corrected herself, "big mistakes, which led me to this point. Do I regret those mistakes? Yes. Do I wish I'd not been on that ridge?" She paused and thought of JD and Win, Kevin and Cliff, even Noah and Nathan. She was surprised at the answer. "No, I don't wish that. I'm glad to have protected them."

Seneca and Robyn looked at each other. Something intangible passed between them. It felt familiar and comfortable, and Seneca was afraid. Robyn knew more about her now than anyone, save her mother. She trusted this woman. She wanted this woman, if only to touch the full beauty of her once in this lifetime. She looked into Robyn's deeply golden eyes and felt such longing that it was hard to maintain the gaze. All reason screamed for her to walk away and save them both deep heartaches. She didn't deserve to be here, to stay here, to stay here in Robyn's life; no matter what Robyn said. She imagined she could see the trust in Robyn's eyes, but she did not deserve to have it. For as much as Robyn now knew, she still did not know the whole story of how she came to be on that ridge. She did not know the bad that dwelled within her, that tainted her. It was an impossible position.

And yet, Seneca could not deny herself a kiss. She pulled Robyn to her and pressed their lips together. It was a fiercer kiss than before. Hungry and urgent in a way that Seneca had nearly forgotten. It felt good. It felt more than good. It felt *right*. This revelation prompted her to pull back and take a breath. One hand still cradled Robyn's face as she stared at her beauty; her soft lips were swollen and parted.

"Robyn, I—"

The sound of the door broke the moment. Robyn and Seneca separated as JD joined them on the porch.

"Hey." He looked at them. "Am I interrupting?"

Seneca could feel Robyn's gaze but did not have an answer. She wasn't sure what she had planned to say to Robyn, anyway. It was a confusing, impossible situation, and she did not have the energy to pretend everything was okay. Robyn replied. "I should probably make sure Dad hasn't had too much to drink."

"I think he's okay, although it looked like he was about to start singing." JD winked.

"Then, it's time to get him settled before everyone has to hear 'Ghost Riders in the Sky' again." With a final look at Seneca, Robyn headed back inside.

❖

Seneca and JD regarded one another. Seneca tried unsuccessfully to shake away the intensity she had shared with Robyn.

"How's that arm, Boss?"

JD lifted his good shoulder in a half shrug. "It's all right. I'm hard to kill; like a cockroach."

She half smiled. "A cockroach?"

"A bear?"

"I was thinking more along the lines of a buffalo."

"Hmm." He smiled. "I like that." JD drew near and propped a boot on the railing to look at the snow-covered courtyard. They were silent again, both adrift in the solitude of the night. "I wanted to apologize, Twist."

"Apologize?" Seneca scanned his profile. "Whatever for?"

"For starting that gunfight. If I hadn't lost my cool and fired my rifle in the first place, we might have made it home without any bloodshed."

She considered this. Though partly true, it was also true the rustlers might have still fired to cover their escape. "Maybe, but I doubt it," she said. "Anyone willing to rustle cattle from under our noses is willing to pick a fight as well. They had to have known we were camping on the ridge. We were making a lot of noise and that fire was bright enough for anyone within a two-mile radius to see."

"I guess that's true."

"It is true. You fired your weapon prematurely. It would have been better to formulate a plan, but it all might have gone to hell anyway with Shep in the mix."

"I still feel responsible."

She looked at the haunted expression on his face. "You probably always will, but no one else holds you responsible." These words echoed in her mind. Hadn't she told Win the same thing about Vallie just a few days ago? It seemed guilt and responsibility would always be a theme in her life. The irony of this struck her between the eyes. "Things could have gone differently, but the outcome might have been the same regardless. It happened and we will move forward."

"Yeah." He looked at her. "I feel bad that I put you in that position. I put the gun in your hands and pointed you toward those rustlers."

"I chose to take the gun in my hands." She shook her head. "It was my decision. A decision I would have probably made anyway." He nodded, but his posture was slumped, and she could tell he was still ashamed. "Look, balance it by helping me get this old cottage into shape. You know I have some basic carpentry skills, but I'll need a little help with the engineering."

After a moment, he rolled his shoulders back, then grinned. "I can do that."

"Good, because I'm liable to make a total mess of things." Seneca chuckled in a self-deprecating way.

"I think you'd do just fine. You're more capable than you give yourself credit for."

These words also echoed something half-forgotten in her past and she was chilled to her bones. Hadn't Hunter said those words to her once? She nodded.

"Tomorrow, then?"

"Tomorrow."

CHAPTER FOURTEEN

Seneca's walk back to the barn was a treacherous one, but more from the turmoil inside her than the weather. It was cold, but the frigid air burning in her lungs was good. It was cleansing. So much had happened she needed space and silence to process. Trekking the road at a consistent speed, her chest constricted as she remembered. The weight of the gun in her hands had been too familiar. Like a headache after a bender. Her calm and control in the face of violence troubled her. Was using violence the only time she was destined to find purpose?

She tried to clear her mind of the chaos of emotions. Any time her feelings threatened to overwhelm her in the past, she had simply pushed them away. She forced them down to remain cool and outwardly in control. This time, it was harder to do. The image of Robyn's eyes filled with concern and then desire surfaced, and she felt a sharp stab of regret. Kissing Robyn was beyond lovely, heated and soothing at the same time, but she shouldn't have done it. She had nothing good to offer Robyn. She nearly stumbled on a slick patch of ice as waves of emotion again overpowered her ability to quash them. She carried too much guilt and regret.

She wiped moisture away from her eyes and huffed impatiently at herself. If tears did any good, she'd gladly succumb, but she had never found any use for them. Seneca pushed a long, frosty breath of air into the dark night. That must simply be the end of it. She couldn't, in good conscience, continue this road of intimacy, friendly or otherwise. It was unfair to Robyn because Seneca knew she wouldn't be able to sustain a relationship long-term, not when it caused such turmoil.

Seneca sent a sad little chuckle to the stars. Oh, but how a part of her longed for a real relationship. She'd had acquaintances and casual flings, but not since her brother had she truly confided in another. Her mother didn't count, she wryly decided. She'd never *had* to confide in her; Rachel Twist had always *known* exactly what was on her daughter's heart.

To trust in another; to go through the trouble of putting into words how she felt seemed impossible. To explain what had happened, how it had happened, and why it all came to pass that she had begun walking in the first place…Seneca was not sure she had it in her to share her full history and bear judgment.

What would Robyn think of her? What would Win and JD think if they knew what a coward she'd been? Their fearless leader on the ridge had been so terrified of failing at college that she'd run away to let the Army determine and train her ambition. She'd run away and taken Hunter with her. She had ripped him away from his goals and future, a future he deserved far more than she. No, she simply would not obliterate their high opinion of her.

The barn was in sight now. She could see it in the valley between the ridge on which she stood and a wooded rise on the other side. She hardly noticed the floodlight on the barn because the emotion had reached a pitch inside her. She cursed into the night at the feelings kicked awake by the recent sequence of events. Events of her own doing.

More tears flooded her eyes, and she wiped them away angrily. As she did, her boots hit a patch of ice and she stumbled sideways into more of it. She reached for something to support her, but the only thing there was the weak branch of a ground shrub. The fragile, spindle-like twig snapped under her grip and there was nothing left but the fall. Over the edge she skidded until her feet were no longer beneath her.

Her instinct was to catch herself, but the ground was closer than she could see in the dark and so when she landed, it was with her left arm underneath her side. Pain flashed hot in her arm. She didn't even have time to grunt in surprise, however, before her left temple connected hard with a substantially sized boulder. Blackness enveloped her.

❖

Robyn wanted to see Seneca again before she went home. She was uneasy about the way they had left things. The kiss, as welcome as it had been, seemed abrupt and unconcluded. Seneca had been understandably rattled by the events on the drive, though Robyn still felt that Seneca was holding something back. She had tasted it in the urgency of the kiss.

She did not wish to minimize Seneca's feelings or analyze her pain, and she did not want Seneca to feel as though she was. Robyn couldn't quite describe what she *was* trying to do, but she felt compelled to do it. As a matter of fact, *compelled* aptly described her reaction to Seneca.

There was something about Seneca that was magnetic. Her mossy eyes were sometimes full of uncertainty, but more often compassionate and kind. The lines in her face spoke of laughter and worry and work. And her hands were so strong and sure, gentle and patient. Seneca's hands were a snapshot of her. As if everything she could ever want to know could be learned by looking at the long powerful digits and the calloused palms to which they were attached.

Yet there were times her shoulders sagged with the weight of a hundred tragedies. Robyn's experience was limited, but Seneca seemed far more burdened than the average soldier. Robyn sensed that Seneca had lost someone important to her. Perhaps a lover or a friend. A friend, she hoped. Thinking of Seneca with a serious lover unsettled her.

She mused on these things as she scanned the crowd for the woman of her intrigue. After several minutes, however, she was forced to accept that Seneca was no longer there. Robyn found her father.

"Where is Seneca?"

He frowned slowly. "I think she left."

"Left? With whom?"

He shrugged slowly. "I didn't see anybody." His eyes scanned the crowd, albeit a bit less steadily than hers had. "Everyone else seems accounted for. You think she walked?"

"I hope not," Joan chimed in. "It's below freezing and she's not accustomed to Idaho cold."

"That's probably just it," Robyn said. She knew her angst and unease made her tone sharp. "She doesn't know any better and she's pig-headed enough to try to walk back." She headed for the door.

"Where are you going?"

"To make sure she gets to the barn safely."

Robyn got to the ranch and idled at the barn. There were no lights on inside. Seneca was probably in bed. Robyn hopped out and banged on the barn door anyway, feeling silly for her overwhelming concern. Seneca could take care of herself.

"Seneca!" There was no answer, save for the whinnying of horses whose rest had been disturbed

Robyn searched for some sign of Seneca's arrival, and noticed her footprints were the only ones visible in the snow. Not so much precipitation had fallen that it would completely cover Seneca's tracks. Robyn's pulse quickened.

Seneca should be here by now. Robyn looked back as though expecting to see her walking on the road with her Montana hat and thick coat. No form materialized. Robyn turned away from the barn, got back into her car, and drove slowly back toward the main road. Taking a right back into town, she put on her hazards and crept along the highway looking for any sign of Seneca. All the while, Robyn fought a mild panic.

After a hundred yards, something caught her eye, and she slowed even more. Robyn stared at the scarf fluttering in the breeze. It was tangled in the bramble of a low shrub on the shoulder of the road and might have been totally insignificant if it hadn't been faded red. The panic she was battling rose into her throat. She pumped the brakes and put the car in park on the roadside, then reached into her back seat to grab her emergency flashlight.

She stepped cautiously toward the bushes on the shoulder. Living in Idaho her entire life had given her the instinct to move slowly and sure-footedly in case of ice and, sweeping her flashlight over the area, ice was just what she found. It gleamed from underneath the dusting of snow in the beam of light, and Robyn measured her steps carefully as she approached the spot.

Parts of Seneca's scarf had solidified to ice. Swallowing another swell of panic, she swung the flashlight over the edge of the ravine and found a boot. The beam followed the boot until she found a leg and torso, too. "Seneca!" She was breathless as she carefully made her way to Seneca. The slope wasn't especially steep or treacherous, but on a cold night it had to be scaled with caution.

Robyn managed to get to Seneca in one piece and knelt beside her; Seneca lay motionless on her side in the snow. There was a boulder near her head. With trembling hands, she removed a glove to press two fingers to Seneca's neck. Her pulse was beating strong, and Robyn sighed her relief. Seneca was cold to the touch, however, and so Robyn prepared to lie beside her to lend her body's warmth. She would not be able to get Seneca to her car, and so she dialed her father's number.

"Robyn?"

"Dad, I found Seneca hurt. We're in the ditch before you get to the ranch turnoff."

"W-what?"

"My car is parked on the side of the road with the hazards on. Please get here with help as soon as you can. Don't drive, Dad."

"We're on our way." He quickly recovered. "Do you want me to call an ambulance?"

Robyn looked at Seneca. Though she knew her face was battered, her breathing was steady, and her pulse was sound. There was no reason to believe she was significantly injured. "No, we can get her to the hospital. She wouldn't want the fuss of an ambulance."

He chuckled. "You're right. Sit tight, we'll be there soon."

She looked at Seneca's pale face in the beam of the flashlight. She seemed so vulnerable and young. Robyn wondered how old she was, surely not far from Robyn's own thirty years. Then again, she had the sort of patience that made JD look like a teenager.

Tightening her grip, Robyn adjusted her position to be a blanket to Seneca in her prone position. She swept Seneca's loose hair back and could not resist softly kissing her cheek and forehead. Robyn felt Seneca stir.

She lifted her head slightly. "Fuck me…"

"Easy there," Robyn said. Seneca stiffened in her arms. Robyn repositioned again to look into Seneca's eyes. "Welcome back. Can you move everything?"

Seneca twisted her head and moved her legs, groaning. More assured of no spinal injury, Robyn levered Seneca to her back, then adjusted them both to lean against the offending boulder with Seneca in her arms. Seneca helped by moving her legs but cursed as she lifted her left arm. She hissed in pain. "I think I did some damage to my arm."

Robyn resisted the urge to caress her face. "I called Dad so he should be here any minute."

"You didn't call an ambulance?"

"Did you want me to?"

"Hell, no."

Robyn laughed softly. She was sorry for the circumstances, but not for having Seneca in her arms. Seneca's solid weight was wonderful to bear, especially considering she'd been so worried about her before. "I didn't think so. What on earth did you think you were doing? Walking alone in the cold darkness?"

"I needed to get back to the ranch."

"I would have driven you."

"I know."

Robyn backed off. Now was not the time to berate her, and Seneca's toneless reply spoke volumes. She was thankful Seneca was okay. More or less. Perhaps she had learned some respect for the winter conditions. The silence stretched as Robyn strained her ears for the sound of approaching vehicles. She was surprised when Seneca spoke again.

"I just needed to get away from everyone. I needed to think. I wanted to be alone."

"Oh." Robyn wasn't shocked at her need for solitude. She was surprised Seneca admitted it. "I respect that, but Idaho can be dangerous, especially when it's cold and dark."

"Yeah, I think I learned that the hard way."

Silence stretched again. "I was so worried about you. When I suspected you'd left alone, I took off after you. I could tell you hadn't been at the barn. So, I drove back toward the bar and by sheer luck saw your scarf in the bush near where you went over."

"I'm sorry to cause you so much trouble." Seneca's voice was raspy with emotion.

"I wasn't looking for an apology. I just wanted you to know that..." Robyn stopped. What did she want her to know? That she cared for her? That she'd been terrified when she'd seen her lying in the snow? That she couldn't imagine Butterbean Hollow without her in it?

The sound of several vehicles approaching broke the strand of their awkward conversation. Robyn and Seneca heard vehicles parking and boots crunching on the ground. Flashlights illuminated the area above them. "Robyn?"

"Here, Dad!" She waved her flashlight.

"It shouldn't take more than a couple of folks to pull me from this ditch!"

"Shut your mouth, Twist." Jack's voice growled in the dark. "Dumbass thing to do, hoofing it out here on your own."

"So, I've heard," Seneca drawled her reply. "Could y'all hurry? I'd like to get discharged before sunrise."

"There's no chance of that." Robyn laughed. "We'll be in the ER all night."

"*We* nothing," Seneca protested. "I'm the one with the busted arm and conked noggin."

"Oh, and are you going to *walk* home from the ER, then?" Seneca didn't respond and Robyn knew she had her. "Like Jack said, Seneca, shut your mouth and accept the help because it's here whether you want it or not."

Chapter Fifteen

"Well," said the emergency room doctor as she came back in and started sliding X-rays onto the viewing box. "It's not broken, but there's quite a bit of swelling. I'd say you have a severe sprain." She pointed at Seneca's radius. "You're lucky."

"Yeah, lucky." Seneca knew she sounded childish but couldn't help but to be sour about the injury, however slight.

"We'll get you a brace to wear for a couple of weeks. Do you want a prescription for pain?"

"No." Seneca shook her head once and stopped. *Ouch.* Robyn and the doctor looked askance. "They don't work anyway. What about my head?"

"Concussion. You may experience a headache and ringing in your ears, but your reactions and speech are normal." She nodded. "Still, I would like it if you stayed with a friend for a few nights—just so there will be someone to watch over you."

"I don't need to be monitored," she said. Her tone was flat. "I just need some sleep."

"She'll be staying with me, Doctor," Robyn said. "Dad has already dropped off her things at my house."

"What?"

"Good. I feel much better knowing she's in your hands."

"I don't need supervision."

Robyn dismissed her petulant tone. "I think I'm the judge of that, Seneca Twist, I am the doctor, after all."

Seneca grumbled under her breath but didn't fuss any more aloud as Robyn and the physician discussed symptoms and remedies and such.

❖

Robyn flipped on a few light switches. Outside, it was the dark just before dawn. She led Seneca to the back of her home and showed her the small guest room.

"The bathroom is across the hall. There are extra blankets in case you get cold. Let me know if you need anything."

Seneca met her eyes. "You didn't have to do all this."

"I know."

"I don't want to put you out."

"I know," Robyn said again and the conversation they'd had several hours earlier echoed in the air. "But I care about you, and you have done so much for me."

Seneca looked at the floor. "I just don't want you to feel like you have to…"

"I don't *have* to do anything." Robyn crossed the space between them and cautiously raised a hand to Seneca's face. "I'm choosing to do this. You've been through a lot. Mentally, emotionally, and physically. Being sucker-punched, being in a firefight, driving those cattle back. And then slipping tonight, spraining your arm, and hitting your head? I should think you deserve a bit of rest, don't you?"

"It sounds a lot worse when you list it all off like that." Seneca's gratitude had turned to grumbles. "I could have gotten rest at the barn."

Robyn simply smiled. "I knew you would say that, but you would not be comfortable—nor safe—swinging in a hammock." She stroked her chin gently. She wanted to kiss Seneca's pouting face, but it was too much, too soon. They hadn't even talked about their interrupted kiss, yet. "There are other spare beds, but I want you here. It's only for a few days. Just to make sure you won't have any lasting effects of the trauma."

"You mean me hitting my head?"

"Sure, what else?" Robyn winked. "If you need something, let me know."

Seneca was convinced she wouldn't be able to sleep. She drifted off as soon as her head hit the pillow.

She held his lifeless body to her breast and cried out in anguish. Her heart was ripped apart. Looking at the face she knew as well as her own, she cradled Hunter as the sand exploded around them. He was gone. Hunter was gone. His body was torn to shreds, and his blood drenched the sand and their uniforms.

A shape appeared over her in the extreme heat. "Twist!" her commanding officer shouted. She raised her gaze to his stricken face. "We need to move now."

"Hunter." Her extreme agony funneled into one word.

"Move, Twist!" Cruso took her arm firmly in his grasp. "Now!"

"I can't leave him."

"You don't have a choice!" Cruso shouted over the gunfire.

"He never would have left me."

The officer cursed. He then bent to lift her brother's body over his shoulder with a grunt. "Move your ass, Sergeant!" They scampered back behind the wall. Cruso placed Hunter on the sand and the other soldiers took a moment to acknowledge his sacrifice.

Seneca looked at her brother who stared blankly at the sky. The world around her came into sharp focus. Explosions jostled her bones, and the corresponding vibration of the ground shook her teeth.

They were in a war zone, and she still had a job to do. Hunter was gone and he wasn't coming back. She would deal with that later. Right now, she could still fire a weapon.

Robyn woke to the sound of yelling. Bolting upright, she blinked in the daylight. Her mind seemed to stop, rewind, and fast-forward in a matter of seconds. The sound of a strangled cry came again, and she remembered Seneca in her guest bed.

She rose from the warmth of her sheets and wrapped herself in her robe while padding across the hall. Pausing at the guest bedroom door, she listened intently. At the sound of groaning, she let herself in to find Seneca flailing.

"Seneca?" Seneca was clearly still asleep, so Robyn kept her voice low, and hopefully soothing. "Seneca?" Robyn approached to put a hand on Seneca's shoulder and her patient was suddenly animated. She sprang from the bed and crouched on the floor as though ready to fight. Seneca's eyes seemed wild. "Seneca." Robyn steadily firmed her tone with each repetition of Seneca's name and hoped she would wake soon. She carefully watched as Seneca turned her head left and right.

"He's dead. He died. It got him more than me." Seneca's husky voice sounded breathless as she raised her eyes unseeing.

Seneca blinked twice before her gaze focused and she seemed to register Robyn's worried face. She looked down, and then slowly stood. Robyn watched her tremble and blink as if coming out of water.

"Nightmare?"

"Something like it."

"Flashback."

Seneca grabbed sweatpants from her bag and pulled them on roughly over her pajama bottoms. "They're so real."

Robyn's heart ached. "I'm sure they are. Do you want to talk about it?"

"No!" She shook her head vigorously but winced and stopped. "I mean, no, thank you. I'm used to my nightmares."

"You've been through a lot in the past few days. That's likely what brought it on. Talk to me about it. Flush it from your system." Robyn watched Seneca worry her lip.

"I don't know."

"Look, wash your face, I'll make a late breakfast and you can tell me over coffee. Nothing seems impossible over coffee."

❖

Seneca was too off-kilter to eat. She did plan to nibble, but it was the coffee she desperately wanted. She watched as Robyn pulled the whistling kettle from the stove and poured the steaming water over the freshly ground coffee in a press. She then placed the top and depressor on it and lowered it slightly so that all the grounds were submerged.

"Fancy." Seneca tried for a bit of humor, but her face wouldn't smirk.

Robyn winked. "It's super simple, and it's the best coffee you'll ever have. You won't be able to drink the slop that machine makes at the barn." Seneca raised her brows.

"That sounded a bit snobbier than I meant," Robyn said a bit more humbly. "I don't have a press at work, so I drink 'that slop,' too. The press does make a wonderful cup, though."

"We all like what we like," she said as she watched Robyn prepare ingredients for a couple of omelets. "I'm sorry I woke you."

Robyn met her eyes for a moment before looking at the whisked eggs. "Don't apologize for something you can't control." She heated butter in her ceramic pan. "Now, I'm assuming it was a flashback from Afghanistan?"

"Yes." Seneca nodded, but she owed Robyn more of an explanation. "It was chaos. We'd been walking toward a little village because we'd gotten word of some suspicious activity. When we were nearly there, a disabled truck exploded. I was close to the IED, and it peppered me with shrapnel, as you know."

"Right."

"What you don't know is…" She hesitated for a moment. "My brother, Hunter, was right beside me when it went off." She let this hang in the air.

"Oh, my goodness!" *He's gone.* "Seneca, I'm so sorry."

She waited for the swarm of emotion, but it didn't come. She took a deep breath and exhaling, continued. "Hunter and I weren't related by blood. He lived next door, and his home life wasn't the best. We grew up together, you know? He spent more time at my house than at his. He was family. My brother. When we were deployed together it seemed like the best luck in the world."

"Did you know what happened immediately after the explosion?"

Seneca shook her head. "No. I didn't know my ass from my elbow. I knew I'd been hit. There was a lot of smoke, so I started looking for survivors. I got two of my group back to safety before I went out again. After the explosion, we regrouped. The insurgents started firing at us. It wasn't until after the firefight was under way that I found Hunter. He and other soldiers who had been closer to the IED were dead." She watched as Robyn poured a cup of coffee. "After I was released from the hospital, I went right back to war. And after that, I trained soldiers. I couldn't sit still because whenever I did, I saw his face."

"Understandable." Robyn nodded and then passed Seneca the ready cup of joe.

Seneca was quiet for a moment, debating again whether to tell her the rest. She feared what Robyn would think, but now wanted to feel the weight of her judgment. It would make distancing herself from Robyn all the easier. "I couldn't forgive myself."

"I can see that in you. But why not? What else could you have done?"

"I could have not brought him there in the first place." Leaning forward to press the heels of her hands into her eyes, she continued. "When Hunter and I graduated from high school, we both had basketball scholarships, but I didn't want to do college. My brother did, though. He was smart as a whip and a hell of a basketball player. Ambitious. I was terrified I couldn't hack it and so the week before we were going to start, I packed a bag and told him I was going to run away and join the Army and was he coming or what?" She rubbed away her tears. "He tried to convince me to stay, but in the end, he came with me. I was always jealous of him and how successful he was, despite his home life. I ruined that for him. I dragged him to the desert where he died. I might as well have assembled the bomb—"

"Stop!" Robyn reached across the counter to peel one of Seneca's hands away from her face and look into her eyes. "His death was *not* your fault."

Those were the words she longed to hear, but she couldn't bring herself to believe them. Seneca snatched her hand away and snapped at Robyn. "Haven't you been listening?"

"I have, but your brother doesn't sound like the type of man who didn't know his mind. He sounds like he made his own decisions. He sounds like the type of man who would have *chosen* to be with you, and to shield you, if he could."

Seneca turned this over in her mind. It was true that Hunter would have made that decision, just as she would have for him. But if he hadn't been there, he wouldn't have had to. "Yes, he was a great guy. But he shouldn't have been in that situation."

"Do you blame JD for what happened in the summer pastures?"

Blinking for a moment at the turn of the conversation, Seneca frowned. "Of course not. I fought because I wanted to." Robyn leaned back triumphantly, but Seneca shook her head. "This is different."

"Yes, your brother died. It is different, but you do his memory a disservice by viewing him as a victim. If the shoe had been on the other foot and you had shielded him, would you want him to see you as a slain innocent? Or would you want him to respect your choice, accept what happened, and move forward?"

"That's easy for you to say."

Robyn took a deep breath. "Yes, I guess it is. I can't understand your pain. But if I were Hunter, I would want to be remembered by how I lived." With this, she turned from the conversation to focus on making breakfast. Seneca stared at her back.

She hadn't thought about things in quite that way. It was true that Hunter would have expected her to move forward. She could picture his easy grin. No, he would not have liked being seen as a victim. Especially by her. Holding on to the image of his smiling face, she tried to push the other images from her mind.

Chapter Sixteen

Later that afternoon, there was a knock on the door. Robyn happily found JD on the other side and welcomed him in.

"Hey."

"Where's the invalid?"

"Pot, kettle, black, old man—I am no more an invalid than you." Seneca grumbled, but Robyn knew she was happy to see him, too. Things had been awkward since Seneca had unburdened herself that morning, so Robyn had called JD to take her on a field trip.

"Old man?" He laughed. "Is that any way to talk to your boss?"

"You're not my boss today."

"Oh? Well, I guess if you don't want to see that cottage in the orchard, I'll just mosey—"

"I'll get dressed." Seneca disappeared toward her room as JD turned to Robyn.

"How's she doing?"

"A lot has happened."

"Yeah." He nodded. "She's okay, though?"

"Physically? Yes, she'll heal just fine."

"And otherwise?"

Robyn looked into the gentle eyes of her father's best friend. She'd known JD since she was fifteen when he came from Oklahoma to take over the ranch. He'd had a lot of hurt he carried with him, but Idaho and the people of Butterbean Hollow had helped him mend. He met Rosemary a couple of years later, and they married and settled into the town.

"She's hurting, JD. I won't tell her story because it's not mine to tell, but she's known loss."

"I get it."

"I know." She put a hand on his healthy shoulder and smiled. "You and Rosemary were there for me when everything happened with Dad and Mom and Joan. You are just as much family as Jack and Sarah."

"We feel the same about you." His eyes flickered to the door through which Seneca had disappeared. "And her too, now."

"She feels it, too." Robyn nodded. "I don't think she knows how to put it into words, but she understands that she has a place here and I think it scares her. She is accustomed to dealing with her struggles alone. She is used to being self-reliant. She isn't ready to stop running; she's terrified that something awful will catch her if she does."

"I can't imagine that girl has done anything to deserve something awful."

She pressed her lips together. "She hasn't. She may be gruff and hardheaded, but she's also tender and patient and kind. I don't think she's truly capable of inflicting pain on anyone she loves on purpose."

"You care about her."

"We all do."

"Yes, but..." He hesitated, then raised his good hand. "None of my business. So, how do we convince her to stay?"

Smiling, she leaned in. "Responsibility."

"Responsibility?"

"Yes. You remember that spring you were ready to leave?"

"What?" His face was shocked. "How did *you* know about that?"

"How do I know anything?" she said. "That was the spring I worked with you on those chicken coops, and you taught me everything you knew about carpentry?"

"Yeah..."

"And Jack got you involved in his illicit distillery?"

"Yes..."

"And my dad and you started doing that kids' rodeo?"

"Ah...I see. You all trapped me here with projects."

"No, we kept you so busy that you didn't have time to feel lonesome. You were so invested in the town and the ranch you felt as though you had been born and raised here. Then you met Rosemary, and the rest is history."

He was quiet for a moment. "So, everyone was in on this?"

"Everyone."

"Rosemary?"

"Except Rosemary. She honestly liked you for some reason."

He gave her a playful punch on the shoulder, and she grinned. "So where do we start with that hard head?" He hitched his thumb toward the guest room.

"Well, the drive is done so we need a project like the cottage to point her toward."

"She won't be able to do much with that bum arm."

"It won't be bum for long. In the meantime, I've got another idea." She wiggled her eyebrows.

"Do I want to know?"

"I don't want to give it away, but you'll know when it happens. How soon can we get her in the cottage?"

"As soon as next week, I would think." He scratched his chin. "The final renovations can be done while she's there."

"Good, a week is good. Her head should be better by then, and that will give me time to get what I need."

JD looked at her suspiciously but did not say anything about her scheming. He nodded toward the guest bedroom. "It's been a minute. Maybe you should go check on her. She's probably having a hard time with one hand."

"Right."

Robyn knocked on Seneca's door. "Seneca? Do you need any help?"

"Uh, yes please." The husky voice was muffled by the door, but Robyn could hear the embarrassment just the same.

She found Seneca facing away from the door with her pants around her ankles. Wow. Those muscled legs were just...yum. Robyn longed to bend Seneca over the bed and bury her face in her backside. "I can't get my jeans with one hand."

"W-what? Oh." Robyn shook herself back into the present and moved behind her. She tried to touch Seneca as little as possible. It was excruciating to be so close to her and not make her desires known. She took hold of the denim and slid the jeans up her amazing legs. She could smell Seneca's musk; she wanted desperately to touch Seneca there. Instead, she slid the jeans past the juncture and over her ass before reaching around her and securing the fly in as professional a manner as she could manage. Her heart rate was somehow only slightly elevated when she finished. "There."

Seneca turned with a blush on her cheeks. "Thanks. I guess it is good I'm here. I can't go outside in sweatpants."

"No, you can't." Robyn looked at the loose chocolate waves framing Seneca's face. "Can I help with your hair?"

"Uh, sure."

"Get on the bed."

"What?!" Seneca sounded panicked.

Robyn almost laughed aloud since both of their minds seemed to be in the gutter. Instead, she waved a hand to the mattress and spoke patiently. "You'll have to sit. I can't reach you if you're standing."

"Oh, right." Seneca sat and Robyn began to braid her hair.

"JD is excited about showing you the cottage."

"Oh?"

"Yeah. He likes building and reno projects. Like you, he's quite the carpenter." She finished the French braid and tied it off before stepping back to study her ward. The swelling in her face had diminished, but the barbed wire scar and smudging of bruises from her forehead to her cheekbone seemed more brutal than ever. Seneca deserved a rest and Robyn would make sure she did so that evening.

"We're having spaghetti for dinner tonight. Do you like spaghetti?"

"You're not going to hide vegetables in it, are you?"

Robyn laughed loudly and Seneca grinned as she stood. "What gives you that idea?"

"You seem the sort to do that."

"You don't like vegetables?"

"I do, with a few exceptions."

"Such as?"

"Anything green."

She laughed again. "Well, I usually put green vegetables in my spaghetti. If you won't eat them, I guess you can find something else for dinner."

"I can just pick them out." Seneca struggled into her flannel shirt over her thermal, careful of the brace on her left arm.

"Then, you won't get dessert." Robyn knelt to help Seneca with her boots.

"Excuse me?" Seneca laughed this time and arched her brows. "I'll do as I damned well please."

Robyn smirked at Seneca as she helped tie her laces. "Not in my home, miss." Robyn shook her head. "If you don't eat your vegetables, you *don't* get dessert." Robyn got to her feet.

Seneca rolled her eyes. "We'll see about that." Seneca also stood and exited the room. Robyn followed. Robyn watched as she reached for her jacket on the coat rack and gingerly pulled it on before struggling with the zipper. Robyn retrieved Seneca's laundered red scarf and wrapped it around her neck before zipping her jacket for her.

"Thank you," Seneca said, "for everything."

Robyn had the overwhelming urge to press a kiss to Seneca's lips, but JD was standing right there pretending to be interested in a loose thread on his sling. Instead, she tightened the band on Seneca's braid. "I'll see you later."

JD led Seneca up the weathered brick steps of the cottage. Barren flowerbeds were in front of the porch. He jiggled the key. The door creaked open and they both chuckled. "Nothing some WD-40 won't fix." He preceded her inside. "Now, this is a two-room sort of deal. Living, kitchen, and mudroom are all on this side." He swept his hand to the left. "And the bed and bath are on the other." He went to check the water was on, boots clumping on worn hardwood. Seneca surveyed the space.

She stood in the living room area. There was a woodburning stove that marked the boundary line where the kitchen started. A sink and an ancient refrigerator stood on a brick floor. The counter space was more than she had expected. She peered into the mudroom where a relatively new washer, dryer, and hot water heater resided. An empty gun rack hung over a bench on a set of hooks.

She turned back to the wall which separated the living area from the bedroom and was surprised to find that the hearth and fireplace led through to the other room. "That's great," she said aloud, forgetting about JD. He came around the wall.

"What's that?"

"The fireplace serves both rooms."

"Oh, yeah. It works because the space is small." JD glanced around. "It's not much, but it's structurally sound. We'll be fine letting you use the truck on permanent loan so you can get to and from the quad. Win can help you load some firewood to haul; but you can scavenge enough in the grove to last a couple of days if needed." He referenced the pecan trees nearby.

"I'll bear that in mind." She smiled. "Thanks, JD. This is perfect."

"Good," he said. "The cabinets need work, and it wouldn't hurt to put a few supports underneath the porch. But overall, it's a sturdy little house." He led her back outside. "No major leaks or anything like that." He showed her where the porch needed work before slapping the key into her hand. "At any rate, it ought to be plenty until you hike out in the spring."

Seneca had already started to think of the cozy cottage as home. She'd forgotten she would be leaving after the thaw. "Thank you." She smiled reservedly, hoping she hid her anxiety.

"Of course. You can move in as soon as next week. There isn't anything that needs doing that can't be done with you living here."

Seneca was happy to hear this news. She could start to put some distance between herself and Robyn. Internalizing her reaction, she pocketed the key. "I need a bed. Got any good thrift stores around here?"

"A few. I'll ask Rosemary to take you around. She's the thrift store queen."

"Good deal."

CHAPTER SEVENTEEN

JD dropped Seneca off, and Robyn met her at the door. "So, what do you think?"

Seneca removed her coat and scarf and hung them on the coat rack. "I think it's solid," she said and toed off her boots after loosening the laces. "It'll do." Sniffing the air, Seneca nodded toward the kitchen. "Something smells good."

"I'm a pretty good cook."

"I would say you're more than pretty good." Seneca smiled at her.

Robyn shrugged her modesty, but she was pleased with the compliment. "I also made lemon pound cake."

"Yum. Lemon is my favorite."

"Yeah?"

"Yes ma'am."

"Well, dinner is ready, but the pound cake will need another ten minutes or so." Robyn teased Seneca while she led her into the kitchen. "If you've decided you *are* eating your vegetables," she said with a grin, "have a seat and I'll start serving." Seneca chuckled.

Over dinner, they chatted about how to fix the cottage and where to find furnishings. "I don't need that much." Seneca shook her head.

"But you'll need a sofa at least. You'll also need a table and chairs."

"What for?"

"Are you going to eat standing?"

Seneca grinned. "I guess not. I just don't want there to be a big fuss."

"Oh, it's too late for that. You have met my aunt and stepmother, haven't you? Rosemary is even worse."

"Well, I don't think—"

The sound of Robyn's doorbell interrupted.

Robyn frowned. She wasn't expecting anyone. She cut her eyes to Seneca, who shrugged. Robyn went to the door and looked through the peephole. With a sigh, she turned back to Seneca. "I'm going to apologize in advance."

Seneca frowned and Robyn opened the door and let her mother in. She came blasting into the room like a cannonball. Her eyes, so much like Robyn's, but somehow frigid, landed on Seneca. "I didn't realize you had company, love." She turned back to Robyn.

Robyn sighed internally. Of course, her mother had known. Otherwise, she would have called rather than drop in unexpectedly. "You remember Seneca? She had an accident and needed somewhere to convalesce."

"Oh? Was it related to the shootout on the ridge?" She turned to Seneca. "I heard you put a young man in a coma, dear."

Robyn flinched, but Seneca merely met her mother's gaze. "Yes, ma'am, I did."

"You were totally justified, of course, but I'm sure you're upset about it."

Seneca responded evenly. "You'd have to be a monster to enjoy causing pain."

Her mother turned back to Robyn. "You must trust this woman to invite her into your home."

Robyn turned to Seneca and met the searching green eyes steadily. "I do trust her. She's proved herself to be a kind and loyal friend." She looked back at her mother. "Was there something you needed, Mom?"

"I can't stop by to see my only daughter?" She glanced back at Seneca. "And I'm glad I did."

"What does that mean?" Robyn stepped between her mother and Seneca. The maneuver was not lost on any in the room.

"She's very attractive, Robyn. And just your type," her mother said. The low volume of her voice accentuated the nastiness it held. "Tall, athletic, mysterious…"

Robyn stood stiffly as her mother smirked. "You don't happen to remember the last time you tried to fix someone, Robyn?"

Robyn fought to control her temper. Her mother's ability to set her off so quickly was astounding. "Seneca doesn't need *fixing*. She's not broken."

"Oh, darling," said her mother as she patted Robyn's face in a patronizing manner and swung her gaze around to stare into Seneca's eyes, "we're all a little broken."

"You would believe that," Robyn said. "I would like for you to leave now."

Her mother looked Robyn over with narrowed eyes. "She's going to hurt you, Robyn." With this, she exited with a flourish and left Robyn and Seneca staring after her.

Robyn turned to Seneca and opened her mouth but was surprised to find that she had drawn close.

"Are you okay?" Seneca's voice was a husky whisper. Her mossy eyes were dark, and her jaw was clenched.

"Yes, I'm used to her."

"I don't think you can get used to that sort of abuse. I think I'd rather be beaten black and blue than spend another minute with her." Seneca bowed her head. "I'm sorry. That's your mother."

"It's an honest assessment of how she makes people feel."

"Yeah, but I was raised better. My mama would kick my ass for being rude."

Robyn led them back to the kitchen counter. "Tell me about your parents," she said with a smile. Seneca beamed immediately. It was a beautiful expression that burnished her face.

"Well, my dad died when I was around eight. I don't remember that much about him except he was a big man with a big laugh. Larger than life, I guess. Oh, and Mama loved him. It was an all-consuming love. She never considered dating again when he passed. It was just me and her and Hunter. She worked two jobs. Taught school and waitressed on the weekends."

"I suppose you get your work ethic from her."

"Yeah, I guess." She chuckled. "She never quit. Tough as nails and just as sharp, too."

"You miss her."

"I do." Seneca twirled a bit of spaghetti on her fork, but never lifted it to eat. "I call her once a week, still."

"How did she feel about you leaving?"

"For the military?"

Robyn nodded.

"Well, she was upset. Pissed that I threw away that scholarship. She was so mad at me and Hunter, she didn't talk to us until after basic training. When we came back home in fatigues, she stonewalled us and wouldn't let us in the house."

She laughed. "I also see where you get your hardheadedness."

"Me?" Seneca grinned. "Anyway, we begged for forgiveness, she finally relented, and she made us our favorite meal."

"What's that?"

"Pork chops, fried taters, and mac and cheese," she said dreamily.

"Sounds like a heart attack on a plate." Robyn rolled her eyes. "Like something my dad would eat."

"Yeah, it does," Seneca said with a grin. "So, after that she was okay. Until I came home without him."

"Did she blame you?"

"No…" Seneca shrugged. "Maybe? I think she did at first because the Army was my idea, but…"

"We all need someone to blame in the beginning." Nodding sagely, Robyn abandoned her spaghetti and dumped the noodles into the compost before putting the leftovers away.

"Yeah, that's true."

"How did she react when you left home to start walking?"

Seneca stood and awkwardly scraped her scraps into the compost, too, before passing Robyn the plate. "She knew it was coming, I think." She leaned back against the counter and watched as Robyn removed the pound cake from the oven and placed it on a cooling rack.

"Oh?"

"Yeah. She helped me pack and gave me a bit of advice before I left."

"Have you followed her advice?" Robyn did not turn from where she was wiping the counters.

"There was a lot of it."

"So, no, then?" She turned around with a grin. She'd felt Seneca's gaze scanning her and was pleased to see a hungry gleam in her green eyes.

"There were a lot of conditions to the advice. Mom always had a way of saying volumes in a few words. The day I left, she was full of insight. I think she knew it would be a long time before we saw each other again."

"You *could* fly her here for the holidays," Robyn said. "I mean, you'll be here until spring, right?"

"That's the plan." Seneca responded slowly.

"Christmas is far too cold, but Thanksgiving would be perfect. You have already seen how beautiful it is in the fall."

"I think Idaho is probably gorgeous all year round."

"Your mother sounds like the sort of person to appreciate that." Robyn had planted the seed and now she backed off. "But, then again, it is a long way to travel."

"It is." Seneca nodded. "But she has always wanted to travel. I think she might like it here."

Robyn turned back to her pound cake. She was anxious to release it from the pan, but it had to cool properly. "How's your head?"

"You know I have a nice goose egg, but I've had—"

"Worse. Yeah, yeah." Robyn finished Seneca's statement with a chuckle. "I know."

"Hey, it's true!" Seneca grinned.

"Yes, but it doesn't mean that *this* isn't bad." She pointed to her head. "Or *that*." She pointed to her arm.

"That's fair, I guess. The hardest part is having to ask for help buttoning my own damned jeans."

Robyn smirked. She couldn't say that she minded. Any excuse to put her hands on the strong woman's body was a good one as far as she was concerned. "Yeah, I guess asking for help is difficult for you."

She had her back to Seneca but watched her reflection in the polished metal hood over her stove. "You'll probably need help unbuttoning them as well."

Seneca's eyes widened slightly, and she stared at Robyn's back. "I think I can manage. But I suppose I should just wear sweatpants for the next few days…until the swelling goes down a bit."

"I don't mind helping you. That is why you're here, after all."

"Well, I don't want you to have to do everything for me."

"You have an injury."

"It's not that bad."

"It's bad enough." Robyn laughed and turned around to look at her. "Buttons and zippers or anything that takes both hands will be difficult for a while. Even showering will be hard."

"Are you offering to help with that, too?" She laughed.

Robyn coyly tilted her head while letting her gaze roam Seneca's muscular frame. "Like I said, that is why you're here." Robyn loved watching the blush that rose from Seneca's collar.

"I think I can manage." Seneca's voice was a sexy whisper to Robyn's ears.

"Well, you know where to find me if not."

Seneca had a difficult time falling asleep that night. She kept picturing Robyn's taunting face. The attraction was undeniable. She'd be lying if she said she didn't want to take her to bed. *Or the sofa, or the floor, or the kitchen counter. I'm not picky.*

She's going to hurt you. Vallie's malicious voice resounded in her head and stopped her fantasies. Vallie was right, of course. Spring would come and she would leave. And it would hurt. It would hurt them both badly. She'd already grown accustomed to life in Butterbean Hollow, had fallen into a comfortable rhythm. *So stay.*

As she lay in the darkness of the room, listening to the wind outside, she tried to picture what long-term would look like in the tiny Idaho town. It wasn't hard to imagine. A permanent place at the ranch. Long days with horses and friends. Coming home to Robyn and her cooking.

She stopped and shook her head. A future with Robyn was easy to picture, too. The chemistry between them was effortless. A simple touch, even an accidental brush of fingers, pushed Seneca's body into a state of soaring sensitivity. She was hyper-aware of Robyn's presence at all times. So much so that she could feel Robyn's gaze like a physical pressure on her body. Robyn was the sort of woman people searched for their entire lives.

More than that, however, Seneca wanted to care for her. To do for her. To provide laughter and comfort and strength. She had wanted to step forward and physically shove Robyn's mother from the house that evening. Vallie had clearly come by for the express purpose of torturing her daughter, and the bitter venom that fueled her nasty words left a stench in their wake. Despite her flippancy about the interaction, Robyn had not seemed quite herself afterward.

Vallie's words echoed again. Seneca wondered what had happened before. Who had Robyn tried to save? Or was Vallie blowing something out of proportion to shake her and Robyn both? Seneca found this easy to believe but tried to convince herself it did not matter. Robyn's past relationships were none of her business anyway. Failing to not care, she rolled over and began counting sheep.

Light streamed into the bedroom where Seneca was resting. She could sense sunshine but didn't care to open her eyes just yet. Her sleep had been peaceful for a change, and she was so cozy under the warm weight on her chest.

Frowning, she cracked a blurry eye to find a single, yellow eye staring back. Seneca's eyes flew open as she stiffened. It was a cat. A large cat. An exceptionally large fluffy cat with one eye and a tilted head. It looked as though it was trying to decide which side of her neck to bite first.

"Nice kitty," she said in her best mega-cat-whisperer voice. The solid black cat blinked its one eye slowly. It tilted its odd head more.

"Please don't eat me." The monster curled its paws into the top quilt and a low rumble began in its chest. It was purring. "Uh, okay." Seneca exhaled a sigh of relief. "I would like to go now," she told the beast politely. It didn't move save to flick its ears backward toward a sound only it could hear. It opened its one-eye wide before Robyn peeked around the cracked open door.

Robyn opened the door fully and just stood there for a year observing the scene.

"Wow, Jinx usually hates strangers." At the sound of its name, the black, shaggy monstrosity rose, stretched, and chirped.

"Come here, my lovely boy," Robyn cooed, and the beast hurried to Robyn's arms. Robyn gathered him to her bosom. *Lucky bastard.* Seneca noticed that one of Jinx's back legs was missing.

"You couldn't have told me you own a panther?"

Robyn laughed. "I didn't expect to see hide nor hair of him while you were here. He's a big scaredy-cat." She rubbed her face on his belly and the cat pawed at her face gently.

"I've never seen a cat that huge, or with that many...afflictions."

"Yeah, I found him on the side of the road when he was little, about four years ago. I think he'd been jumped by a coyote or something." She set Jinx on the floor, and he hopped back on the bed to rub on Seneca's covered knees. "Anyway, he'd lost an eye, a leg, and an eardrum or something because his head is always tilted, but he is very affectionate and fluffy."

"Jinx is definitely fluffy." Extending a hand, Seneca watched as the beast sniffed and then rubbed his face along it. Smiling, she petted him. "He is sweet. He just scared the shit out of me."

"Yeah, that surprises me. He must have been in here already, or was curious because your door was cracked? Jinx hardly likes anyone but me. He likes Sarah, but there isn't anyone who doesn't. That's about the extent of his social circle."

"Sounds more like a triangle."

Robyn laughed again. Seneca and Jinx played a few minutes while Robyn looked on. "He likes you though. He must recognize a kindred spirit."

Seneca stood and looked at Robyn. "How's that?"

"Well, you're both introverts and have both been through a lot. But neither of you has become bitter because of it. You're still good people." She glanced at Jinx. "Well, not *people* exactly, but you know what I mean."

The cat looked at Robyn in an affronted sort of way, chirped, and preceded them out of the room. "I don't think he liked you calling him inhuman." Seneca watched him trot with his tail high in the air.

"Neither do I." She laughed. "Breakfast?"

CHAPTER EIGHTEEN

Seneca rose with the sun to set about getting ready. By the time she was lowering the depressor in the French press, Robyn was stirring. Minutes later, she walked into the kitchen, still stretching away sleep.

"Good m-m-morning." She sniffed the air mid-yawn. "Coffee?"

"Yeah, I've been watching you and figured I could handle it."

"That's awful nice of you," Robyn said and watched the rich brown liquid as Seneca poured her a cup and put a bit of honey in it. "And you remembered I like honey?"

Seneca blushed a bit. "I pay attention to details."

"You certainly do." She brought the cup under her nose and sniffed. "Mmm. Thank you." Robyn looked at her. "So…" Her look turned somber. "You're not to get on a horse today."

"How can I work if I can't ride?"

"There are plenty of other things that don't require riding, Seneca." Robyn's tone was terse. Coming around the island, she softened. "Look, I get it. This is the thing that you're amazing at and you don't like not doing it."

"It's not exactly that." Seneca leaned against the counter and shook her head. "I just…" She took a deep breath. "That was what I was hired for. If I can't do the job…"

"You're worried about job security?" Robyn's tone was incredulous. "Don't."

"But—"

"Seriously." She reached for Seneca's hand. "You may not be ready to hear it yet, but…. Seneca, you have a place here, and you always will."

Seneca looked into the golden eyes and held the gaze until she was breathless. "Thanks," she said softly and leaned over to give her a gentle kiss. The press of Robyn's lips grounded her. She was much less unsure of her place at Butterbean as she broke the contact and backed away to get ready.

❖

"Tell me about the drive, Noah." Robyn smiled at the young man. He flashed a charming smile back at her. His large brown eyes, curly blond hair, and dimples made him look angelic. Robyn knew otherwise.

"It was good."

"Yeah? How so?"

He rubbed the back of his neck with a hand. "I don't know, it just was. It was good to put what I've learned to use."

"You mean what you've learned about horses?"

"And working on a ranch. I even got to help Seneca drive the cows a little bit."

At the mention of Seneca's name, Robyn's heart beat a little faster. Trying to keep her voice neutral, she prodded him gently. "Did you like working with Seneca?"

"Oh yeah." He nodded. "She knows what she's doing. And she shot those guys when they tried to take our cows. She's badass. Did you know she was in the Army and a war?" Noah spent the next ten minutes of the session describing, in detail, the amazing Seneca Twist. Robyn hid her amusement.

"Where were you during all the action?"

"Cliff dragged me and Nathan to the wagon and shoved us under it. We couldn't see what was going on, but we heard all of it. We weren't scared. Me or Nathan."

"I think I would have been." Robyn's admission was sincere.

"We knew Seneca would take care of it."

The confidence in his voice made her smile. "She sounds like a great person to have on your team."

"Yeah." Noah nodded absently, then turned to the window. "And Nathan's not so bad. He did good driving the cart and all with Cliff."

"It sounds like you both learned a lot from the experience."

"I guess we did." Noah's tone of voice suggested his surprise.

Once her session with Noah was concluded, Robyn had three others. By lunch she had formulated a plan about how Seneca could spend her time at the ranch while she was healing. She called Kevin.

"Hey." Kevin's friendly, drawling voice answered her call. "How can I help, Dr. Mason?"

"Would you mind popping over during your lunch break? I'd like to hear the latest on the equine therapy program, and I have an idea I'd like to run by you."

"Sure. I've got a few things to finish and then I'll be over that way."

"Thanks, Kevin. I'll have my door closed working, so just knock."

True to his word, there was a knock on Robyn's door a little after noon. "It's Kevin."

"Come on in." Robyn stood and came around her desk to gesture him to a seat on her leather couch.

Kevin collapsed his lanky frame onto the cushions. Robyn compared him to a marionette whose strings had been cut. He took off his hat and placed it on his knee before leveling his gaze at her. His freckles stood out on his face.

"Right, so the program is doing great despite the nasty business on the drive. I thought Nathan and Noah were going to be scarred for life, but they seem to have taken it in stride." He shook his head. "These kids are funny. One comment about someone's mama and they lose their shit, but ducking for cover under a wagon as bullets fly is just another Saturday night."

Robyn laughed. "I was pleasantly surprised there were no lasting traumatic impressions as well. I think the situation was handled well enough that the boys felt secure."

"We have Seneca to thank for that."

"True, and actually," Robyn tried desperately to keep her tone neutral, "that's what I wanted to talk to you about."

"Yeah?" He rubbed a hand over the lightly graying stubble on his jawline.

"I think pulling her into the therapy program would be a good idea. The kids already respect her, she's a good teacher, and she has more time than before because of her arm."

Kevin considered the idea. "I like it. I don't know why I didn't think of it first." He looked her over shrewdly for a moment. "Have you talked to Seneca about this?"

"No, you're the program coordinator."

"Yeah, but you two—" He looked at her. Robyn felt the air leave the room.

"What?"

"Aren't you?"

"Aren't we *what*?"

His crystal blue eyes looked at her dumbfounded as he frowned. "Surely, you are?"

Robyn could feel the heat in her face. Of course, she understood his meaning, but didn't want to be crude.

"Oh, come on!" He laughed. "You mean to tell me you've had her *at your house,* and you haven't slept together?"

"Um, no." Robyn's tone was brusque. She stood. Her cheeks were aflame as she walked around her desk to safety.

"Why not?"

"It's complicated."

"You lesbians always make things harder than they have to be." He stood, put his hat on his head, and adjusted the brim.

"Excuse me?" Robyn turned, fighting a grin. "That is an over-generalization, friend."

"But I'm not wrong," he asserted. "You want her. She wants you." He snapped his fingers. "Simple."

"Whatever is between Seneca and I, it is *not* simple."

"But there is something between you." Kevin grinned again. "Don't fight it."

"I'm not the one fighting it," Robyn said before she could stop herself.

Kevin laughed. "Oh, so that's the way it is? I thought it might be." He looked back as he stepped to the door. "Don't worry, Robyn, she'll come around." He walked into the hallway, leaving Robyn frowning after him.

❖

Seneca felt little more than useless. She had thought, erroneously, that Win and JD would understand her need to get on a horse. Unfortunately, Robyn had gotten to them first. For the first few hours of her first day back, she had sullenly managed inventory in the barn.

After lunch, Win called her to the loft where he'd been meeting with Kevin. "Seneca." He greeted her as she approached. "Kevin's got something he needs your help with."

"Sure thing." Seneca smiled. "How can I help?"

"Well, I lost Stephen to the field crew when Shep got fired, so I need another set of hands with the equine therapy program. I think you would do."

Seneca was caught off-guard. "Equine therapy? You mean working with the boys?"

"Yeah. I mean, you've already got the respect of Nathan and Noah, and they're two of the hardest knuckleheads to win over."

Her pulse quickened. Hard work didn't bother her, but she was unsure about this specific responsibility working with their young charges. She wasn't a psychologist and wasn't keen on putting in extra emotional work. "I'm not looking to win a popularity contest—"

"Hear him out, Seneca."

Win's voice broke through her anxiety. Seneca nodded. "Right, sorry, Kevin. I'm listening."

"Like I was saying, you're a good teacher. You're trustworthy. I could use your help."

"And this is only temporary?"

"Well, yes—at least until your arm heals, but maybe a brief time after. We're looking to hire some folks full-time, but that might take a minute," Win said.

Seneca considered the situation. She was bored to tears only a few hours into her first day back at the job. If she had to spend each day doing inventory or other "light-duty" tasks, she would really lose her mind. She couldn't lift anything heavy, mend fences, or ride—if everyone had their way—for maybe a couple more weeks. What the hell. At least she'd be near the horses. Honestly, the young men she'd met thus far were not that bad. And there was no chance of them following her into military service, she thought wryly.

"Uh, okay, sure. If you think I'd be useful. When do you want me to start?"

"Tomorrow, if possible. Like I said, I need the help."

Seneca looked to Win. "Does that timing suit you, Boss?"

"Suits me fine. Any of these cowhands can clean tanks and feed, and you can't do either right now. The therapy program is a more specialized job."

"Specialized?" Seneca laughed. "All I know is riding. Are you *sure* you want me?"

"Absolutely certain," Kevin said in a way that warmed her heart.

Later that evening, Seneca rode home with Robyn, and it was strangely quiet in the car. Her usual chatter was missing and instead, she seemed absorbed in her thoughts. The silence was disconcerting. Seneca was accustomed to conversation when Robyn was around.

"So, how was your day?" The words sounded stupid, and Robyn must have thought so too because she looked at her with a strange expression. Seneca plowed forward. "I took another look at that cottage today to make sure all the appliances worked. A few bulbs need to be replaced and I did find a tiny leak under the bathroom sink, but everything else seems to be in order."

Robyn smiled faintly. "Thank you."

"What?" Seneca frowned in confusion.

"You are perfectly at home in the silence, but you tried to initiate small talk."

"Okay…"

"You were checking on me."

Seneca looked at her. "What?"

"You noticed that I was far too quiet. You were checking to see I was okay. Thank you."

"I don't know about all that," Seneca huffed, disconcerted.

"Well, I do." Robyn laughed. "And my day was awful, but you already knew that."

After a silence between them, Seneca probed. "So, what made it awful?"

"Just one thing after another. We had one resident run away last night."

"Run away? Where the hell did he go?"

"Into a passing car."

"Ah."

"Some of the boys don't like the rules or the work. Or..." She exhaled. "Then a couple of the apprenticeships fell through. I mean, they always do, but it hurts every time. It's difficult to remember that we play a long game on days like today. The best we can do is provide resources and try to influence the residents to make the right call. We can't force them to do it."

"I'm sorry."

"It's okay." Robyn sighed tiredly. "The topper was my mother leaving a message with my secretary about a casserole dish she claims I have never given back to her."

"What?"

"Yeah. She evokes that casserole dish every now and then. Usually as a segue into something else like, *Robyn, I need that dish I lent you and oh, did you hear about Barney Miller's daughter? She got mugged by a guy she met in a bar.*"

"Is that what she said?" Seneca tried not to laugh at the imitation of Vallie's haughty voice. It was spot-on.

"Something to that extent, yeah."

"She's trying to warn you about me."

Robyn glanced at her before returning her eyes to the road. "Don't take it personally. My mother has hated every woman I have ever dated." There was silence in the car as both of them studied the implications of this statement. "Not that we're dating," she amended. "But that doesn't matter to her. She hates any woman friend, too."

"So, she usually runs your girlfriends off?"

"Anyone I've been serious about, yes. She's never accepted that I'm gay."

Seneca could hear the frustration and sadness in Robyn's voice. She wanted to soothe her, but she was also curious about something Vallie had mentioned.

"I'm sorry. That's got to be tough. When she said I was your type…"

"She was referencing the last serious relationship I was in. Honestly, I've dated all sorts of women. Tall, short, thick, thin—whatever. But Michelle was a bit like you, I guess. On the surface anyway." Robyn glanced at her, and Seneca lifted her brows. "She was tall, cool, and lean. She didn't have near the amount of muscle tone you do, though."

"Oh?" Seneca smiled. "You find me appealing?"

"I'm not sure who wouldn't find you appealing."

"So, she was like me?"

"That's just it, though. She wasn't. Michelle had a complicated history."

Scoffing, Seneca looked out the window. "Oh, and mine is so straightforward."

"Do you want to know, or not?" Seneca raised her hands in a placating gesture.

"Michelle's *was* different. There was abuse and hard drugs. She was clean when we met, but only just. Anyway, she had a lot of turmoil, but instead of using it as motivation, like you do, she used it as an excuse."

"How did it end?"

"It ended when she was hospitalized for attempting suicide in my apartment in Boise. She realized she needed to help herself and got into a program. I moved back here. It's been five years since I've seen her, but I hear she's doing well."

Seneca digested this. "Wow."

"Yeah."

"Thank you for telling me that. You didn't have to."

"I don't want to keep anything from you." Robyn glanced her way. "You are my friend, and maybe more, soon. It's important to me you know my history."

Friends. She liked the sound of that. They'd discussed it before, but it meant more now after all that she had shared with Robyn. Things she'd not shared with anyone else. "Well, I'll order pizza when we get back, and you can go take a bath."

"No, you're the guest."

"I think prisoner is the more apt term." Seneca grinned.

Robyn looked over at her and a slow smile spread over her face. "Prisoner? How kinky."

Blushing, Seneca looked out of the window. This woman sure could press her buttons. "You know that's not what I meant."

"Oh? That's a pity. I rather like the image of you chained."

Seneca's mind flashed an image of *Robyn* in restraints, smiling at her coyly. *Is spontaneous human combustion a thing?* "Uh, that's not going to happen."

"No, I suppose not. What would I chain you to?"

She squirmed in her seat. Her body reacted to more sensual images surging in her head. "I don't think you *could* chain me."

"And why is that?"

"I'm much larger than you."

"I would caution you not to underestimate my experience."

"I'm sure your *credentials* are impressive," Seneca fired back. Robyn laughed delightfully. "However, it's your stature that is less than intimidating."

"Perhaps." Robyn tilted her head and looked at her in a way that caused Seneca's pulse to jump. "I've found that knowledge is power."

There was a tick of silence as the tension between them built. She was sensitive to Robyn's needs because they were the same as hers. Finally, Seneca responded in a calm voice.

"Clever and experienced, or not, you cannot replace your bravado with physical matter."

"We will see." Robyn waggled her eyebrows suggestively.

"Maybe we will." Seneca tried to reply evenly but heard her voice quaver. Her body was a quivering mess of angst. Robyn was driving her insane. For each delicate touch, there was a steamy look or word. Seneca remembered vividly the kiss they had shared on the back deck of Jack's after the drive. The hunger. She remembered Robyn's body pressed against hers, the quiet sighs and swollen lips. It had been so long since she had felt such *need*.

Seneca looked out the window. How did that make her feel? She glanced to Robyn, whose eyes were on the road. *Disconcerted. Anxious. Hungry.* Seneca focused on the mountains they traveled past as she questioned every decision she'd made since following the little state highway crossing I-90. Could this work? Could she stay in Butterbean Hollow? She'd faced more demons in the past few weeks than she had in nearly five years. She'd also been more at ease here among these people than she had anywhere else.

So far, she'd not *needed* to move, winter notwithstanding. The first few days after she'd realized she couldn't walk any farther, she had expected that itch to come back. She'd expected to feel trapped. But the truth was that she'd been too busy with the ranch and horses to feel any such thing. Preparing for the drive had preoccupied her. And now that she didn't have the drive, she had the cottage to repair. And although it scared her some, the equine therapy program. There was plenty to do here, fulfilling things for her to do here, and there probably always would be.

She glanced at Robyn. Was she willing to take the chance on a relationship? She wasn't sure. She didn't want to hurt Robyn; it was the last thing she wanted to do, in fact. But how she wanted her. Even now, sitting in total silence, Seneca could feel the desire pulsing between them as distinctly as she could feel her own heartbeat.

She looked at her mending wrist. It wasn't as if she could do the thing properly now, anyway. When she took Robyn to bed, she wanted to be sure to have two, well-functioning hands to pleasure her with. Thinking she could put off her decision for another week, Seneca leaned back in the seat and tried to ignore how poignantly aware of Robyn's every breath she was.

CHAPTER NINETEEN

It had been three days since Seneca had moved into the cottage. Robyn's father had loaded the porch with a neat stack of firewood and Robyn had helped Sarah and Joan clean the little house from top to bottom. They had bought all the furniture second-hand at a thrift store and had made the little home as comfortable as possible.

Still, Robyn dwelled on Seneca's well-being. Did she have enough firewood? Was she eating properly? Robyn tried to keep her distance. She shouldn't hover; Seneca would not tolerate it. But her concern got the better of her, and so she found herself at the corrals checking in with the equine therapy program earlier than usual.

As Robyn approached, Seneca was working with a younger boy. He sat astride a docile gelding as she patted different locations on the horse. Whatever Seneca said, the boy seemed engrossed. It seemed, whatever Seneca's earlier reservations, she found herself equal to the task. Robyn smiled at the irony. She wondered if this was where Seneca had imagined she would be just a couple of months ago. Surely not. Tearing her eyes away, she spotted Kevin and waved.

He made his way over as she slipped between the metal bars of the round pen fencing. "You'll get those fabulous heels dusty."

Robyn looked at her shoes. "Dirt washes. How's everything going?"

"Got a couple of those new boys here today. Seneca is giving one the rundown. Says he's been on a horse before, but I'm not convinced."

"You know how these kids like to seem in control," she nodded. "That's normal given the various circumstances bringing them here."

"Yeah, I overheard Seneca and him talking as she was explaining posting, and he wanted to know what fences had to do with riding."

"Wow!" Robyn laughed. "She's got her work cut out for her, doesn't she?"

"I think she's up to it." He smiled and spotted a couple of boys loitering. "Excuse me."

"Of course." Kevin strode off on his long legs. Robyn watched his interaction with the boys for a moment before turning back to Seneca. As she watched Seneca gesture for the boy to dismount and take hold of the saddle as though she planned to climb astride the horse, Robyn felt her feet moving. "Ms. Twist!" she called over the din.

Seneca turned with surprise evident on her face. The surprise turned to chagrin and then to frustration. "Dr. Mason," she said coolly.

Robyn drew Seneca away from the boy.

"Were you about to mount that horse?" She purposefully kept her voice low.

"Only to demonstrate posting."

"I don't think that's wise."

"He needs a demonstration."

"Someone else can do it."

"Who?" Seneca challenged. "You?"

Robyn took in Seneca's taunting face. "Sure," she said brusquely. Robyn stomped over to the horse sensing Seneca close behind. She removed her heels, thrusting them at Seneca. "Hold these, please." Before Seneca could reply, Robyn stretched to mount the gelding, thankful for her choice of an emerald pantsuit that morning and not the ochre skirt she'd been contemplating. She smirked at Seneca's stricken face before turning the horse about and entering the arena.

It had been a while since she'd been on a horse, and she was reminded how much she loved it. The gelding responded well and moved quickly into a trot. Robyn patted him approvingly. Unfortunately, the stirrups meant for the boy were far too long for her. Rather than fight with them, Robyn kicked her feet free and pressed her soles against the horse's ribs.

It felt good. The velvety smooth of the horse's muscled ribcage beneath her instep reminded her of early summers at the ranch. When she'd been young, she had pulled herself astride any horse. Robyn looked at Seneca standing with her mouth open. A small chuckle escaped her throat, and she urged the horse into a canter. She used her best form while posting along with the rhythm of the gelding. After a few minutes, she slowed him back to a walk and approached Seneca again.

Robyn dismounted smoothly and handed the boy the reins. "I hope that was helpful." Her toes were cold, and her face flushed, but the much-improved expression on Seneca's face made it all worth it. "May I have my shoes?"

"Oh! Yeah." Seneca handed them over and Robyn put them back on, ignoring the dirt between her frozen toes. "Nice work, Dr. Mason. I think we *all* learned a great deal today."

"I hope so."

After the boy was mounted and had headed to the arena, Robyn stood by Seneca and watched. Seneca's voice broke the silence. "His posting looks better now."

"He'll find his rhythm." Robyn nodded. "Now, be honest, Seneca. How surprised are you that I can ride?"

Seneca's eyes sparkled looking at her. "I'm not surprised you can ride, Robyn. I *am* surprised you can ride barefoot in business attire."

"I told you before that you were not the first female cowhand here."

"I know. I'm sorry. I learned my lesson."

"Did you?" Robyn raised a brow. "You're not going to try to get on another horse?"

Seneca had the decency to look chagrined. "I guess not. But you understand my dilemma, don't you?"

"I do." Robyn sympathized. She'd been hired to ride and yet had to keep her feet on the ground. "You feel ineffectual."

Seneca scratched her arm in the brace. "I hate this thing."

"It will be well soon. Then you can go back to breaking horses, hitching wagons, and demonstrating all manner of things for these kids."

"Yeah, not soon enough."

Robyn smiled at the grumble in Seneca's voice. "At least you can button your own pants now."

Seneca smirked. "Don't pretend you minded helping."

Robyn laughed loudly. "Oh, I definitely did not." She was pleased to find Seneca's hungry gaze on her face. "I mean, you were such a *terrible* inconvenience, but we are called to help our neighbor, are we not?"

"I suppose so." Seneca's face was flushed.

"Speaking of neighbors," Robyn said, "how is it that I have not yet been asked to your place?"

"You didn't get the housewarming invitation?" Seneca asked with a mocking note in her voice. "Hmm, I can't believe it got lost in the mail."

"No matter. How about this Friday? Around five?"

Seneca's eyes opened wide in pretend shock. "Did you just invite yourself to my house?"

"You were going to anyway."

"Maybe."

Robyn smiled. "I'll bring the food if you can manage the beer."

"I can probably handle that."

"Good. Friday night, then."

Robyn turned and walked away. She could feel Seneca's eyes on her back. Well, not her back exactly. If she turned around, she would see desire in Seneca's face. The dirt between her toes was enough to drive her crazy and Robyn knew she would be sore from riding without stirrups, but it had all been worth it to see Seneca gaping at her from the fence. Perhaps, once Seneca's arm was better, they could take a little trail ride. The idea of tumbling with Seneca in the great outdoors filled Robyn with lust. She expected more of their relationship and this knowledge filled her with an almost painful longing. She sighed. She was needlessly torturing herself. Seneca might indulge in a fun roll in the hay but may never be ready for more. She had to decide if she could accept a casual good time while waiting for a real opportunity for intimacy. An opportunity that might never present itself. She crossed the yard, her head bowed against the cold wind.

❖

It was impossible for Seneca to get the image of Robyn riding out of her head. She was certain she'd never seen anything sexier. The ease with which she had kicked aside the stirrups and the confidence with which she rode had Seneca's head reeling. She had assumed Robyn was comfortable on a horse simply because she was Win's daughter and had grown up at the ranch, but Seneca had not been prepared for the sheer pleasure she'd seen on Robyn's face as she'd sat astride the gelding. Her face had reflected the same joy Seneca experienced riding.

Friday couldn't come soon enough. She agonized over the beer until finally deciding on a warm stout with a smooth finish. She wanted to ask Robyn what she was cooking so she could pick a complementary beer, but she didn't want to seem overeager.

Eager she was, though. Less than a week in her cottage, and she had *missed* Robyn. It was a hard thing for Seneca to admit as she sat on her front porch steps, breathing in the autumn air and scratching absently at her arm. The sun peeked out weakly from behind thin, gray clouds and Seneca automatically lifted her face to it. It wasn't warm, exactly, but it was welcome against her skin.

Seneca loved her little house. It was cozy and solid. It was also isolated by trees that helped break the worst of the wind. She hadn't minded the barn, but it was wonderful to have a home. Even a temporary one. Still, Seneca deeply felt Robyn's absence, more than she could have imagined. She'd grown accustomed to their routine and meals and conversations. She'd gotten used to Robyn's laughter and to watching her in the kitchen. She missed the golden eyes roving over her hungrily and the after-work chats about what made their days good or challenging.

Comfort. I got comfortable. It had been so easy to settle in and be comfortable, too. Robyn had made it easy. Robyn. Robyn had taken care of her, had listened to her darkest secrets. Robyn, who kicked her ass on occasion. Robyn, her friend. Robyn, who she wanted to be more than a friend—and who did not deserve to be hurt, least of all by a wanderer who somehow still could not make up her mind to stay put.

Seneca heard tires on gravel. As Robyn's car appeared, Seneca rose and leaned against one of the posts on the porch, hooking her thumbs gently in her belt loops.

Robyn stepped from her car and checked her out. Seneca felt the scorching path of Robyn's eyes on her body. She was suddenly unsure if it was a great idea to have Robyn at her house.

"Hey." Seneca took a step off the porch to help her bring in the groceries. Seneca gave Robyn her best bear hug, and sweetly kissed her on the cheek in greeting. She was careful not to do more. Forcing herself a small step back, she smiled.

"What's all this?"

"Dinner."

Seneca peeked through a bag containing produce. "Tomato, lettuce...uh...this isn't a salad, is it?"

Robyn stopped her pilfering through the back of her car. "And if it is?"

"Well, you know, I just...I'm just not a big salad person."

Robyn arched a brow. "Are we doing this again?" Robyn's voice was usually soft, but something about the quiet put fear in Seneca's heart.

"Please remember you inhaled my spaghetti, veggies and all. Do you honestly think I would come all the way over here to make a salad?" In the brief silence, Seneca heard Robyn huff from the energy it took to deliver Seneca's well-deserved chastisement. There was no way in hell Seneca was going to answer that question. Robyn was doing the major lift on this meal, whatever it was. She would force down a head of lettuce and be grateful.

Robyn then proffered another bag full of ground beef.

"There's charcoal in the trunk. I'm making cheeseburgers. There's a little grill station in the back."

"Oh, that sounds great," Seneca said, relieved.

Robyn rolled her eyes. "Yeah, and you thought I was going to make a *salad*."

"Right." Seneca laughed while she took the ground beef from Robyn and placed a mandatory make-up kiss on her cheek. "I'm truly sorry, Robyn. I'll just take this stuff inside."

"You do that."

Seneca put the bags on the small table in the kitchen and went back to retrieve the charcoal. As she hoisted it onto her shoulder and began to carry it around the house, Robyn called to her.

"Is this all the wood you have?"

Seneca turned to find Robyn gesturing to the firewood on the porch.

"Oh, yeah. That should last me a while. Until Cliff can get here, anyway."

Robyn frowned. "That won't even be enough for the next couple of nights. It's supposed to drop to eighteen tonight."

"I'll make do gathering from the orchard."

"No, don't bother. I'll chop some while I'm here."

"You're going to chop wood?"

Robyn narrowed her eyes at her. "What is that supposed to mean?"

Backpedaling quickly, Seneca tried to slap on a casual expression. "Nothing. I just thought we were going to make dinner." She dropped the bag of charcoal by the grill.

"We are, but how are you going to stay warm tonight without enough wood?"

Seneca grinned. "I have comments I'm not going to share."

Robyn smirked. "Oh? Perhaps you ran out of wood by design."

"I don't think so."

"Then, you won't mind me chopping some." With this, Robyn tossed aside her gloves and retrieved Seneca's work gloves laying nearby.

Robyn took up the ax. "I'll just split enough to get you through the weekend." She lifted a small log, hefted the ax, and brought it down swiftly. The log split right down the middle and Seneca felt her knees go weak.

There was absolutely nothing Robyn could not do. She was amazingly strong, smart, and sexy—and all woman. Seneca realized her mouth had been hanging open, so she shut it abruptly as she watched Robyn work. Maybe she should run out of wood more often.

Once Robyn had split quite a pile, Seneca began loading the wood underneath the porch. After a few trips, she heard a strange noise. She stopped her work. The noise seemed to be coming from the tree line. Robyn didn't seem to notice. "Do you hear that?"

Robyn stopped chopping and turned her perspiring face. "Hear what?"

The sound came again. It was a high-pitched call, like a tiny bark. "It sounds like a dog. A puppy."

Robyn frowned. "A dog?" She rested the ax on the stump.

As Seneca stepped toward the woods, the bark came again, and she pointed in its direction. "Hear it?"

Robyn abandoned the ax. "Yeah, I did that time." She stood beside Seneca.

Seneca whistled loudly and there was a brief pause before the leaves to their right started rustling. A loud yip sounded. "Come here, pup! This way!" Seneca encouraged the animal as the sounds moved closer.

Out of the tree line tripped a multicolored mutt. It face-planted in the yard before finding its feet and rushing toward her. Seneca hoisted it and it licked her face.

"Aww!" Robyn laughed, but Seneca frowned.

"Skunky puppy breath." Even so, she cradled the mutt to her chest while she headed indoors. She filled a bowl with water and set the pup on the brick floor of her kitchen. The animal nearly dove into the bowl.

"Gosh, he's cute." Robyn stooped to ruffle the pup's ears.

"Weird-looking, though." Seneca squatted to examine him. He seemed to be about eight to ten weeks. His ears pointed but flopped at the tips. Most of his body was white, but it was mottled with brown, silver, and black. He had blue eyes set on either side of a wide, white blaze and a vaguely heart-shaped black spot halfway up his snout.

"I think he's perfectly handsome."

The puppy yipped in agreement before turning to Seneca as if sensing she was the one who needed convincing. Seneca stood. "Don't look at me. You're not staying here." She glanced at Robyn.

"And just where is he going?"

"With you, of course."

"No way, I can't take care of a dog." Robyn protested. "Besides, Jinx would eat him for breakfast. The poor thing wouldn't be safe at my house."

"Well, I can't keep him."

"Why not?"

"Because…" Seneca struggled for a reason. "I'm still planning on leaving here in the spring." Even as she said it, she noticed the statement didn't have the same confident ring it once did.

"He could go with you. Wouldn't a dog be the perfect companion on the road?"

There was merit in the idea, and it gave Seneca pause. Even during the spring, it was cold at night, and a dog would be a good bed warmer. Plus, he'd be a great alarm system when she had to pitch her tent in less salubrious locations.

"I don't have anything for him. Don't you have to train them to pee outside?"

"He looks intelligent enough," Robyn said as the pup, which had resumed its drinking, dribbled water all over the floor.

"And messy enough." By this time, the pup had drunk his fill. He turned to her and plopped his butt on the floor, tail wagging. "He is cute…" Seneca considered the shaggy, multicolored mutt. "He can stay for now. But if he's too much trouble, I'll find another home for him."

Robyn smiled. "Sounds reasonable." Her eyes twinkled.

"Now, what do you need from me?"

"What?"

"For dinner?"

"Oh. You could start the grill and pour me a beer. I'll handle the rest."

"Sounds good."

After the charcoal was smoldering, Seneca went back inside to grab another beer. She fed a few small logs into the fireplace and stood at the mantel for a moment, watching Robyn.

Her auburn hair was pulled back into a half ponytail, but Robyn still looked glamorous in her snug, dark denim jeans and forest green sweater. She was chopping potatoes for home fries and feeding raw scraps to the puppy dancing happily beneath her feet. There was something so deeply domestic and adorable about the scene that Seneca found it almost painful. This was what she wanted every day for the rest of eternity. She wanted every moment to be a moment with Robyn and their family. The admission scared her. Trying to regain her footing, Seneca focused back on the pup as he hopped up to retrieve a fallen morsel.

"Aww, don't do that. He'll be underfoot all the time now."

Robyn grinned. "That was bound to happen, anyway," she said. They both watched as the puppy rushed Seneca and tugged on her pant leg with small teeth.

"Hey, you quit that." She picked him up again. "Where did you come from, all the way out here on your own?" Seneca mused over him and then put him back on the ground.

She washed her hands and turned to Robyn. "What else can I do to help?"

After dinner, they sat on the couch, still nursing their second round and playing tug-of-war with the puppy and an unmatched old sock. Finally, the dog went to the rug in front of the fireplace and flumped across it to rest. Minutes later, his breathing deepened, and his paws twitched in sleep.

"Look at that booger." She grinned. "He just put himself to bed."

"He seems to be the *goodest* boy." Robyn laughed. "He'll make a great companion for you."

"He just might." Seneca put her beer on the end table and leaned back into the cushions of the couch. "Might even bring him to the ranch. He looks to be a working dog."

"He does."

"Maybe I can train him that way. It's good for dogs to have a job." Seneca looked at Robyn. "Thank you for dinner. I haven't had a meal like that since I moved in here."

"So, you missed my cooking?" Robyn smiled.

"And your coffee."

"Is that all?"

Seneca watched as Robyn leaned forward, her head tilted, smile sexy, and her eyes sparkling. The air between them was charged. "No, that's not all."

"Oh?" Robyn's brow raised.

"I also miss Jinx."

"Jinx?" Robyn repeated with a smirk on her face. "That's what you miss about my home? My cooking, my coffee, and my cat?"

Seneca grinned. "Yeah, I think that about sums it up. What else is there?"

One moment, Robyn was sitting stone-still beside her, the next, she had straddled Seneca's lap and taken her jaw in hand. "What else, indeed?" Robyn's lips crashed into Seneca's.

Seneca responded to the urgency of Robyn's mouth. Her nipples pebbled and her gut clenched as Robyn pressed against her. Seneca wrapped Robyn in her arms to draw her as close as possible. She trailed her hands down Robyn's back to worshipfully take hold of her bottom. A small moan in Robyn's throat encouraged Seneca, and then there was too much clothing between them in the too hot room.

Seneca felt Robyn plucking deftly at her shirt buttons; soon after, Robyn's fingers caressed her stomach and her slightly calloused palms touched her breasts. A growl worked its way up her throat. Robyn's touches were fire, and Seneca's center was wet. The heat built between them until Seneca thought she would burst. Just as she'd decided to take Robyn there on her couch, her left thumb got hung in a belt loop and a twinge of pain shot through her arm. Seneca stiffened and Robyn pulled back, peering at her in concern.

"Are you okay?"

"Yes, I just…" Seneca was panting and took a few breaths to even her breathing. "It's my damned arm."

"Oh." Robyn sat back in her lap. "I was afraid…"

"No. You are perfect." She kissed her again to reiterate her point. "And I want this." She gestured between them. "But not while I still have a brace on this arm."

Robyn moved slowly to recline on the sofa. "How long until you can go without it?"

Her tone of voice caused Seneca to grin. "Another week, maybe."

Robyn sighed. "Well, this should give you a good reason to behave yourself."

"How's that?" Seneca laughed.

"The quicker you heal, the quicker I can have you."

Leaning over, Seneca kissed Robyn again and grinned.

"We both want that. So, I'll try my hardest to be the *goodest* girl."

CHAPTER TWENTY

"Angus!" Seneca whistled sharply. The dog had been sniffing a tree but swung his head around quickly. She opened the door of the old loaner truck and gestured inside. "Ride!" Angus gave a jubilant little hop before running full tilt and careening into the truck. He missed the jump and slammed into the side of the bench seat. With a sigh, Seneca gathered him up and placed him on the seat. "Klutz." She grinned at him as he panted happily beside her.

Angus had quickly made himself at home in the week since he'd found her. His potty training was going well, and he was eager for her attention. She'd even begun letting him sleep in the bed as the temperature had continued to sink at night. Overall, Seneca decided he was a perfect four-legged companion.

As she drove the path from her house to the barn, Seneca contemplated the drastic changes in her life. Five weeks ago, she'd been a solitary nomad backpacking across the country. She'd thought of little else but putting one foot in front of the other and finding a good campsite for the night. It was easy now for Seneca to recognize how problematic that pattern had been. She had convinced herself she was dealing with her trauma in her own way, when in fact, she had not been dealing with it at all.

Since Hunter's death, she'd been stuck between two worlds. In the first, she carried her pistols strapped to her person everywhere she went. Her nightly routine of cleaning them had become almost a ceremony of preparedness. In the second world, Seneca loathed her talent for violence. She loathed feeling most in control in situations where she had a gun in her hands. These two worlds had seemed at odds.

Recently, the line between these worlds had faded, and Seneca found she could both be good with a weapon and hate using it. It didn't have to be one way or another. Conflict and confidence could exist in the same place.

Seneca's thoughts turned to Robyn and the corners of her mouth lifted reflexively. Robyn seemed an embodiment of that. Seneca had never been more confident in her desire for a person, but prospective intimacy with Robyn also had a weight that was conflicting for Seneca. She just knew she would always want more. More than a friend. More than a fling. She would also need to stay in Butterbean Hollow to have a chance at what she wanted.

Turning to Angus, she stroked his thick, wavy hair. This was the first day she would trust him off-leash at the ranch. "Ready, boy?" He looked at her eagerly, his tongue lolling. "Don't get kicked, all right? You can't afford to lose any brain cells."

"Aroooof," he agreed as she parked at the barn.

Seneca slid out the door with the pup scampering behind her. "Now, let's see what we can get into today."

Her first stop was the loft where Win was pouring what Seneca judged to be his second cup of coffee. "Morning." He nodded to her, then greeted the dog. "Good morning to you, Angus." The pup went to rub catlike against Win's legs. Win chuckled while patting him affectionately with one hand. "Damn fine dog here, Seneca."

Seneca smiled. "Yeah, he'll do." Angus returned to sit on her right boot. "Anything you need help with today?"

Win stroked his mustache, pondering. He took a sip of his coffee. "Not that I can think of. Aren't you busy with the horse therapy program?"

"Pretty busy, yeah." She shrugged. "But it's been a while since I've been out riding fences."

"Are you telling me you've missed being in the cold wind cleaning tanks and dealing with ornery cattle?"

"Yeah, I have."

Win laughed. "That's cause there's something wrong with you, Seneca." He pointed at her brace. "You get that arm better and we'll talk cattle. In the meantime, the way I hear it, you're awful good with those boys."

Seneca was proud. "Who have you been talking to?"

"Who do you think?" He raised his bushy eyebrows.

"Robyn is just trying to keep me from trouble."

"Well, we ought to be paying her double, then."

Seneca laughed. "I reckon so."

The barn door opened, and Cliff called a greeting. Win and Seneca called back as he stepped into the loft. "Hey, uh, Mr. Mason, we had that appointment—"

"Whose dog is that?"

"Mine. Why?"

"He looks just like my uncle's dog."

"Earl?"

"Yeah." Cliff took a knee and Angus sniffed him over. "Is this one of her pups?"

"I don't know. He was in the woods by the cottage. He just found me."

"Weird." Cliff stroked the blaze between Angus's eyes. "I wonder how he got so far away."

"Maybe somebody else got him and he went missing?" Win's voice sounded casual, but Seneca could see his face was tense. Given her musing on the subject, she was suspicious.

"I think all the others were adopted by out-of-towners." Cliff gave the pup one last pat before he stood again. "He's the spitting image of Earl's dog. She's got that wide blaze and that spot on her snout." Cliff looked from Seneca to Win. "I wonder if—"

Win cleared his throat loudly. "That appointment, right?"

"Oh, right!" Cliff shifted from one foot to another. He looked nervous.

"You head on over to the offices and I'll meet you there."

"Yes, sir." Cliff left.

Seneca turned to Win. "Is Cliff interviewing?"

"Yeah, he's been working part-time and as needed, but we need him to take on more responsibilities now. He's pretty much got the job; we just want to be official about it."

"Oh, right." She smiled. "Cliff is one of the good ones."

"He sure is."

"Weird about Angus, right?"

Win turned to the sink to dump the rest of his coffee. "Yeah."

Seneca suspected he might be avoiding her gaze. "You wouldn't happen to know anything about it, would you, Win?"

"About what?" At Seneca's raised eyebrows, he rubbed both sides of his mustache at the same time. "Oh, about him being in the woods?" Win regarded Angus who watched the discussion as if he understood every word. "I didn't drop him out there."

"I guess I should talk to Robyn about it."

Win nodded. "Uh, maybe you should." He grabbed his hat from the drafting table and settled it onto his head. "I've got to be going." Win strode quickly from the barn.

"*Maybe you should*?!" Robyn pinched the bridge of her nose as she unlocked her car. "Dad! I knew you wouldn't be able to keep it from her." Win had called her as she was leaving the office to tell her the jig was up with Angus.

"What was I supposed to do?"

"Play dumb!"

"She's too smart for that, Robyn. I think Seneca knew it the moment Cliff was so familiar with the pup."

Robyn suspected Seneca had known the moment the dog came tumbling adorably out of the woods. "Look, it doesn't matter she knows I was behind it. What matters is she loves Angus now."

Win's sigh sounded relieved. "So, I'm off the hook?"

Robyn laughed. "Of course, Dad. I shouldn't have roped you in to begin with."

"Oh, I didn't mind keeping Angus for a few days. As a matter of fact, I think Joan enjoyed it a bit too much. She's been talking about getting a dog now."

Robyn paused in surprise before cranking the car.

"Wow, he made quite the impression, it seems." Robyn smiled as she remembered watching from a distance as Angus toppled from the truck cab that morning. "He is the best boy."

"He'll be a damn sight more useful than Shep ever was."

"Speaking of Shep, did Cliff sign an official contract today?"

"Oh yeah, I thought the young man was going to float away, he was so happy." Robyn heard her father's whistling chuckle.

"Good." She glanced to the back seat where she had a box of sundry items for Angus. "I've got to go, Dad, but I'll see you this weekend for dinner. Please make sure you let JD know about Seneca and Angus. And thank him again for getting the pup pointed in the right direction through the woods."

"Right, kiddo. Love you."

"Love you, too."

Robyn guided her vehicle up the rutted road to Seneca's little house. As she parked, Angus came bounding out the front door, barking and circling excitedly. "Hey there, handsome!" She ruffled his ears as Seneca stepped on the porch. Robyn was strangely turned on at the sight of Seneca's smirk. "I brought you a few things," she said to Angus. She retrieved the box from her back seat.

"What's all this?"

Robyn put the box on the porch step and began rummaging through it. "Well, I know Angus gets plenty of exercise at the ranch, but he will gnaw your boots if you don't watch it. I got him some chew toys, a couple of stuffies, and some old blankets."

Seneca grinned as Robyn touched a choice of each item in turn. "I see." She grabbed one of the stuffed animals. "It doesn't make noise, does it?" Seneca asked just as she squeezed the rabbit. It produced a high-pitched squeal and Angus sat at attention.

Seneca cut her eyes from Angus to Robyn. "Absolutely not."

"Why not?"

"That sound will drive me insane. No." Seneca tried to hand the rabbit back to her.

Robyn crossed her arms over her chest as Angus panted between them, watching the rabbit closely. His tail thumped loudly against the porch where he sat. "Look at him! He loves it already!"

Seneca sighed. She dropped the toy and Angus snatched it. He jumped around with it in his mouth before he settled to chew on it between his paws. "Thanks. I guess." Seneca rolled her eyes.

Robyn chuckled. "How did he do at work today?"

"He was perfect." Seneca grinned. "But you already knew that."

"That he's perfect? Yeah, I am aware."

"I guess that was why you picked him out of the litter, huh?"

Robyn looked at Seneca. She didn't seem upset. "No, I chose him because of the little heart on his nose."

"Ah, yes, that is cute."

"So, you're not mad?"

"Mad?" Seneca frowned. "No, I love the little booger."

Robyn exhaled, relieved. "I was afraid you would be lonely here, but I knew you wouldn't admit it."

"You act like you know me or something." Seneca grinned and pulled Robyn closer with her good arm. "I think I would have been a little lonely. Especially after being used to having Jinx around."

Robyn rolled her eyes but lifted her smiling face just the same when Seneca leaned in to press a gentle kiss to her lips. Robyn found Seneca's hips with her hands and grabbed denim to pull her even closer. Seneca trailed her hand up Robyn's spine and then rested it on the back of her neck. She pressed herself against Seneca's long frame and shuddered with need.

Seneca eased back. She raised her arm.

"How long?" Robyn grumbled.

"Soon."

Robyn pulled away. "You'd better rest while you can, then." As she snapped her car door shut, her car mirror reflected Seneca smirking from the porch. While she drove away, she smirked at the many delights to come.

CHAPTER TWENTY-ONE

Halfway back to the ranch, Seneca's phone rang.
"What's up, Boss?" She spoke to Win through the magic of Bluetooth.

"Just calling to check on that arm. You ready to ride some fences?"

"Hell, yeah." She'd just received the all-clear from her doctor, with permission to return to normal duties at the ranch. No more brace. She smiled into the phone and twiddled the loose steering wheel of the borrowed old truck. "I'm about ten minutes out."

"See you when you get here."

Seneca ended the call, but the smile on her face did not diminish. It touched her that Win had reached out. He had other cowhands to ride fences, but he'd made a point to call her just the same. Robyn might have had a hand in it, but it didn't dilute the warmth in Win's gesture.

Seneca parked in the gravel front of the Old Barn to find several cowhands milling about. Frowning, she addressed Cliff.

"Hey. Why are y'all hanging 'round?"

"Hey." Cliff stood tall where he'd been leaning on the bucket of an ancient tractor. He scowled. "We were supposed to finish worming the cattle, but Shep showed and told us all to wait outside."

"Shep?" Seneca's jaw tightened.

Cliff nodded. "We were all so surprised to see him we—"

"I'll be back." Seneca strode quickly inside.

Anger seeped into her limbs from a frigid place in her chest. Fucking Collin Shepherd. Seneca found Win, JD, and Shep standing at the foot of the loft stairs. They turned to look at her.

"Seneca Twist." Shep grinned easily.

"Did you tell the cowhands to wait outside?" she asked without preamble, her tone icy.

Shep's eyes slid from her face to the open door behind her. "I might have," he drawled, "but it was only so I could have a quick word with my boss."

"I'm not your boss, anymore, son." JD spoke softly, but sternly. "I made that much known to you weeks ago."

"Well, now that tempers have cooled—"

"Temper had nothing to do with it," Win said gruffly. "Us letting you go was a direct consequence of your actions."

"Actions which I deeply regret." Shep had the gall to act abashed. Seneca's brain absurdly conjured the image of a five-year-old asking forgiveness for coloring on the walls. "However, I hope forgiveness can be granted." With this, he turned to her. "What do you say, Twist? Seems you healed fine."

Seneca was stunned. She stared at Shep. Did he truly believe all was well just because she had mended, and he had arrived hat in hand? She sensed JD and Win stiffen as she stepped forward.

"Forgiveness is for the gods. I hold no grudges." Shep smiled until she continued. "But the thing is, Shep, I can't trust you." Seneca shook her head. "I will never count on you or expect the others to do so, and I certainly will never present my back to you again." His face fell. "Those are the facts, Shep. There's no place for you here."

After a tense moment, Shep shrugged. "It's a good thing you're not the boss, then." He turned back to JD and Win, who were sharing a quick glance.

"I think it's time you left, Collin," JD said. "Twist is right."

Shep was angry. "I—"

"Leave now." Win's low voice sounded like a growl.

"You'll regret this." Shep walked away and pushed roughly out of the door. They stood looking after him.

Seneca still reeled. "I can't believe that just happened." Win grunted and JD shook his head.

"That was ridiculous, even for Collin Shepherd," JD said. "I couldn't believe my damn eyes when he walked in here. If Win hadn't spoken to him first, I would've thought I was hallucinating."

"Just the absolute—"

"Audacity." Win finished the sentiment. "I know, Seneca. Anyway, if I were him, I'd be thoroughly humiliated. He surely won't show his face on this ranch again."

"Surely not." Seneca agreed the theory was sound, but a bit of her tingled with doubt.

Seneca awoke with a vague feeling of unease. She glanced at the clock: oh three hundred hours. Pulling the blanket around her shoulders and rolling over, she came face-to-face with Angus, who lay on his back with his paws to the sky. Taking in the rise and fall of his chest, she was a bit jealous the pup slept so deeply when she was wide awake. The night was quiet, but like the remnants of a bad dream, something foreboding tugged on her consciousness.

Seneca placed her socked feet on the worn boards and padded into the kitchen. She filled a small glass with cold tap water. Sipping, she leaned her bottom against the sink to watch Angus trot into the kitchen.

He stopped in the doorway and cocked his odd-looking head as if to say, *"What's this about?"* She grinned at him and patted her leg. The pup came to her at once but sat on top of her right foot. Seneca chuckled softly and reached to pat him lovingly. "You're all right, aren't you?" He met her gaze with a lolling tongue.

She drank more water and turned again to look out the window. She stared at the glowing horizon in confusion. It was too early for the sun. With a frown, she leaned closer and examined the strange light that was cast against the underside of the dark clouds. Seneca set her glass in the sink and hurried outside to stand on her porch facing southwest. She heard Angus start to whine inside the cottage, then bark. A restless wind rustled the leaves of the orchard and brought to her a familiar smell. It was faint, but unmistakable. Smoke.

Seneca dashed back inside to grab her cell phone.

"Nine-one-one, what's your emergency?"

Seneca replied while hastily pulling on her jeans. "I'm Seneca Twist at Butterbean Hollow Boys' Ranch. Something's on fire out here."

"I'll get an engine to your location right away, ma'am."

"Thanks." She ended the call, buttoned her jeans, and dialed Win's number. She was just about to end the call when his groggy voice answered.

"Something is on fire. I can see it from the cottage. Maybe the barn."

"Call nine-one-one—"

"Already done. I'm going to meet the fire truck. I'll call JD—"

"No, I'll call JD," Win said. "You go see to the horses."

"Yes, sir."

"And Seneca...Be careful."

"Yes, sir." She wasn't certain he'd heard her soft response before she disconnected. She was touched by the tenderness in his voice.

She didn't bother to button the flannel shirt over her thermal as she shoved her feet into her boots, grabbed her coat and sprinted from the house, skidding slightly on a small patch of ice at the bottom of the steps. She heard Angus barking frantically as she dove into the work truck and cranked it. It came to life with a stuttering complaint as she tried to fight the sour fear in her stomach. She uselessly shouted to Angus that it would be okay and for him to settle. She heard him whining loudly as she accelerated on the rutted road. If only she could believe all would be well and settle her heart's rhythm. It would take the fire truck at least fifteen minutes to get to their location. She gritted her teeth as the wind blew leaves across her windshield. Wind was not a blessing in a fire. At least the boys knew to stay at the residence hall after curfew, no matter the trouble.

When she got through the gate, she could see the Old Barn's front wall was engulfed in flames. Somehow, the front corner of the building opposite the ancient tractor had caught fire. She could faintly hear the horses neighing in the other barn. Thank goodness they were far enough away to be okay. With her driving the truck, she didn't think there was enough gas or oil in any of the machinery to do much more damage. Still, she parked away from the fire to burst from the cab and stand outside the burning barn. A sound and movement at the other side of the structure caught her attention.

A man stumbled to the ground and then scrambled to his feet. She automatically reached for the Browning in her holster. It wasn't there. She hadn't grabbed her gun before leaving the house.

"Shep!" He whirled toward her, then took off. Seneca sprinted after him for a few steps, but the roaring sound of the fire demanded her attention.

Springing into action, she ran to the spigot on the backside of the barn and divested it of its winter covering to turn it on full blast. Seneca wasn't delusional; she could not extinguish the flames. She could soak the ground around the barn so the fire wouldn't spread. She grabbed a feed pail and began running between the well pump and the barn, filling the bucket, and then tossing the water at the base and sides of the burning building.

Win arrived with JD just behind him. He leapt from the truck cab and took a few quick steps to the barn which now had flames licking the roof. She watched Win stare at the building. "I don't believe this…" he said. Win finally turned to Seneca. "How long ago did you call nine-one-one?"

"About ten minutes? They should be here soon."

JD came to stand beside him. His entire body seemed to radiate sadness and frustration. "You opened the spigots. Good thinking," he choked out as they stood and watched the barn burning to the ground. "What's the bucket for?"

"I was drawing water from the pump and…" Her voice was weirdly calm. "It was stupid."

"It was something," JD said. "Let's start a line." He took the bucket from her hands. "I'll draw the water on account of you've got the quickest feet."

"Yeah, you run the water to me." Win's mustache bristled as he grabbed another pail. "I'll toss it on the barn. We can't just stand 'round and watch it burn."

Seneca followed JD to the field pump with the second pail. There was a strange understanding among them. They were fighting a fruitless battle and would not win or make a difference, but *something* must be done.

It wasn't long before they heard sirens and halted their efforts. The fire truck arrived, and several men and a woman jumped out clad in bright, reflective suits.

"All right! Let's get to it!" The authoritative voice with a thick twang was attached to a stocky, dark-haired man. The firefighter strode to the group. "Anything we need to know?"

"I saw the fire from my porch, smelled the smoke, and called you all. There's machinery inside, but not much in the way of oil or gas." Seneca stepped forward. "We tried to wet the ground so the fire wouldn't spread."

"Thanks, we'll do what we can."

She retreated to give the firefighters room to work. She motioned Win and JD over. "I'm pretty sure someone set the fire."

Win blinked and JD stared at her blankly.

"Set the fire?"

"Who?"

"I saw Shep."

"Shep?!" Win growled.

JD grabbed her shoulder. "Are you sure, Twist?"

Seneca met his eyes steadily. "Certain."

"We'll need to tell the police when they get here."

Seneca watched as the firefighters hooked the hose to the pump truck and began spraying over the mostly burned barn. "I know."

JD turned to Win. "What's in there that we can't replace?"

He watched the commotion for a moment before he responded with a sigh. "You mean besides years of hard work?" Win shook his head. "Nothing, I don't think. There was a fire-proof safe in the loft that had copies of documents and such, but everything is replaceable, I suppose."

JD sighed as another car traveled the driveway and parked nearby. Rosemary, Joan, and Robyn emerged. Rosemary ran directly to JD.

"Oh, my word..." She put a hand on his arm and covered her mouth with the other. JD hugged her with one arm but remained silent.

Win put his arm around Joan as she approached. "Will it spread?"

"Hopefully not. Seneca started soaking the ground as soon as she got here."

"That was a good call," Joan said to her.

Seneca hesitated. Her actions felt so insignificant as she stood by the burning building. She wanted to say *thank you* but couldn't quite manage the words. Finally, she managed a nod to acknowledge Joan's kindness.

A form sidled to stand next to her. She didn't need to turn to know it was Robyn.

"I can't believe this," Robyn said.

"Yeah, coming back from this will be..." Seneca glanced where JD and the others stood and clenched her jaw. "It's just a goddamned mess."

Win's phone rang. "This is Win." His voice was gruff when he answered.

"...Jack...Yeah, it's a total loss..." He glanced at JD.

"...No, no one got hurt...Just the one building..."

He cut his eyes to Seneca as the police arrived. "...We can talk about causality later," he said.

Seneca nodded, then turned her back on the barn. She stepped over to lean her forearms on the truck. Her sweat was now cold on her body and her fingers were icy from handling water. Stuffing her hands into her coat pockets, she turned to find Robyn close. So close. Her eyes glittered in the cold light of dawn. Seneca knew she was a mess. She felt the gritty soot that streaked her face, and she was certain the smell of smoke and charred wood was emanating from more than the destroyed building.

"You're exhausted," Robyn said. Robyn's always soft voice sounded softer still.

"I'm okay." Seneca answered automatically, but she knew Robyn knew better. "I've still got to talk to the police about what I saw."

Robyn narrowed her eyes. "What did you see?"

"Collin Shepherd."

Robyn seemed to reel. "Surely not…"

"He looked me square in the eye before he ran away." She remembered the fleeting moment she'd decided to not give chase and to try to salvage the barn. Shaking her head and turning back to the building which stood like a jagged, black monument against the silver sky, she sighed again. "I wish I could have stopped him."

"That's not your job."

"Isn't it?"

Robyn shook her head. "Give me your keys," she gently demanded.

"What?"

"Give me your keys. I'll go check on Angus and start some coffee. When you're done speaking with the police, meet me there. You more than deserve a shower and rest."

"You don't have to do all that—"

"Stop talking, please." Robyn frowned. "For once, just do as I ask."

Despite her weariness, Seneca grinned. "Yes, ma'am," she said in her best drawl. She glanced at JD who motioned her over. "I've got to go."

"I'll see you at home," Robyn said to her back as Seneca retreated.

The domestic sound of it rang in Seneca's ears. A flash of what could be skittered across her mind. She mentally shook her head. No sense dwelling on that when she wasn't certain what the spring would bring. She joined JD and Win as another police cruiser pulled in.

Seneca was exhausted. The sun was rising, she had gone over her story multiple times, and the civil servants still milled about investigating the fire. JD patted her on the back and sat beside her on the tailgate of his truck. "You could probably go if you want, Twist."

"I do want." She rolled her shoulders. "But I'd rather answer all the questions now than be called back in today." She thought about her warm house filled with the scent of coffee and Robyn's reassuring presence. Her mouth lifted in a smile, but she cleared her expression as Win approached. Her thoughts about his daughter were unfortunately ill-timed for circumstance.

"Well, the police say they'll review the video footage to see what they find. Unfortunately, your word is not good enough for an arrest."

"I figured as much, Win." She nodded. "It was him."

"We believe you." He stroked both sides of his mustache with one hand. "Let's hope they can find something on the recording. In the meantime, go home, Seneca. You look like hell."

CHAPTER TWENTY-TWO

S eneca's feet thumped loudly on the steps of her porch. She heard Angus's quick bark and Robyn's soothing voice. The door opened before she could reach for it and Robyn stood in the doorway. "Can I come in?"

"Can you go around back?"

"Huh?"

Robyn answered with a small smile. "The laundry room is in the back. We need to put your clothes directly in the washer or they will stink up the whole house."

"Oh, right." Seneca circled the house to mount the small back stoop. Robyn was there ushering her inside after a brief, tired kiss.

"Put your clothes in the washer and head to the bathroom. I'll start the washer after you finish showering."

"Yes ma'am," Seneca murmured. She waited until Robyn turned her back to start stripping. She didn't mind being in her underwear in front of her, but the act of undressing was somehow too intimate. Once she had divested herself of her clothing, she scuttled to the bathroom with Angus on her heels sniffing behind her.

❖

Robyn fought back a tiny giggle as she watched Seneca skedaddle to the bathroom. To be so headstrong and stubborn, she was a bit prudish. She wasn't sure why this was so funny to her.

She listened until the water started. Angus came trouncing back and she petted him lovingly on the head before pouring herself a cup of coffee. She sat at the little table in front of the window that looked over the orchard.

Robyn saw wispy remnants of the black smoke traveling with the wind in the cold, gray sky. A small sigh escaped her. She pictured Seneca running back and forth with useless buckets of water, doing all she could to contain the raging flames despite the insurmountable odds. It was a sad image, a portrait of futility and tragic bravery. Robyn shook her head as she pushed a hand through Angus's silky fur when he propped his head on her denim-clad thigh.

Seneca baffled her in many ways. She was all at once quiet and reserved, and then open and full of wry humor. She felt so deeply and cared so much, but she was hesitant to commit to her place or person. Robyn believed Seneca longed to feel at peace and to settle in somewhere, but she wondered at her motivation in having that belief. Maybe she was seeing what she wanted to see or was finding patterns that did not exist. Seneca might just be making the most of her stay and would happily march out of here come spring.

The unwelcome idea of Butterbean Hollow without Seneca Twist pitted her stomach with emptiness. It was as if their little family had not been whole before she hiked into town. Seneca brought a sense of completeness to the community, to the ranch...to Robyn.

Robyn considered that trying to convince Seneca to stay in Butterbean Hollow might have been a mistake. Not because she didn't want Seneca to stay, but because she was now so invested in the idea that when Seneca left, she would be devastated. She would miss her reluctant half-smile and eyes that seemed to absorb every detail. She would miss the capable hands and solid, reassuring presence. She loved Seneca Twist.

Great. *Now what?*

Seneca wrapped herself in her thick robe and toweled her hair dry. She retreated to her bedroom only to find she'd left her meager stash of clean laundry in the dryer. "Damn." She cinched the belt on the robe and padded back toward the kitchen.

Seneca found Robyn sitting at the small table, staring out the window with Angus at her feet. Robyn seemed to be lost in thought and, as she came into the room, she heard a little sigh. There was something melancholy in the air.

Seneca yearned to comfort Robyn. The impulse filled her with warmth and terror. She longed for the sort of intimacy that could only be had in Robyn's arms. She was selfish for wanting to possess Robyn's time and affection, but she could not deny her feelings. Neither could she deny how the idea of intimacy with Robyn terrified her. She and Robyn were already too close. What if Robyn realized she wasn't good enough for her? There were too many potential complications for her to feel at ease with her longing for Robyn. How could she commit to remain in Butterbean Hollow when she was so conflicted?

Robyn is enough reason for anyone to stay anywhere.

Seneca cleared her throat and Robyn turned. She stood and crossed to the counter to pour Seneca a cup of coffee.

"Do you feel a little better?"

"I do, thank you. It's amazing what a shower can do." Seneca smiled. "I forgot I left my clean clothes in the dryer, though."

"Don't feel the need to get dressed on my account." Robyn winked.

Seneca looked at her with a teasing grin. "Me in only a robe doesn't make you uncomfortable?"

Robyn stepped toward Seneca. "Seneca, you in a robe makes me many things, but uncomfortable is not one of them." Robyn rose on her tiptoes so they were barely a breath apart. She grabbed her shoulders. "Kiss me."

Seneca lowered her mouth to capture Robyn's. The kiss was soft and pleading, and Robyn sighed into her quietly before gripping the back of Seneca's neck and drawing her closer. Seneca registered the pressure of Robyn unwinding the tie of her robe.

"Robyn, wait—"

But Robyn would not be persuaded. "We've waited long enough. I want to feel you."

Seneca moaned when Robyn pulled the robe open and pressed her body to her bare flesh. "Yes," Seneca whispered before she deepened the kiss. Robyn gripped the curve of her hip. Seneca had never known such need. Every stroke of Robyn's fingertips and the press of Robyn's body ratcheted her own desire higher. Who knew of tomorrow? Seneca wanted this to last forever.

"There's no hurry," she said. Her breath hitched as Robyn's hands trailed her ribs to stroke the undersides of her breasts. There was a furious fire in her belly and Seneca longed for the contact of Robyn's skin.

Robyn smiled against her mouth. She drew back long enough to pull her sweatshirt over her head. "Not hurry, urgency. I want you now." She tossed her shirt across the back of a chair in the kitchen before returning to Seneca's mouth.

Seneca slowed her. "I want you in my bed."

"Then, let's go." With a smile, Robyn took Seneca's hand to lead her the few steps to the other side of the house. Seneca watched her strip off her remaining clothes and slide between the sheets. Seneca dropped her robe and joined Robyn.

"I want you to know—"

She lost her train of thought as Robyn rolled to straddle her. Robyn's hot, wet center connected with her lower belly, and Seneca stumbled on the words. "I—it's been a long time since I've been with anyone." She felt her face flush with the admission.

"Me, too." Robyn lowered her mouth to Seneca's nipple. Seneca jerked as the electric connection between her breast and center ignited. Robyn stroked her other breast and stomach as she pleasured Seneca with her mouth.

Seneca grasped Robyn's bottom, grinding upward into Robyn's heat. "Mmm…"

Robyn moved restlessly against her, straddling one of Seneca's legs to slide her pelvis into the juncture of her thighs. Seneca groaned as her swollen center met Robyn's. She grasped Robyn even tighter and, with one hand on Robyn's hip and another on her thigh, set a steady pace with her hips. Pressure built deep inside, and her breath came faster.

"Yes, right there." Robyn braced a hand on Seneca's chest and thrust her hips to meet Seneca's, beat for beat.

Seneca pressed her lips together. She pumped into Robyn's heat, watching her face as it flushed brighter. Seneca's stomach clenched as her control wavered. Not yet. Not...yet. "You are so beautiful," she gasped. She held Robyn closer with one arm while she trailed her fingers over the curve of Robyn's breasts and gently pinched her nipple.

"Oh!" Robyn's eyes widened. "I'm—" She stiffened and moaned, shuddering as she rocked against Seneca.

Seneca held her breath, mesmerized as Robyn trembled in pleasure. The sensation of Robyn coming in her arms brought Seneca to the edge. She rolled them over, hips flexing desperately, a light sheen of sweat sliding between them. Robyn's hands stroked her back rhythmically. She let herself fall. When the flood of her release ebbed, Seneca collapsed with her face pressed into Robyn's shoulder. Trembling, she fought to regain her breath.

Robyn stroked her shoulders and back and kissed any part of her she could reach. Seneca floated for a time in the wonder of Robyn. When Seneca rolled off Robyn, she snuggled her into the crook of her shoulder.

"That was incredible," Seneca murmured.

"Hmm, yes. It was."

"I'm afraid I'll do something stupid now."

Robyn smiled against her arm. "I'm sure you will."

"What?"

"I'm sure you'll do something stupid. Like regret it and try to rationalize and justify it to yourself. Then you'll process it and come back around, and we'll be all right."

"Oh?"

"Yes." Robyn rolled to lean on her elbows and locked eyes. "So why don't we skip all that?"

"Skip it?" She stroked the curve of Robyn's jaw. "What are you talking about?"

"Yes, skip all the wallowing and self-loathing. Let's process it here and now."

"I don't know how to do that." *And I'm not sure I want to.*

"Well, I won't pretend it will be easy." Robyn laid her head back down. "But I think it'll be worth it."

"Yeah?" Hope filled Seneca's heart. *Robyn thinks we can have more. Robyn thinks we are worth having more.*

"Yeah." Robyn traced her abs. "I mean, that was mind-blowing sex."

"It was." She chuckled softly. It was hard to voice her feelings, and even more difficult deciding how to say what she felt. "I don't want you to think that I'm desperate to get away. But staying in one place means building relationships and, eventually, losing relationships. That terrifies me."

"Yes, I know that. I see that."

"I did not want to get involved with you because I knew it would be torture to leave."

"And you believe your desire to leave will be stronger than the connection you feel for me?"

Seneca did not hear any judgment in Robyn's question, so she answered as honestly as she could. "I don't know." She considered the question more deeply. "I know that every other time, the drive to walk has overwhelmed any friendships I've made."

"Have you had connections with others like you've found in Butterbean Hollow?" Robyn tilted her head up again. "Have you been as invested anywhere else?"

"No…" Seneca captured Robyn's hand which had somehow found its way back to her breast. "Stop, I'm trying to think."

"I don't want you to think." Robyn rose to straddle her waist. She pulled the covers around her shoulders so that she could snuggle down on top of her. "I want to stay like this forever." She rested her head on Seneca's chest.

Seneca smiled into her tousled auburn hair. "They'll come looking for us."

"We'll hide."

She laughed. She stroked down Robyn's spine and then up again. She smiled as Robyn shivered. She rolled them over to look into her gorgeous eyes. Bracing herself on the mattress, Seneca instinctively ground herself into the slick heat below her. Robyn squirmed and grasped her back. "Like we did under the table at JD's birthday?"

"Oh, wow! Yes." Robyn smiled. "My heart jumped right to my throat when you grabbed me."

"Yeah?" Seneca pumped gently with her hips against Robyn's center.

Robyn wrapped her legs around Seneca and clutched at her. "I had just decided that I found you very attractive and then there I was in your arms, in your lap, under that table."

"It definitely wasn't what I planned, but I am not sorry for the experience." Seneca reached down to part Robyn's slick folds and tease her entrance with a finger. Robyn gasped.

"Me either." Robyn caressed Seneca's breasts. "After that, all I could think about was how good it felt."

Seneca groaned as Robyn slipped a hand between her thighs to palm her sensitive folds. Robyn spread her legs a bit before Seneca slipped one finger into her velvet heat. "Yes…" Seneca resumed the slow rhythm of her grind against Robyn's hand.

"More…"

Seneca slipped a second finger inside Robyn and pressed their foreheads together. Robyn trembled but thrust against Seneca's digits with the same slow rhythm. "I don't know how long—" Seneca began.

"Not long." The pressure built. Robyn's chest and face were flushed with heat and her movements became agitated. "So good," she said as she quickened her pace.

The low hum of Robyn's voice pushed Seneca higher. She dipped and ground her hips firmly against her hand and used her thumb to stroke Robyn's clit with every slick pump of her fingers into Robyn's heat. Suddenly, the climax was upon her. "Oh, G-God—" She shuddered as she peaked. Robyn's orgasm followed soon after, and she cried out while thrusting against Seneca, clutching tightly.

Seneca did not stir for several seconds. When she finally rolled over, Robyn snuggled into the crook of her arm once more. "Mmm…"

She stroked from Seneca's jaw, through the valley of her breasts, to her belly button. "That was pretty great."

Grinning, she pulled her closer. "That *was* pretty great."

"I think it could be better, though?"

"Oh, yeah?" Seneca frowned and looked at her. "How's that?"

"Practice," Robyn said. "Lots and lots of practice." She laughed and climbed astride her.

"I think I could make time for that." Seneca grinned and met Robyn's mouth with her own.

Afterward, Seneca lay awake in the semi-darkness. The silvery gray of morning came through the windows and lit on Robyn's bare back. Seneca longed to run her fingers down each exposed vertebrae, but this would likely wake her. She was too restless to lie next to Robyn for the next hour. She rose from bed and slipped on her robe to cover the goose bumps on her arms. Angus's ears perked, but she waved him down and motioned for him to stay put. He dropped his fluffy head back to his paws and gave an almighty sigh.

Seneca slipped from the room. She squatted at the fireplace to shuffle the logs as Robyn's words circled in her head. Admitting the relationship scared her had been a big step, and Robyn's reassurances had soothed a bit of the fear. She added a couple of new logs as she kindled the sleepy embers from their ashen bed. The dry wood quickly crackled in the grate.

She pulled a large, multicolored throw about her as she sat on the small sofa and watched the hungry flames. She was far more invested in Butterbean Hollow than anywhere else she'd passed through. The loss of the barn felt personal and Shep's involvement, as much as she was repulsed by him, felt like a betrayal to the ranch. The people here had become *her* people and their struggles had become her struggles. When had that happened? After the drive? After the cattle penning? Or had some small part of it happened the moment she set foot on the ranch?

She couldn't point a finger at the specific moment, she knew only that it had happened. Her work at the ranch hardly felt like work at all. Her relationship with Robyn brought her happiness and contentment. How could she walk away?

The room was warming from the flame in the hearth and the subtle silver of early morning had given way to a golden line on the horizon. It would be sunrise before long, and she would have to face Robyn in the light of day. The prospect of this made her uncertain and anxious. What did Robyn expect from her? For them? Seneca thought she knew, but delivering it was easier said than done. There were a million ways she could fail. She resolved, however, to try to be the woman that Robyn deserved.

CHAPTER TWENTY-THREE

It took a week to clear the wreckage. They had their own equipment and used their own labor, so they were only out the price of gasoline for their trouble. The rebuilding would be the expensive part. Not to mention the time lost working on other projects. The truth of the matter was that the barn *had* to be rebuilt. They did not have an operations hub or maintenance shop without it. In the meantime, they had rented a mobile trailer, and this put everyone in a foul mood.

Seneca had nightmares the evenings she was away from Robyn. It was as if her subconscious couldn't let her be happy. Most of the nightmares consisted of burning buildings, but last night, she and Robyn had been trapped inside the barn as it collapsed into flames around them. She had woken that morning in a pool of sweat with Angus pawing at her anxiously.

The lingering emotion of the dream had her disoriented. She was struggling to focus, and the confining space of the small modular unit made the experience much more difficult.

She sat at a desk reviewing the equine therapy schedule Kevin had handed her that morning. Win turned away from the drafting table and knocked his coffee off his desk with his tool belt. Seneca and Angus jumped when he exploded.

"Damn it all! This is the biggest pile of horseshit!" He slammed his fists into objects randomly, and Seneca quickly ducked outside with Angus. Win sure made losing his temper count.

JD parked his truck as she stepped down the trailer's rickety steps. He stepped out and pulled on his jacket.

"I'd wait a few minutes before going in there."

"Did you clog the toilet?"

She tried to smile despite her rattled nerves. "Win is throwing a hissy fit about the office space."

"Ah." JD nodded. "I did that yesterday. Put a hole clean through the wall. We won't be getting the deposit back." He leaned down to pet Angus.

"Well, I'm going over to Robyn's to steal some of her coffee. Give him time to calm down." With this, Seneca tucked her head against the November wind and began the trek across the quad to Robyn's building.

"Oh, Seneca." She turned back to JD. "What are your plans for tomorrow tonight?"

"Uh…" she cast about as though thinking, because she couldn't just say *spending all evening in bed with Win's daughter.* "I don't have anything planned."

"How about you come over around five? We've got some meetings in the morning with the finance people, and I would like to discuss stuff with you and Win afterward."

"Sure. Need me to bring anything?"

"Just you and an open mind."

She grinned. "Right." She watched as JD ducked into Win's trailer before setting out again for the office building.

Seneca took the steps two at a time. Robyn's door was cracked, but she knocked anyway.

"Yes?"

"It's me." Seneca poked her head in Robyn's office. "Your dad is pitching an unholy fit in our trailer. Mind if I get some coffee?"

Robyn glanced at her with a smile before returning to her notes. "It's not as strong as you usually like, but you're welcome to it."

"You know I'm not picky." Seneca ambled in to study the selection of ceramic mugs.

"Oh? And I haven't spoiled you with my brand of…coffee?"

Seneca wondered how in the hell Robyn managed to make coffee sound suggestive. Images of her draped over her kitchen table from two nights before swept through her mind like wildfire, burning away any coherent thought. "Ah, I don't think you've managed it quite yet."

"I shall have to try harder." When Seneca looked at her puzzled, Robyn cleared her throat and clarified. "To spoil you."

"Is that what you're trying to do? Spoil me like a fat house cat?" Seneca poured a cup of coffee and let it steam into the air as she tried to decide her feelings about Robyn's declaration. *I have been jealous of Jinx, but something about deliberate spoiling isn't quite right.*

At this, Robyn pushed away from the desk and stood; Seneca admired her perfectly coordinated blouse and pencil skirt. "Would that be so bad?"

She answered automatically. "I don't like for things to be too easy."

"Right." Robyn smiled. "It makes you nervous. You're a bit of a masochist." She rounded the desk and stood close as she poured hot coffee into her half-full mug. The corners of her mouth turned up as she sipped. Seneca was now jealous of the mug, which showed a print of Robyn's lips when she lowered it.

"Perhaps I could torture you a bit to keep things interesting?"

This woman is going to kill me. Seneca looked at Robyn's red, smirking lips. She wanted to pin her to her desk right now. Stepping back, she narrowed her eyes. "It amazes me that you could be so cruel as to goad me in your place of work."

Robyn laughed. "If only it weren't so easy." She winked and then retreated to her desk. "Did JD invite you to his brainstorming session?"

"He did. I assume it's about raising money for the barn?"

"I think so."

"Good, we need a new one before your father completely demolishes the modular unit," Seneca chuckled and took a sip of her coffee.

"What could he possibly be so upset about before nine o'clock in the morning?"

"Well, it's simple," Seneca said with a wry smile. "We took two cowboys accustomed to open spaces and crammed them into a tiny-ass trailer."

"Ah, yes, I suppose it's been a difficult transition for all of you."

"Not so bad for me." *Nightmares aside.* "I've done the tiny space thing before, but JD and Win are a different matter. It's been a harder adjustment." She looked out the window to the space where the barn once stood. "That's a drawback to being in one place for so long."

"What is?" Robyn's curiosity abruptly seemed wary.

Seneca had said more than she meant. She met Robyn's eyes. "I just mean that you can get set in your ways. It makes it hard to adapt."

"I should think it's normal to have difficulty adapting when something like this happens."

"All I'm saying is that when you move constantly, you don't run the risk of getting trapped in—"

"Is that how you feel here? That we've trapped you?"

The nightmare she'd had of being in the burning barn with Robyn resurfaced violently. Seneca fought a shudder. "That's not what I said."

"No, but isn't that how you feel?" Robyn rose again from her seat.

Seneca sipped her coffee to slow the tempo of the conversation. Her palms were sweating. "I don't want to do this with you."

"That's too damned bad, Seneca Twist." Robyn leaned in, pressing her palms to her desk. "Because we are doing *this*"—she waved her hand between them—"and we're doing it right now."

I would have lost her at some point, anyway. Robyn had misunderstood her statement, but Seneca suddenly wondered if her nightmare had foreshadowed her destruction of their relationship. She tried to hold on to their week of happiness. Seneca adopted an impatient tone to hide her weakness. "I knew this would be a problem. I knew I shouldn't get involved with you. That I would regret it." Seneca put the coffee down on the counter.

"What exactly is it that you regret? The sex? The intimacy?"

"I regret…that you've fallen in love with me."

Somewhere below someone hummed a tune, and the person down the hall typed aggressively. Robyn's office was silent. Seneca could not believe the cruel words that had come from her mouth. Robyn looked stricken before her gaze dropped to the desk. Robyn came around her desk slowly. Rather than look angry or hurt, as Seneca had expected, she seemed sympathetic.

"Robyn, I'm—"

"Is that your true—your greatest fear? That someone will love you?"

"Don't do that shrinky thing." Seneca retreated to the door, but Robyn followed.

"I don't think it's the love that scares you."

"Oh?" Seneca turned around. "Then, what is it?" Her heart hammered in her chest. She was on the edge of a great precipice. The ground beneath her was crumbling and would force her fall into darkness. She had lost again. "What is it I'm afraid of, Dr. Mason?"

"That love hurts."

Again, silence. "I know love hurts. I watched my mother mourn my father. She and I both mourned Hunter. I'm familiar with pain."

"Let me rephrase." Robyn cleared her throat. "You are afraid love *always* hurts. You keep everyone at a distance and keep moving around so that you won't continue to love and lose. It's not the love that scares you, it's that the love won't be worth the pain."

Seneca opened her mouth to argue but found she couldn't. What Robyn said was true. This didn't make her easier to face, however. Quite the contrary. The fact Robyn had gotten so quickly to the heart of her fears and motivations unnerved her in the extreme.

"So what?" Seneca finally said, shoving her hands into her pockets. "Let's say that is my fear. Doesn't that prove I'm not fit for this relationship?"

Robyn shook her head. "I think it demonstrates the opposite."

Seneca huffed, frustrated. "Look, I get you want this to work. Hell, I wanted this to work. It was a beautiful dream." Her voice thickened momentarily, and she looked away from Robyn, who was so open and vulnerable. "But I'm just not built for this sort of thing. I think it's a good idea if we end it here before either one of us has the chance to be hurt too badly."

"It's too late for that, you fool." Robyn's sadness was evident. It was shared.

"I truly am sorry, Robyn."

"I believe that."

Seneca had nothing more to say. She stared at Robyn looking tired. "See you later." She hurried away, pausing only to grab her jacket and hat.

Seneca was miserable the entire drive to Jack and Sarah's house. She was heartsick about the way she had left things with Robyn. This meeting would be torture. *What am I even doing?* She would keep her word with JD, help the ranch determine how to get the barn rebuilt. She would keep her head down and work hard. She would work harder. Maybe she could find a kinder way to end things with Robyn.

She pulled into the driveway of the modest, brick home. Robyn's car was in the drive. She parked beside it, then swung down from the cab and stomped on the steps to dislodge any muck on her boots. Sarah met her at the door. Seeing Sarah's tamed wild gray mane again momentarily lifted Seneca's spirits.

"Hi, Seneca. Dinner will be ready after the meeting. Just hang your coat on the peg and grab a drink."

"Damn, Sarah. If I had known there was going to be dinner, I wouldn't have come empty-handed." Seneca hung her coat.

"Two things you ought to know by now, Seneca." She smiled kindly. "First, there is always going to be a meal with this family. And second, we will never consider you empty-handed."

Seneca smiled back, but a sudden swelling of emotion constricted her throat. She tried to swallow it away, but knew Sarah saw it. "Thanks," she whispered.

"What's this?" Sarah was obviously concerned. "Are you okay?"

"Of course." Seneca shook her head, then cleared her throat. "I don't know why I was so touched by that." She laughed weakly while wiping her face with a shaky hand.

"There's a bathroom down the hall if you need it."

"Yes, thanks." She quickly headed down the hallway scolding herself. What must Sarah think of her? A voice that sounded much like Robyn's answered in her head. *That you have emotions like any other person.* Shaking this away, too, she let herself into the bathroom to compose herself.

❖

Robyn had heard Seneca's voice in the kitchen, but when she didn't appear in the den, the knot in her stomach twisted. It wasn't like Seneca to not greet everyone first. Her father seemed to note the oddity, too. "Was that Seneca I heard?"

"I think so." Robyn took a sip of her beer. "Should we get started?"

"Not without Twist," JD said. "We should all be on the same page." He tapped the drafting paper spread over the coffee table. "It will be easier if everyone is here from start to finish."

"I agree," Jack growled as Sarah returned to the den.

"Dinner will be ready in an hour."

"Thank you, Sarah." JD smiled. "We should have made some headway by then."

"It's no problem, JD." Jack rubbed a hand down his stubbled face. "Y'all take the time you need. There's not a last call here."

"That was the wrong thing to say." Seneca's voice called from the doorway as she stepped into the den with a foaming beer. "Win and JD will be here all night." She winked and took a seat next to Robyn.

Determined to be as normal as possible, Robyn gave her as warm a smile as she could muster. It seemed they had both come to the same conclusion regarding how to interact this evening. It wasn't necessary for everyone to know they'd had a falling out, especially since they had not known how close they had been. They would be discreet. "So, now we're all here. What's this big plan you and Dad have cooked up?"

❖

Seneca was impressed. Win and JD seemed to have ironed out all the details. It was a great plan, though a huge part of it depended on her participation, and she wasn't sure if she could still be around to see the project's completion. Her quarrel with Robyn had brought her fears to the surface.

"How about it, Seneca? You're awful quiet over there."

She leaned forward. "I think it's solid, Win. A rodeo carnival? I've never seen anything like it. Should be a huge success." She sipped her beer. "The only problem is what we will do in the meantime."

"In the meantime, we have to have a new barn." JD sighed. "Those modular buildings are not cutting it in the way of size or comfort. I think getting another barn standing as quickly as we can is the right call."

"And as much as we all loved that old barn, it wasn't much in the way of energy efficiency or sustainability." Win sipped his beer.

A tick of quiet filled the room.

"Wow," Robyn said. "That's not anything I ever thought I would hear you say."

He smiled. "Nor I. But I recall a conversation I had with this trailhand about the solar energy they used on base." He gestured to Seneca. "I thought why not try to incorporate some of those type things in the new building?"

"It would be cheaper in the long run," JD said, pitching in.

Seneca grinned and looked at Robyn for a moment. For the barest hint of time, nothing was changed between them. Remembering their argument, she averted her eyes. "It sure would be, Boss," she said.

The sounds of Rosemary coming through the back door could be heard from the living room. JD stood from the couch to greet her. Sarah stepped into the doorway. "Dinner is ready."

Seneca hung back to allow Robyn time to get her plate and find a seat. She avoided Win's curious glance by reviewing the drafting sheet. It wasn't until Jack growled from the kitchen for her to come eat that she stepped into the crowded room and took a plate.

Over dinner they rehashed a few details and discussed the efficiency of different building plans and materials. It was a loud affair and there was some good-natured banter. Seneca did the best she could to explain how solar energy was used and what she knew about the general construction, but her knowledge was limited.

"Well." Sarah smiled at her. "I suppose we can let you off the hook until Thanksgiving."

"Thanksgiving?" Seneca nearly snorted her green beans.

"Yes. You can do some research and educate all of us then."

"Oh…"

"You are coming to Thanksgiving?" Jack grunted his question.

"Well, I hadn't considered it…"

"But you must come!" Rosemary smiled at Seneca and turned to Robyn. "Tell her, Robyn."

Robyn and Seneca contemplated one another, and an awkward, interminable silence filled the room.

Robyn cleared her throat. "Seneca knows she has an open invitation to every dinner at this house," she said. "She can do as she wishes."

"What the hell sort of convincing was that?" Jack's usual growl sounded like a rumble. He frowned as the table at-large looked on.

"Ms. Twist is a grown woman—"

"Ms. Twist?" Win repeated.

"I appreciate the invitation." Seneca quickly disrupted the current flow of the conversation. Robyn had turned bright red. Seneca was somewhat annoyed with how Robyn had bumbled the situation, but also realized her part in creating the awkwardness between them. If the family didn't know before they were on the outs, they surely did now. So much for keeping their relationship details discreet. "What should I bring?"

Robyn was loading the dishwasher when she heard Seneca's footfalls at the kitchen door. She didn't turn as Seneca thanked Jack for the hospitality, and he bid her good night. As the door shut, her uncle stepped over to her. She was just starting the dishwasher's cycle.

"What's going on with you two?"

She looked at Uncle Jack, contemplating how much to share. She realized she could use some advice. "We've argued."

"Clearly."

Helpful. Robyn frowned at him. "What would you have me do?"

"Go after her."

"I've already done that."

"Do it again."

"And when she pushes me away again?"

"Do it again."

"That's not healthy for either of us." She wiped her hands on a dishtowel while they both heard the strains of Seneca struggling to start her truck.

"I suppose not," he said. "But you love her."

Robyn tried to be dismissive. "I've loved a lot of people."

"Not like you love her."

This was true. Her feelings for Seneca were more intense than anything she'd felt before. It was terrifying and exhilarating and completely illogical. "I'm not sure she feels the same."

"She does, or she wouldn't have pushed you away."

"That doesn't make any sense—"

"You know it does." Jack's gruff interruption was incredibly gentle.

They both listened to the continued noise of the loaner truck not starting.

"So, are you going out there, or what?"

Robyn stepped to the door to grab her coat.

Robyn could hear Seneca cursing the cold as she tried to turn the truck's engine over. Seneca stepped out of the truck and slammed the door as Robyn came down the porch steps.

"Is everything okay?" Robyn cringed at the question because it clearly wasn't.

Seneca huffed. "The truck won't start."

"It's so cold—"

"I know." She looked at her. "I'm sorry." Seneca seemed to speak through clenched teeth. "It's not you I'm mad at."

"Isn't it?" Robyn laughed humorlessly into the frigid air.

Seneca opened her mouth to speak. She shut it again. Robyn waited. Finally, Seneca shook her head. "I don't know what you want me to say."

Robyn smiled sadly. "I only want you to say what you feel."

"Oh, is that all?" Seneca sighed. "Okay, I feel like you want something from me that I can't give."

"Like what?"

"I don't know. Everything?"

This word hung between them. "I don't want everything." Robyn stepped closer. "I just want to be with you." She felt the words lay her bare as she waited on Seneca's response.

"I…"

Robyn went even closer so she could look into Seneca's mossy eyes. "Why can't you let me love you?"

Seneca looked to the stars. "It's not that simple." She sniffled.

"Isn't it?" Robyn traced her jawline tenderly. "I love you, and, unless I'm much mistaken, you love me."

"I do. I do love you, Robyn."

"Then why—"

"Because love is fragile," Seneca huffed, pulling away. "What happens if you fall out of love with me? What happens if I stop loving you?" She took a step back. "And I'm stuck here? The awkwardness in there tonight"—she jabbed her finger toward the house—"would become the norm. I can't do that to either of us."

Robyn drew away from the bitterness in Seneca's voice. She didn't stop her when she swung back into the truck's cab to try the ignition again. Robyn listened to her pumping the accelerator repeatedly, almost frantically. The engine caught. Seneca glanced at Robyn once more before she drove away.

Robyn stared after Seneca, at a total loss as to how to move forward. Robyn was angry at herself for being so vulnerable, and she was angry with Seneca for refusing to be. As Robyn dried her eyes, her father stepped out onto the porch. "Robyn? Did Seneca get away all right?"

She cleared her throat. "Yes, she escaped safely."

She had meant to sound joking, but something in her voice must have given her away, because her father made his way down the steps and onto the gravel drive. His concern was evident in his eyes. "What's going on?"

"Seneca and I have had a disagreement, that's all."

"Disagreement?" He grunted. "Must have been a hell of one for you two to have been acting so strange tonight." He took in the stars and then her face. "Do you mind if I ask what it was about?" Her eyes filled with tears again. "Oh, it was like that, then? I see." He stroked his mustache. "I suspected that might be the case."

"Well, your suspicions were correct." She could hear the ice edging into her voice and willed its faster injection into her veins. It would hurt less to be angry and numb.

He patted her shoulder. "You know people like Seneca take a long time to trust—"

"Don't do that, Dad." She put distance between them. "Don't take her side."

Win raised his arms in surrender. "I'm not taking sides."

Robyn had already begun walking to her car but stopped and turned back. "I don't know where you get the gall to lecture me about relationships after that clusterfuck of a marriage you had with Mom, anyway." With this, she turned back around and got into her car. She left her father staring after her just as Seneca had left her moments before. As she got down the road, the stricken expression on her father's face haunted her. She owed him an apology. "Damn," she murmured.

Chapter Twenty-four

Robyn arrived at her office to find a fresh box of doughnuts by the coffee maker. With a contrite smile, she put down the container of sausage bread and went to lift the lid. The doughnuts were from her father. Just as she had brought him his favorite sausage bread, he had ordered doughnuts as an apology.

Booted steps could be heard in the hall and so, firing up the coffee maker, she called out. "Thanks for the doughnuts. I've got some sausage bread here if you're interested."

The footsteps stopped at her office door. "I can't honestly take credit for those doughnuts, but I might lie for sausage bread." Instead of the tall frame of her father, JD poked his head into the room, grinning.

"Oh, JD." She smiled. "I thought you were Dad."

"Nope, just this dusty, old cowboy," he said. "Is there some sort of breakfast food exchange happening? If so, I'd like to be dealt into that."

"No, I—um…" Robyn sighed. She looked at him closely. "I'm sure you noticed the weirdness at the meeting."

He shuffled more fully into the room and took the coffee cup she offered him. "I might've noticed something off between you and Twist, yeah." He ran a blunt fingertip around the rim of the ceramic. "Might've noticed Win's been in a mood, too."

"Yeah, I'll bet he has." Robyn sat down in a chair wearily and JD followed her lead. "Seneca and I had a…relationship."

"We figured that."

"We?"

He shrugged. "We."

Robyn shook her head dejectedly. Of course, everyone would know. "Right. Anyhow, I think it's over now."

"That's a shame," JD said. "Did that hardheaded ranch hand get cold feet?"

"Something like that." She leaned back into the chair. "She's afraid she's not enough."

"Does this have to do with her buddy? The one who was killed?"

"Partly, yes, it does." She was surprised JD knew about Seneca's history, but it helped to be able to talk without breaking Seneca's confidence. "She feels responsible and it's understandable, but she can't not live her life because of her past. She's stuck in this cycle of cut and run and she's convinced herself that is who she is. But if that were true, she wouldn't feel so at home here." Robyn gestured around the room with a hand. "Her instinct is to come to the aid of others and to establish friendships."

"But she's afraid she'll ruin it and so she runs before she can."

"Precisely."

"And you holding her here with projects hasn't worked?"

"It has, but, as you said, she's hardheaded."

"I know a few people like that." He grinned. "*You* can be mighty hardheaded. So can Win." He looked down at his hands. "So can I." JD lifted his head, smiling sadly. "You know, I had a daughter."

Robyn tilted her head. "Yes, I remember. She passed away, didn't she?"

He nodded. "She would be a few years older than you. Thirty-four next month." He sighed. "She killed herself going on seventeen years ago."

"I'm sorry," Robyn said softly and meant it. "I hope I haven't been insensitive."

"No, it's just there's not a day goes by that I don't think about her. For a long time, I felt responsible." JD shrugged. "It's common, apparently. Survivor's guilt and all that."

"It is, yeah." She leaned into JD's pain.

"I was angry for a long time, too. Kept thinking it was unfair. Kept feeling like I needed to keep people at arm's length."

"What changed?"

"You and Win did." He grinned. "The ranch did. You see, I did a lot like Seneca did. I started traveling. I didn't strap on a backpack or anything. But I started hopping around from one place to the other until I landed here. Then y'all wouldn't let me go."

"We weren't about to do that." Robyn smiled. "You were one of us."

"Just like Seneca is."

"Yes." Robyn stood to pour the coffee. "So, what am I to do? Jack thinks I should club her and drag her back to chain her to the wall of my cave."

"There's an idea." He watched as she filled his cup with steaming liquid and handed him a doughnut.

"Do you have any? Ideas?"

"Don't chase her. Give her some space to realize she's exactly where she needs to be."

"Is that how it happened for you?"

"In a way." He smiled. "I was getting ready to leave and y'all sprung all those projects on me. Within a couple of months, I met Rosemary and convinced her to love me. 'Round about that time, I realized I was home." He grinned again. "It just came on me gradual like that."

Robyn shook her head. "I wish I could be as optimistic about it as you, JD." She sighed. "Seneca fights it so damn hard."

"That's how you know she knows." He nodded. "Give her some space. She'll realize what she's got to lose. Then, the fear of losing you will be greater than her fear of loving you." He sipped his coffee.

"And if that doesn't work?"

He took a bite of his doughnut, chewed it thoughtfully, and then swallowed. "If that doesn't work, Jack and I will find you a good club."

Robyn smiled and bit down on her own breakfast.

❖

"So, you're telling me you don't want me to come?" Seneca's mother's disbelieving voice was sharp over the cell phone.

Seneca pinched the bridge of her nose. "It's not that I don't want you to come, Mom. The barn burned down, remember? There is too much going on here for me to give you much attention."

She looked at Angus, who was greeting the horses at the fence line. Training him to work with her had been a spectacular idea. So far, he'd been the picture of professionalism. Just in that moment, however, he was lifting his leg on the tires of Win's truck. She motioned him back to her as her mother continued.

"I don't understand, Seneca. Last week you called me gushing about Thanksgiving and the beautiful Idaho landscape. It was the happiest I've heard you in *years*. Now, you're telling me not to come. What has changed?"

"The barn burned down—"

"No, that's not it. I am sorry for the loss of what was clearly an important piece of property, but you know damned well that has nothing to do with your sudden change of heart."

"I don't know what you mean—"

"It's a woman." Her mother's voice softened. "You've finally met someone and now you're scared. It's that psychologist, isn't it?"

"Mom—"

"I knew it."

"Mom!" Seneca raised her voice in frustration. This was not going how she wanted. She had hoped the arson explanation would persuade her mother that their reunion would have to wait. Indefinitely.

"Don't take that tone with me!" Seneca sighed softly as her mother reprimanded her. "I've already bought a plane ticket and made arrangements to board Ralphy."

She must be serious if she's boarding her precious corgi. Seneca plowed on—albeit much more respectfully. "Mom, I will not have any time to spend with you."

"But you have so many friends I can spend time with. Sarah and Jack and Win and JD..." She recited a few more names as Seneca clenched her jaw in frustration. "I feel like I know them all already."

"I—"

"And I cannot *wait* to meet Robyn!"

Oh God. "This is not a good idea—"

"Well, that's too bad, Seneca Twist. I am not going to be persuaded to cancel," her mother said with a note of finality. "I'll see you in two weeks. I love you."

"I love you, too." Seneca had barely said the words when her mother ended the call.

"Damn it all!" She would not be able to avoid an awkward Thanksgiving with Robyn. She resigned herself to her fate.

Seneca opened the door to the modular unit to find JD and Win sitting at a folding card table, reviewing blueprints. The sight of them crammed into the tiny space and squinting in the fluorescent overhead lights was incongruous to the work of the ranch. Her anger toward Collin Shepherd surged. He had put them in the current situation.

They had found enough evidence on the video footage to arrest Shep for arson. From what Seneca had been told, he'd gotten liquored up and had come to the ranch to see what he could get into. Setting the fire had not been, according to Shep, the original goal. Neither had he intended to destroy any property. He'd simply wanted to cause a ruckus and the whole situation had escalated.

Not unbelievable. Shep was an asshole for sure, but he was also impulsive and seemed to get into the most trouble when he *wasn't* thinking. He hadn't come to the ranch to burn the barn down; unfortunately, the fact remained.

Ignoring Angus, who had bounded in and made a beeline for JD and Win, she strode to the coffee pot and poured a mug to warm her hands before sitting down to look at the blueprints for the new barn. It looked like a modernized version of the old one, everything in the same place, but adding energy-efficient construction. She was glad for this.

"I'm happy to see you're adding back the loft."

Win joked. "Of course. Where else will we hide when everyone else is working?" He removed his hand from Angus's half-floppy ears to rub his shoulder with kneading pressure.

"Sore muscle?"

"It's old age," JD teased. Win scowled.

"I may have pulled something chucking hay. Or maybe while throwing water buckets at the fire. But the pain just started this morning. It's the damnedest thing."

JD nodded. "I put my back out like that once," he said. "Lifted something wrong and grew stiffer each day until one morning I could not stand. You should put a heating pad on it later; helped me tremendously."

"No kidding? I'll try that then."

She smiled at the banter and sipped her steaming coffee. The cowhands milled about outside the window. "Well, what's scheduled today, Win?"

"A couple of boys are headed to the corrals to check the fences and Cliff is taking Noah and Nathan 'round on cleaning duty. Kevin might need some help haying the pastures."

"Sounds good."

Win readied himself to leave and nodded his farewell. "I'm going to meet with the contractors."

"Good luck," Seneca called, and he tipped his hat. She turned back to JD who was watching her. "If he's not feeling better by tomorrow, he needs to have that shoulder checked sooner than later."

"That's unlikely to happen." JD refilled his coffee. "He'll limp along with it troubling him until he retires in the spring. Then, *maybe* he'll get to a doctor."

Seneca was surprised. "I didn't know Win was planning to retire."

"Oh, yeah. This May." He shook his head. "I don't know what we will do with both you and him gone."

She felt a sinking in her stomach. "I could stay a while after the thaw, I suppose. Until y'all hire someone else."

"Oh, we won't wait long for all that. Don't want to keep you from your journey."

"I wouldn't mind—"

"Nah, no, don't you worry about it. Really. We'll hire someone soon, then you and Win can train them to do the job before spring. That way, when Win retires and you leave, we'll be all set."

"Right." She was unmoored. "I guess that makes the most sense."

"I don't suppose anyone could ever do the work as well as you two, but I'm sure we'll find someone who will do a good enough job."

"Right," she said again with a melancholy air. JD stood and took a last sip of his coffee.

"Right, well you might want to get the keys to the tractor and meet with Kevin before that sharp wind kicks up later today."

"Sure." She nodded to him and put a hand on Angus. "We'll get there, shortly." JD left. The idea of walking away from the ranch and leaving her job in the hands of a stranger bothered her immensely. She'd assumed Win would always be here. He was a fixture of the ranch. Like the sharp prairie wind. And Robyn. Seneca got her coat and hat and exited with Angus close behind her.

❖

As JD had predicted, Seneca spent the better part of the day outdoors. When she finally returned to the modular building, she was surprised that Win wasn't there. She wanted to speak with him about the duties to impart to a new employee. She'd not been able to stop thinking about it.

She peered into the second room where they had been keeping paper files, but Win wasn't in there, either. Thinking that maybe he'd gone to visit Robyn for lunch, she relaxed to warm herself. Angus whined at the door.

She grumbled at Angus. "We were outside for hours. You couldn't have gone then?" He whined again and pawed at her leg. She stood with a grunt. "If I go back in the cold and you don't do your business…" She let the threat hang in the air as she opened the door.

The mottled mutt bounded to the fence and lifted his leg. Just as he finished, the wind changed, cold and biting against her face. Angus turned his head sharply and whined. Without so much as a bark, he ran away.

"What the hell? Angus!" She watched as he rushed down the trail toward the Old Barn site. "Damn it! Get back here!" Angus didn't even look back. Instead, he disappeared behind a tack shed.

"Damn it all," Seneca whispered before following him.

She marched quickly down the trail and around the tack shed toward the large dumpster they had filled with trash from the burn site. Straining her ears, she heard Angus whining on the other side of the massive bin. She rounded the corner of the rusted metal container to find her dog pawing at a body.

Seneca froze. "Win?"

He didn't move from his slumped position against the dumpster. Seneca phoned JD as she rushed to kneel beside Win. "Win! Wake up!" She shook him, but he didn't respond. Seneca removed her gloves and checked for a pulse as Angus paced anxiously. JD answered.

"Hey—"

"Win doesn't have a pulse." She interrupted immediately. "He's on the ground by the big dumpster. I need you to call an ambulance and get the defibrillator. I'm starting compressions."

"Compressions..." He seemed stunned. "I'll be right there."

Seneca pulled Win away from the dumpster so that he lay on the hard gravel surface. She positioned her hands and began compressions. It could have been two minutes or ten by the time JD arrived with a defibrillator. "Do you know how to set that up?" She panted between presses.

"We all got trained on them." He set about removing Win's many layers of shirts. "How did you find him?"

She cut her eyes to the dog still pacing. "Angus found him."

"Angus?"

"Yeah..." She was breathless as she continued the compressions. "Ready?"

"Let me get the pads on." JD's voice shook, but his hands were steady as he placed the wired pads. "Sit back," he warned and then pressed the button. The machine detected no heartbeat and administered the first shock. They waited as the AED failed to detect a heartbeat and advised another shock.

"Do it." JD pressed the button again and Win's body flinched again, but the machine still didn't find a pulse. "Damn it, Win! Come on!" She shared a look with JD beside her. "Again."

"Twist—"

"Do it again."

JD pressed the button a third time just as the wail of sirens met her ears. *You're too late.* The AED administered another shock. Win's body flinched before his chest heaved, and an alarm went off on the machine. *How will I tell Robyn?*

"Heartbeat detected," the robotic voice intoned.

"What did it say?" Seneca asked over the machine's noise as she pressed two fingers against Win's carotid artery.

"He's got a pulse, Twist! Seneca!" JD grabbed her in relief as the ambulance screeched to a stop. A man and a woman hurried toward them. JD rose to answer their questions as another EMT unloaded a stretcher.

The care team soon had Win loaded in the ambulance. JD turned to her.

"Go with him," she said. "I'll get Robyn. Call Joan as soon as you can."

"I'm glad you were here, Seneca. And Robyn will be, too."

"Right." She nodded. *Maybe.* "Call me with any news."

CHAPTER TWENTY-FIVE

Robyn had just finished a client's session and had fifteen minutes before the next one. It was enough time for a cup of coffee while she typed her notes. She had just lifted her mug when she heard striding boots in the hallway. *That sounds like Seneca.* Confused, she met Seneca at the door.

"Seneca?"

"We need to get your coat and cancel your patients. Win is headed to the hospital."

Robyn was stunned. "What?"

Seneca took Robyn's heavy coat from the rack. She shook it out and helped Robyn into it. She then strode to her desk and reached into the bottom left drawer to retrieve her purse. "Phone?"

"In the top drawer." Robyn answered automatically. "What happened? Is he injured?"

Seneca dropped the phone into Robyn's bag. "I'm not sure." She returned to stand at the door. "I found him on the ground. We got his heart going—"

"His heart stopped?" Her legs trembled, but Seneca was there to catch her. Robyn was vaguely aware of strong arms around her as she was helped into a chair.

Seneca knelt before her and reached for her hand. "Robyn, look at me." She met the mossy gaze. "I don't know what happened. Angus found him on the ground. When I realized his heart wasn't beating, I called JD and started compressions. JD brought the AED, and we got his heart going as the ambulance arrived."

"Oh, my God." She leaned into Seneca's open arms. Robyn pressed her face into Seneca's neck and breathed her in. The warm, solid presence was just what she needed. "We argued the night of the meeting. After you left, he came outside. He was trying to give me a pep talk, I think…" Her voice cracked.

"That sounds like him."

Robyn took a deep breath. "But I blew him off. No." She sat back with a shake of her head. "Worse, I said some awful things."

"We all say awful things when we're upset." Seneca wiped away Robyn's tears. "Win knows you love him, and you know he loves you. The ambulance may already be at the hospital and those EMTs know their stuff. Are you ready? Do you need another minute?"

"I'm ready." She stood. "Oh, somebody should call Joan—"

"JD is on top of it."

"Someone should call Sarah—"

"I'm sure Joan will do that."

"Right." She looked at the weather-worn and weary woman before her. The large, designer purse hung awkwardly from her right arm, and she had Robyn's cream and gold scarf in her left hand. "Thank you." Her throat constricted.

"Of course." Seneca handed her the scarf and held her hand as they left the building.

By the time they reached the hospital, Win had been taken back and JD was pacing in front of the ER. Seneca watched as Robyn reached him. He took her into his arms and pulled her tight. "I'm sorry."

"Let's get inside," Seneca said as the wind snatched her breath away.

They headed through the sliding doors as JD filled them in. "They took him for an angiogram." He led them to a relatively quiet corner of the waiting room. "They said they would know more after that."

"Why was he by the dumpster?"

"He had to meet with the contractor, and I reckon he probably walked there afterward. There was no telling how long he had been down." Seneca remembered their morning conversation. "He complained about his shoulder. Remember, JD?"

JD frowned before his face dawned with comprehension. "That son of a gun was having a heart attack right in front of us." He shook his head. "Shit." He looked at Robyn. "Win was complaining about his shoulder bothering him. Seemed to think it was something he did last week or the night of the fire. None of us thought much about it."

"No, you wouldn't." Robyn sighed. "With a physical job like his, a stiff shoulder is all in a good day's work." She looked at Seneca. "Tell me about Angus."

"Well, it was the damnedest thing. We'd been working and when we got back to the trailer, he acted like he needed to go again. Whining and pawing and such." She rubbed her face, trying to fight the surge of fear and helplessness she remembered at seeing Angus lying beside Win's crumpled form. "As he's doing his business, he just ran off. I followed him to Win. I guess he smelled him or something." Seneca rolled her shoulders. "If it hadn't been for Angus..." She trailed off, and then smiled. "I reckon I've got to keep him now, don't I?"

"Absolutely." Robyn returned the tired grin. Her gaze slipped to the door. "Joan." She stood abruptly and strode to meet her stepmother. Robyn and Joan embraced. JD and Seneca stood to welcome her. Moments later, Sarah came in. There was another round of hugs before they all settled in and persuaded Seneca to tell the story about Angus once more.

The waiting was unbearable, but an hour later, a nurse explained Win had been taken back for angioplasty and stenting. They would move him to his assigned room once he was stable and he would probably be in the hospital a couple of days.

The group decided Joan and Robyn would stay at the hospital, at least until Win was roomed, as they were closest of kin. Sarah invited JD and Seneca back to the house for an early dinner. Jack and Rosemary were already preparing for their arrival. Seneca accepted and then turned to Robyn, who was preparing to follow the nurse to Win's assigned room.

"You call me if anything changes." Seneca's hands dwarfed Robyn's as she held them. She stared intensely into Robyn's eyes. "Or if you need me for anything." She paused. "Or if you just need to cry."

"I might take you up on that."

"Do," Seneca said and then started to pull away, but Robyn stopped her.

"Thank you, Seneca. I don't know what I would have done without you."

Once, the sentiment of that sentence and the responsibility it held would have scared her, but no longer. "I'm here," she said and leaned down to press a chaste, but loving, kiss to Robyn's lips. Seneca gathered Robyn into a hug. *I love you.* Seneca then looked at Joan, who was trying, along with everyone else, to act uninterested in the interaction. "Call me if you need absolutely anything."

"Thank you, dear." Joan patted her arm and then took Robyn's hand. "We will."

She nodded, turned, and exited with JD and Sarah.

At Sarah and Jack's, Seneca sat with Angus on her lap. The dog had been receiving a plethora of praise and affection, and he was exhausted by the events of the day. She absently caressed his silky fur as she sipped her beer. Robyn had just called to relay that Win was now resting in his room. JD and Rosemary had volunteered to bring some clothes for Win and Joan so Robyn could come home and go back the next day. For the moment, Win seemed stable.

"How's Robyn?" Jack sat down beside her and propped his feet on his coffee table.

"Exhausted. Anxious…"

"Relieved that it wasn't worse."

"Yes." She patted Angus as he stretched. Smiling down at the pup, she took a sip of her beer. "The doctor told them that if we had been even a minute later, Win might have died." She sat up straighter on the sofa. "Apparently, Win started feeling woozy after walking to the barn site, and so he leaned on the dumpster. After that, he reckons he passed out. The doctor thinks he was unconscious for a while before he…" Her voice caught in her throat unexpectedly.

"Before his heart stopped."

"Yeah." They sat quietly for a moment, sipping their beer. Seneca shook her head. "Well, Robyn said JD and Rosemary were going to drop her back at the ranch so she could get her car and head home."

"You should go be with her," Jack said. "She'll need you."

"Yes, she shouldn't be alone." Seneca stood and Angus yawned. "Besides, she'll want to thank the hero." She ruffled the pup's ears.

"She sure will." Jack stood, too, as Sarah came into the room.

"Leaving?"

"Yeah."

"Well, remind Robyn we love her and that we're here if she needs us," Sarah said. "We're here if either of you need us."

Seneca took her hand. "Thank you, Sarah," she said with a smile before grabbing her hat and coat and whistling for Angus.

Robyn collapsed onto her sofa. She was in a light sleep when she heard the crunch of tires in her gravel driveway. She sat up to a dark living room. She rose unsteadily and flipped on the outside light to see Seneca and Angus on the porch steps. Robyn opened the door before Seneca could knock.

"Hey."

"Hey."

Robyn let them in and watched Seneca remove her hat, coat, and red scarf. "How are Jack and Sarah?" Robyn knelt eye-level with Angus, who was sitting at Seneca's feet.

"They said to remind you they love you."

She smiled. "I love them, too." Robyn scratched behind the dog's ears as his tongue lolled from his mouth happily. "Thank you, boy," she addressed the animal. "You and your mama make a great team." She stood again, slightly trembling. Seneca helped her up with a frown.

"When did you last eat?"

"Breakfast, I guess?"

She led her to the sofa. "Sit. I'll make you a sandwich or something."

"There's some leftover pizza in there. I wouldn't mind a bite of that."

"Sure."

Robyn sat down on the couch, and Angus immediately crawled into her lap. "Someday you'll be too big for my lap." She smiled and petted him.

"As if that will stop him." Seneca grinned. Robyn watched as Seneca preheated the oven and rummaged under the counter where Robyn kept her liquor. She found a bottle of bourbon and a snifter glass, and she poured an inch of the amber liquid into the vessel. This, she delivered to Robyn before returning to the kitchen.

"Thanks."

She must have sounded as exhausted as she felt because Seneca frowned in concern. Seneca sat down and held Robyn's hand. "Why don't you go take a bath? I can manage heating leftovers." She smiled reassuringly. "Take the bourbon with you and try to unwind."

"I don't want to leave you alone."

"I'm not alone." She pointed to a corner above the refrigerator where one yellow eye was peering down at her. "Jinx is here."

"Ah." Robyn followed her gaze. "Well, in that case." Smiling, she stood and leaned over to press a grateful kiss to the top of Seneca's head. "I think I will. Let me know when the pizza is done."

"Sure." Seneca reached above the refrigerator to give Jinx a scratch under the chin. "We'll be right here."

Robyn went to her bedroom with her drink and a smile. *What would I do without you, Seneca?* She hoped she never found out.

Hours later, Robyn woke again from slumber. This time, she had drifted off while snuggled in Seneca's warm embrace on the sofa.

Seneca sat asleep with her head leaned against the back of the couch and her arm around Robyn. Even in slumber, she looked exhausted. Robyn was just about to stroke down Seneca's cheek when her mossy green eyes opened.

"Hey." Robyn breathed.

"Hey." Seneca turned to look at her. "How are you feeling?"

"Better."

"Yeah?"

"Yeah." Robyn looked her over. "How are *you* feeling?"

"I'm all right."

"That's not good enough."

Seneca frowned. Something in her face must have told Seneca she meant business. Seneca sighed. "I'm tired. Finding Win like that was plain awful." Seneca leaned her forearms on her thighs.

Robyn stroked Seneca's back. "We're all grateful you found him."

"He was just totally limp, you know? I've never seen him *not* moving. It scared me so bad." Robyn caressed Seneca's face when she fell silent, troubled. There was nothing to be said, they just needed to be there for each other.

"The whole time I was doing compressions, though, I wasn't thinking about Win. I was thinking about you." Seneca glanced at her and then down at her own hands.

"Me?" Robyn was surprised.

"I kept wondering what I was going to tell you if he didn't make it. How could I comfort you? How could I say anything at all to you after I left things between us as they were?"

Robyn longed to comfort her, but, instead, she let her talk. Part of her needed to hear Seneca's apology. "That's valid," she said softly.

Seneca made eye contact. "I am sorry I was an asshole."

"You were afraid," Robyn murmured as her heart lifted.

"It sometimes seems easier to walk out than to wait around for someone to walk out on you." Seneca sighed.

"But I'm done walking, Robyn."

Robyn's heart soared. She leaned forward to give Seneca a loving peck on the cheek.

Seneca grinned and then tilted her head from side to side as though to stretch her neck. "You should go to bed."

Robyn considered her for a moment. "You should, too."

"Yeah, I'm good."

"Come to bed with me."

"*With* you?" Seneca tilted her head with the question.

"Yes, Seneca." Robyn smiled. "Come to bed and make love to me."

Seneca stood, pulling Robyn to her feet.

Robyn led her into the bedroom, both of them stripping along the way. They slid into bed nude and Seneca rolled her over to fall between her thighs. Robyn arched at the pressure on her swollen sex. "Oh, Seneca…" She moaned softly.

Seneca captured her mouth briefly and then kissed down the column of her neck. Seneca roamed Robyn's body with her lips and hands and caressed her tenderly. She ran her fingers along Robyn's side, gently glancing the outer swell of her breast. Robyn's breath hitched.

Robyn shifted restlessly beneath her.

"Does that tickle?"

"No…" Robyn murmured in reply and grasped her back. "I just want…"

"What?" Seneca took one of Robyn's nipples between her thumb and forefinger and rolled it.

"That." She arched into her, rolling her hips so that Seneca could feel the slick heat between them.

"Slow—"

"I don't want slow." Robyn raked her fingernails down Seneca's back until Seneca hissed and pinned Robyn's wrists above her head.

"That's too bad." Seneca captured her mouth before she could protest. With her other hand, she softly stroked the tops of Robyn's thighs and the apex of her legs.

Robyn groaned and writhed beneath Seneca but did not protest any longer. Her body burned from the inside. Seneca released Robyn's wrists and turned her mouth on her breasts. She closed her lips around Robyn's nipple and sucked and laved until Robyn threaded her fingers in her chocolate hair and wrapped one leg over her back.

After giving her other breast the same attention, Seneca slid down and nuzzled Robyn's thighs with her open mouth. Robyn clutched at the strong shoulders between her thighs. Seneca slid her hands underneath the back of Robyn's thighs and pressed gently. Spreading her. Baring her.

"Mmm…" Seneca seemed to pause before lowering her mouth.

When Seneca's tongue connected with her swollen folds, Robyn gently pulled on the silky tresses still threaded through her fingers.

"Ah…" Robyn sighed and shifted her hips restlessly, driving toward the heat of Seneca's mouth.

"You taste so sweet and—"

"Stop talking." Robyn groaned. The vibration of Seneca's laughter under her clit only excited her more.

Then, Seneca wrapped her arms around her thighs and buried her face between Robyn's legs, covering her sex with her mouth completely. Robyn cried out and threw her head back at the intense stimulation. She writhed beneath Seneca as she licked through her folds with the broad flat of her tongue. Seneca sucked at the pearl between her lips. Robyn thrust her hips against Seneca's mouth, desperately seeking release. She felt her climax dawning on the horizon.

"Come for me," Seneca murmured. Seneca pressed two fingers inside Robyn to accompany the laving of her tongue.

"Yes!" Robyn cried out, clutching and arching against her. "Oh, God." She shuddered as she rode the current of ecstasy coursing through her.

Seneca moaned quietly before surfacing to wipe her face inside Robyn's thighs. She looked down at her before pulling her body up to straddle Robyn's thigh. A low groan escaped Robyn's lips as Seneca's slick thighs and engorged clit connected with her quadriceps. Seneca thrust against her rhythmically and leaned over to capture her mouth. Robyn could taste her own arousal on Seneca's lips.

"Oh…" Seneca moaned as Robyn brought her hands to her breasts.

Robyn marveled at how quickly Seneca came undone. Her wet folds ground on her thigh as Seneca arched and moaned in release.

After she came hard in her arms, Robyn stroked Seneca's back lovingly until her breathing evened out.

Seneca rolled to the side, and Robyn followed her to throw a leg over her strong torso. "Stay with me?"

"Of course, Robyn." Seneca took one of Robyn's hands in her own to bring her knuckles to her mouth. "I'm all yours."

Robyn smiled and nuzzled into her side. "I like the sound of that." She rested her head on Seneca's chest. Robyn could hear the strong, and still excited, beat of Seneca's heart. Robyn smiled when Seneca's breathing deepened and slowed.

All mine. Contented, Robyn drifted.

CHAPTER TWENTY-SIX

Robyn cracked a bleary eye at the sun coming in the windows of her bedroom. She was the big spoon of the pair and, as she rolled away, Seneca grumbled softly. Smiling, she rose, wrapped herself in a robe, and padded to the kitchen to start the kettle for coffee.

Her phone screen was uninteresting, but Robyn didn't want to wait for there to be a problem before calling the hospital. As she set out two mugs, she called Joan.

"Hello?"

"Hi, Joan."

"Hey, honey." She sounded tired, but not distraught.

"How's Dad doing?"

"Ask him yourself." There was a pause on the line.

"Hey, girl." Her father's voice came over the phone, and she exhaled, relieved. Robyn smiled.

"Hey, Dad." Robyn leaned on the counter as a tousled Seneca ambled into the kitchen wide awake. "How are you feeling?"

"Like a horse kicked me in the chest."

Robyn laughed in relief. His sense of humor was reassuring. "I'll bet."

"They said if I do well today, they'll let me go home tomorrow." He huffed slightly. "They've got all these rules they want me to follow."

"I imagine so." Robyn sighed. "And you'll follow them."

"How do you figure that?"

"Because I'll set Seneca loose on you if you don't."

He paused. "Is she there with you?"

Robyn met Seneca's eyes. Seneca nodded. "Yeah, she's here." Robyn switched to speakerphone.

"Tell her thanks for saving my life." He paused. "And that mutt of hers, too."

Seneca grinned. "I wasn't about to let you sleep easy, Win."

He laughed. "It looks like he'll be taking an early retirement," Joan said.

"That's fine. I can manage things." Seneca went to the kettle on the stove to check its progress.

Robyn smiled at her and turned off the speakerphone. "I'll be by today to relieve Joan and to check on you, Dad. Is there anything you need?"

She spent the next few minutes sorting details with her father and stepmother. Seneca managed the coffee and had just retrieved the pan for fried eggs when Robyn disconnected. Robyn stood behind Seneca and, putting her arms around Seneca's waist, she leaned her head against Seneca's back.

"Is there anything you need me to do?"

"Exactly what you're doing." Robyn sighed a small sigh.

She turned around to take her in her arms and kiss her on top of the head. "He seems in good spirits."

"Even knowing he can't return to work." She looked at her. "You'll take his job, then?"

Seneca shrugged. "I guess JD might want someone else."

"I doubt it. You've proven yourself."

"Then, yes. I will."

"And you'll be staying? Past the spring?"

Seneca looked at her for a moment. "My people are here. My place is here. I think I've known that for a while now. It just took almost losing it to put it into perspective."

"Well, however it is you've arrived at that conclusion, I'm glad for it." She rose on tiptoes to kiss her gently. "I love you, Seneca Twist."

"And I love you." She took Robyn's face in her hands and captured her mouth for a moment, "A whole lot." Pouring her emotion into the contact, Seneca didn't release her until they were both a bit dazed. She returned to the eggs with a smile.

❖

"Twist! Help with this damned bird," Jack growled from the kitchen.

Seneca rolled her eyes. "Sounds like I've been tapped in, Mom." She patted her mother's hand. Rachel watched her stride into the kitchen. The conversation flowed around her as Robyn recounted the time Seneca's team had won the penning competition.

"She made it look easy. It is disgusting how good she is with these horses."

"My mother and father had a small farm. She just grew up around them. After her father passed, she spent a lot of time with them and learned all manner of skills." Rachel smiled. "I'm certain she and Hunter skipped school once in a while to ride."

Robyn grinned. "That sounds about right." She paused for a moment and looked at Rachel, marveling at how much she looked like Seneca. "I wish I could have known Hunter."

Rachel smiled broadly. "He would have been just as in love with you as my daughter is."

Robyn blushed but did not respond. Sarah called from the kitchen. "Thanksgiving dinner is ready! Come help yourselves."

❖

Seneca's mother joined her and held her hand. "You have special people here."

"I do."

"And Robyn is amazing."

Seneca smiled at her mother. "She is."

"I'm glad you've found your home, here, baby girl. It's a wonderful place."

"You're okay with me not coming back to Alabama?" This, above all, had concerned Seneca. She knew her mother wouldn't stand in the way of what she knew brought her contentment, but Seneca needed to know her mother wasn't against it.

Her mother regarded her quizzically. "Why would you?"

"Well, because you are there?"

"But I'm going to retire soon."

"Okay…"

Rachel smiled. "There's nothing stopping me from moving here in a few years with you."

"You would move here?" Seneca was stunned. She had not been expecting that.

"Why not?" Rachel looked around. "I already know people here. There's nothing in Alabama keeping me there." She looked at her. "You're here. Why not?"

Seneca grinned at her. "Why not?" Laughing, she got in the buffet line behind Robyn, who was helping herself to a healthy serving of dressing.

"Leave some for the rest of us."

"Hush. There's always plenty. You know that by now."

"That's true." Seneca smiled at Robyn even as Win drew her attention. She smirked as she saw him sneak a piece of turkey skin into the waiting mouth of Angus under the table.

"Seneca, come sit over here," Win said. "I want your ideas about the upcoming rodeo—"

"No work talk," Joan cut him off sternly. "Today is about family."

"But the rodeo—"

"Can wait," Joan said.

Win looked ready to argue more, but Seneca mouthed "Later" to him with a smile from across the room.

"Right." He casually dropped another scrap to Angus. "It's not like Seneca is going anywhere."

Seneca smiled at Robyn and gave her a soft peck on the lips. "Certainly not."

About the Author

A former English teacher and current homemaker, Jo Hemming-wood lives in an enchanted wood in rural Alabama with her wife and son and a menagerie of animals. She was published twice in her college's literary collection and enjoyed being an educator for six years, winning teacher of the year in 2020. Jo's writing is often humorous and personal, drawing from her varied life experiences. She pulls from her Southern rural upbringing to craft stories about community.

Books Available from Bold Strokes Books

Broken Fences by Jo Hemmingwood. Former army sergeant Seneca Twist has difficulty adjusting to civilian life until she meets psychologist Robyn Mason and has a place to call home. (978-1-63679-414-3)

Never Kiss a Cowgirl by Ali Vali. Asher Evans dreams of winning the National Finals Rodeo in Vegas, and Reagan Wilson wants no part of something that brings back the memory of what killed her father. (978-1-63679-106-7)

Pantheon Girls by Jean Copeland. Cassie Burke never anticipated the detour life was about to take when a meeting with a prospective client reunites her with a past love and reignites the star-crossed passion they shared twenty years earlier. (978-1-63679-337-5)

Roux for Two by Aurora Rey. For TV chef Chelsea Boudreaux and hometown boy Bryce Cormier, love proves as tricky as making a good pot of gumbo. (978-1-63679-376-4)

Starting Over by Nance Sparks. Jennifer has no idea if she can mend Sam's broken soul after the sudden loss of her wife, but it's never too late for starting over. (978-1-63679-409-9)

The Accidental Bride by Jane Walsh. Spinsters Miss Grace Linfield and Miss Thea Martin travel to Gretna Green to prevent a wedding, only to discover a scandalous passion—for each other. (978-1-63679-345-0)

Three Wishes by Anne Shade. A magic lamp, a beautiful Jinni, and a cursed princess make for one unbelievable story. (978-1-63679-349-8)

Undiscovered Treasures by MJ Williamz. For Cyl and her friends Luna and Martinique, life's best treasures often appear when you're not looking. (978-1-63679-449-5)

Curse of the Gorgon by Tanai Walker. Cass will do anything to ensure Elle's safety, but is she willing to embrace the curse of the Gorgon? (978-1-63679-395-5)

Dance with Me by Georgia Beers. Scottie Templeton mixes it up on and off the dance floor with sexy salsa instructor Marisa Reyes. But can Scottie get past Marisa's connection to her ex? (978-1-63679-359-7)

Gin and Bear It by Joy Argento. Opposites really can attract, and as Kelly and Logan work together to create a loving home for rescue cat Bear, they just might find one for themselves as well. (978-1-63679-351-1)

Harvest Dreams by Jacqueline Fein-Zachary. Planting the vineyard of their dreams, Kate Bauer and Sydney Barrett must resist their attraction while battling nature and their families, who oppose both the venture and their relationship. (978-1-63679-380-1)

The No Kiss Contract by Nan Campbell. Workaholic Davy believes she can get the top spot at her firm if the senior partners think she's settling down and about to start a family, but she needs the delightful yet dubious Anna to help by pretending to be her fiancée. (978-1-63679-372-6)

Outside the Lines by Melissa Sky. If you had the chance to live forever, would you take it? Amara Rodriguez did, and it sets her on a journey to find her missing mother and unravel the mystery of her own heart. (978-1-63679-403-7)

The Value of Sylver and Gold by Michelle Larkin. When word gets out that former Boston homicide detective Reid Sylver can talk to the dead, the FBI solicits her help on a serial murder case, prompting

Reid to assemble forces once again with Detective London Gold. (978-1-63679-093-0)

When It Feels Right by Tagan Shepard. Freshly out of the closet Marlene hasn't been lucky in love, but when it comes to her quirky new roommate Abby, everything just feels right. (978-1-63679-367-2)

Lucky in Lace by Melissa Brayden. Straitlaced stationery store owner Juliette Jennings's predictable life unravels when a sexy lingerie shop and its alluring owner move in next door. (978-1-63679-434-1)

Made for Her by Carsen Taite. Neal Walsh is a newly made member of the Mancuso crime family, but will her undeniable attraction to Anastasia Petrov, the wife of her boss's sworn enemy, be the ultimate test of her loyalty? (978-1-63679-265-1)

Off the Menu by Alaina Erdell. Reality TV sensation Restaurant Redo and its gorgeous host Erin Rasmussen will arrive to film in chef Taylor Mobley's kitchen. As the cameras roll, will they make the jump from enemies to lovers? (978-1-63679-295-8)

Pack of Her Own by Elena Abbott. When things heat up in a small town, steamy secrets are revealed between Alpha werewolf Wren Carne and her human mate, Natalie Donovan. (978-1-63679-370-2)

Return to McCall by Patricia Evans. Lily isn't looking for romance—not until she meets Alex, the gorgeous Cuban dance instructor at La Haven, a newly opened lesbian retreat. (978-1-63679-386-3)

So It Went Like This by C. Spencer. A candid and deeply personal exploration of fate, chosen family, and the vulnerability intrinsic in life's uncertainties. (978-1-63555-971-2)

Stolen Kiss by Spencer Greene. Anna and Louise share a stolen kiss, only to discover that Louise is dating Anna's brother. Surely, one kiss can't change everything...Can it? (978-1-63679-364-1)

The Fall Line by Kelly Wacker. When Jordan Burroughs arrives in the Deep South to paint a local endangered aquatic flower, she doesn't expect to become friends with a mischievous gin-drinking ghost who complicates her budding romance and leads her to an awful discovery and danger. (978-1-63679-205-7)

To Meet Again by Kadyan. When the stark reality of WW II separates cabaret singer Evelyn and Australian doctor Joan in Singapore, they must overcome all odds to find one another again. (978-1-63679-398-6)

Before She Was Mine by Emma L McGeown. When Dani and Lucy are thrust together to sort out their children's playground squabble, sparks fly leaving both of them willing to risk it all for each other. (978-1-63679-315-3)

Chasing Cypress by Ana Hartnett Reichardt. Maggie Hyde wants to find a partner to settle down with and help her run the family farm, but instead she ends up chasing Cypress. Olivia Cypress. (978-1-63679-323-8)

Dark Truths by Sandra Barret. When Jade's ex-girlfriend and vampire maker barges back into her life, can Jade satisfy her ex's demands, keep Beth safe, and keep everyone's secrets...secret? (978-1-63679-369-6)

Desires Unleashed by Renee Roman. Kell Murphy and Taylor Simpson didn't go looking for love, but as they explore their desires unleashed, their hearts lead them on an unexpected journey. (978-1-63679-327-6)

Maybe, Probably by Amanda Radley. Set against the backdrop of a viral pandemic, Gina and Eleanor are about to discover that loving another person is complicated when you're desperately searching for yourself. (978-1-63679-284-2)

The One by C.A. Popovich. Jody Acosta doesn't know what makes her more furious, that the wealthy Bergeron family refuses to be held accountable for her father's wrongful death, or that she can't ignore her knee-weakening attraction to Nicole Bergeron. (978-1-63679-318-4)

The Speed of Slow Changes by Sander Santiago. As Al and Lucas navigate the ups and downs of their polyamorous relationship, only one thing is certain: romance has never been so crowded. (978-1-63679-329-0)

Tides of Love by Kimberly Cooper Griffin. Falling in love is the last thing on either of their minds, but when Mikayla and Gem meet, sparks of possibility begin to shine, revealing a future neither expected. (978-1-63679-319-1)